PENGUIN METRO READS
THE LEGEND OF PARSHU-RAAM

Dr Vineet Aggarwal is a doctor by qualification, manager by profession and artist by temperament. Born in a family of doctors, he successfully completed an initial stint with the family occupation before deciding to venture into pharmaceutical management. He pursues writing as a passion and is an avid travel photographer as well.

His literary repertoire extends from politics to poetry and travel to terrorism but his favourite genre remains the amalgamation of science and mythology. He is the author of the popular online blogs Decode Hindu Mythology and Fraternity Against Terrorism and Extremism. *Vishwamitra* was his debut novel. This is his second book.

THE LEGEND OF
PARSHU-RAAM

DR VINEET AGGARWAL

Penguin
metro reads

An imprint of Penguin Random House

PENGUIN METRO READS

USA | Canada | UK | Ireland | Australia
New Zealand | India | South Africa | China | Singapore

Penguin Metro Reads is part of the Penguin Random House group of companies
whose addresses can be found at global.penguinrandomhouse.com

Published by Penguin Random House India Pvt. Ltd
4th Floor, Capital Tower 1, MG Road,
Gurugram 122 002, Haryana, India

First published in Penguin Metro Reads by Penguin Books India 2015

ISBN 9780143423454

Typeset in Minion Pro by R. Ajith Kumar, New Delhi
Printed at Manipal Technologies Limited, India

To my teachers
Who taught me the difference between Desire and Duty,
May I prove worthy of your teachings

Author's Note

Legends, they say, are hyperbolic versions of historical events. Yet, they remain far more popular than authentic, verifiable history. Throughout the world, stories of legends occupy more mind space than the lives of historically documented people.

The exploits of Robin Hood and King Arthur are arguably more popular than those of Churchill or Thatcher from Great Britain and the labours of Hercules and Hanuman excite a greater number of children in Greece and India respectively than those of Alexander or Chandragupta. As the title of this book suggests, this too is an effort to bring to my readers one such powerful legend that has fired the imagination of thousands of people since time immemorial.

Parshu-Raam is recognized, and even dreaded, as the man who decimated the entire ruling class in a bygone age. His name was whispered in hushed tones by Kshatriya kings till not very long ago and the Bhaagvat Purana mentions him as a Shaktyavesh Avatar of Lord Vishnu—a human invested with special powers of the Supreme Lord.

You may have heard of him from your grandparents or seen a brief glimpse in some television mythological but seldom is his life story detailed to an extent that it could become an epic by itself. The purpose of this book is not to harp on his later achievements that many of us are aware of, but to bring to readers the events from before his birth that slowly but surely led this simple Brahmin boy to become the legend that fate forced him to become.

Since a protagonist's story does not get a complete perspective till it is compared with that of the antagonist or the anti-hero, this book would be incomplete without the inclusion of the travels and travails of his arch enemy, the man who, according to scriptures, was an incarnation of Lord Vishnu's Sudarshan Chakra himself! Hardly anyone would have heard of him before, but I must mention that this extraordinary man is considered one of the very first humans to rule over a global empire—a dream many colonial powers cherished in a previous century and a few harbour even today.

The struggle between the two men is a reflection of the fight for supremacy between two powerful classes of ancient India—Brahmins and Kshatriyas—and their ideologies. It can be seen even today, especially in countries where the intelligentsia and military exist at loggerheads. Even as you read this, some military leader somewhere in the world is surely planning a coup to snatch power from the bureaucrats while somewhere else, the literati is preparing for a protest against the authoritarian regime in their country.

In this book I shall introduce you to the clash that completely transformed India's social structure in a bygone age. I have merged some true stories about the lord of Lanka taken from the Ramayana to help me arrive at this sequence of events. You may be surprised to know that Ravan was also defeated by someone other than Shri Raam!

Like the demon king Ravan and his own grand-uncle

Vishwamitra, Parshu-Raam also makes an appearance in that grand epic, although briefly. When Shri Raam breaks Shiva's bow in the Swayamvar for Sita's hand, Parshu-Raam arrives on the scene like a storm and challenges the prince for a duel. As far as I am aware, this is the only instance where two different incarnations of Lord Vishnu have come face-to-face as adversaries!

Parshu-Raam also finds mention in the Mahabharata as the guru of Kuru patriarch Bhishma as well as the ill-fated Karna. Since Parshu-Raam was opposed to Kshatriyas, Karna had to lie about his identity in order to receive martial training from him, a subterfuge that ultimately led Karna to be cursed to forget the very knowledge he had acquired when he needed it the most. In Kerala, Parshu-Raam is believed to have imparted similar training to Swami Ayyappa, the lord of Shabrimala, and developed the martial art of Kalaripayattu along with Rishi Agastya.

His influence though is not restricted to great personalities of the past. He is still believed to reside on earth, awaiting the arrival of Kalki, the tenth avatar of Lord Vishnu, who will receive training in the martial knowledge Parshu-Raam has perfected, in order to help the final incarnation of this yuga fulfil his purpose. You may wonder how one man's lifespan could transcend that of three different incarnations of Vishnu but then, as the scriptures tell us, the gods grant special powers to humans who are needed to carry on their work. The mission of Parshu-Raam's life is to help humanity find its way whenever it gets lost and thus he is counted as one of the seven immortals or Chiranjeevis.

Besides all these military accomplishments, he is also destined to become one of the Saptarishis in the next Manvantar along with Vishwamitra, who is related to him by not just ties of blood but also a powerful bond of magic. This book is my attempt to bring to you the legend of the only Brahmakshatriya known in the history of India, a fitting companion to the saga of Vishwamitra, the only Kshatriya in history who became a Brahmarishi.

It is the story of a boy who was forced to take difficult decisions in order to fulfil his duties not just to his parents but also to the idea of a fair and just society. It is the story of a man who rose to the level of divinity, the story of the making of a legend.

NABHIVARSH

N
E
W
S

Kailash

Kashyap-mir

Gandhar

R. Brahmaputra

Kamarupa

Ayodhya

Kanyakubja

R. Ganga

R. Saraswati

R. Sindhu

R. Charmanvati

Janapav

Mahishmati

R. Narmada

R. Tapti

R. Godavari

Dandak-Aranya

R. Krishna

R. Kaveri

Parshuram Kshetra

Varun's Domain

Varun's Domain

Lanka

Family Chart of Chandravanshis

Brahma
- Marichi
  - Kashyap
    - Other Adityas
      - Indra
      - Surya (7th Manu)
        - Ikshvaku
          - Vikushi
          - Dand — Created Dandak-Aranya
          - 9 more sons
          - Nimi
    - Daityas
    - Danavs
      - Nagas
      - Apsaras
      - Gandharvs
      - Yakshas
      - Birds
      - Aquatics
      - Flora
      - Fauna
- Pulatsya
- Pulah
- Daksh
- Narad
- 1st Manu
- Atharva
  - Durvasa
- Atri
  - Chandra
    - Budh
      - Ila/Sudyumna
      - Pururava (Urvashi)
        - Ayu (Amavasu)
          - Nahush (Kush)
            - Yayati (Kushanabh)
              - 4 more sons
              - Haiheyas (Kadhi)
                - Kirtivirya (Vishwamitra)
                  - Arjun (Deval)
                  - Other Yadavs
                  - Padmini
                  - Manorama
- Angiras
  - Dattatreya
- Vasishth
  - Shukracharya
- Bhrigu
  - Chyavan
    - Ruchik (Satyavati)
      - Yamdagni (Renuka)
        - Parshu-Raam

SURYAVANSH

CHANDRAVANSH

Prologue

It was a pleasant, sunny day in Kailash when its residents returned from a visit to Brahmalok.

Lord Brahma, the First Mortal Being of the universe had stepped into the fifty-first year of his life, officially hitting middle age and there had been a huge celebration in his honour. All his offspring, including the four Kumars, the ten Manas-putras, the Devas, Asurs and Pitris were present with their spouses, children and extended families to make Brahma feel special, and he deserved every bit of attention he was getting.

For the past five decades of his incredibly long lifespan that ran into trillions of human years, Brahma had been creating and recreating galaxies, stars and planetary systems along with numerous life forms that could strive for salvation. His efforts had resulted in the appearance of dynasties, civilizations and interstellar alliances, which was a matter of pride for him, but on the other hand, had also led to conflicts, subjugation and galactic wars which gave him a lot of heartburn, causing a sort of midlife crisis.

The celebration was a way to remember all the good work he had done and, for the first time in years, Shiva had seen a smile light up Brahma's four faces. He knew how deeply the creator god wished for someone else to take over the responsibility so that he could just spend his days lazing around on the golden lotus, listening to the divine notes of Saraswati's stringed veena but creation was a task meant for him alone just as Shiva himself was responsible for destruction.

Shiva knew that gave him a lot of heartburn. He had asked Brahma to forget all those worries and enjoy the moment by lighting up a chillum, and to his surprise the creator god had given in to his suggestion, taking a drag from each of his four mouths. He had been much better company since then and they had lost all sense of time, immersed as they were in the cosmic trance of Shiva's special concoction. In the relaxed mental state induced by the contents of the chillum, Brahma had shared with his friend the brief glimmer of hope he had felt when the Manav king Vishwamitra had audaciously dared to create a new star system. It had been a stupendous feat since even demigods were not capable of accomplishing such a task without Brahma's help. However, this was not a task for a mortal since their short lifespans made it practically impossible for them to help Brahma consistently.

Shiva turned his gaze towards the eastern end of the Himalayas, where the star of their discussion, the man who had dared to challenge the gods was meditating. He remembered the time when Vishwamitra had been conceived by means of a magical potion. The joyous moment had been mired by controversy though—Ruchik, the rishi who had prepared the potion, had divided it in two parts for his wife, Princess Satyavati and his mother-in-law, Queen Ratna.

But the latter, suspecting that her son-in-law may have saved the best portion for his own child, had convinced her daughter to exchange their potions. When Ruchik found out, he had quite understandably felt betrayed and in his anger, had decided to leave his family and head to the Himalayas. Before leaving though, he had revealed to the women the blunder they had made by doubting his integrity. The two portions had been imbibed with different character-enhancing herbs—one with those that encouraged Brahmin virtues of scholarship and the other with those that promoted aggression fit for a Kshatriya. By switching their portions, they had ensured that the queen would be giving birth to a child with scholastic tendencies while Ruchik's son would be born a warrior.

Satyavati had begged for forgiveness for she did not wish to have a combative child and her husband had finally given in to her request by making the Kshatriya trait skip one generation. Fortunately, the boon had turned out well for Prince Vishwamitra but what came out of the second part of the boon remained to be seen.

Shiva had a feeling he would have a role to play in the events that would transpire but he was glad that, for now, things seemed to be stable. On earth, the Ice Age had ended and human civilization seemed to be prospering under the leadership of Vaivasvat Manu. On the other lokas, the Asurs and Devas were also experiencing a rare phase of tranquillity after Lord Vishnu had forbidden the Asur king Bali entry into higher lokas for one whole Manvantar. Devas, Asurs and Manavs were all related to each other through Rishi Kashyap, the grandson of Brahma and the progenitor of most species populating the world, yet they seldom saw eye to eye. While Brahma had always fretted about this scenario Shiva knew that the rise and fall of different species was a way for nature to find a balance.

Bringing his attention back to Kailash, he noticed Parvati asking the children to take a dip in the Ganga to get rid of the interstellar dust and, quite predictably, Ganesh, their younger son, was throwing a good-natured tantrum. Shiva watched with a smile as Kumar, his elder son, managed to convince his brother by turning it into a competition—whoever got to the river first would get to eat from their mother's hand that night.

His heart brimmed over with love watching the mundane affairs of a householder's life and he realized that he had come a long way from Sati's death. It seemed like he had lived the life of an ascetic for almost an eternity before Parvati had come marching into his boring life and turned everything upside down. She had broken down the defences he had built around his heart with her care and affection and opened his eyes to the realization that it was possible to love again..

From an austere yogi, he had turned into a householder, looking after his family and attending functions such as the one for Brahma, and could now balance the two roles with perfect ease. Contrary to what many believed, his involvement in the functioning of the universe was not limited to destroying it alone.

Yes, he wouldn't deny that that was the highlight of his day but the dance of destruction, the Tandav, was not enacted just at the end of Brahma's day; rather it was taking place every single moment as one grain of time turned into another and the old gave in to the new. Destruction and creation existed in tandem and each depended on the other for it to become possible. For the same reason, Shiva made sure he helped one or the other species of life at regular intervals with a benediction that could keep the process running.

He knew he would have to intervene in the life of the yet-to-be born grandchild of Satyavati and Ruchik as well but till then, he would let life take its own course. A lot had to happen before the Brahmin child with the destiny of a Kshatriya could come into this world and he felt a frisson of excitement run through his chakras.

He was the Supreme Yogi Shiva, the perfect householder Shankar, the easily pleased Bholenath, yet it was his fierce Rudra avatar that would get expression through this yet-to-be-born child and he loved the chance it provided for him to get rid of all his anger.

Shiva, the destroyer of the world, was ready for the next adventure.

Ruchik

Adhyaye 1

Kanyakubja was flushed with the faint light of the winter sun.

Satyavati, the queen regent of Mahodayapur, sat inside her spacious chamber that was illuminated by the numerous brass lamps that adorned the alcoves. Wrapped in a shawl made of the finest wool from Kashyap-mir, she held a manuscript in her hands that she had been working on. As a child she had loved listening to the stories of her ancestors, narrated by her father and grandfather. Now that she was the eldest in the family the responsibility for continuing the tradition fell on her shoulders. And though she regularly regaled the children in the palace with the anecdotes and legends of the Chandravanshis, she wished to put them down for posterity in case her memory failed in the years to come.

Her bronze skin glowed in the light of diyas that lit the chamber as well as her deep brown eyes as she reflected on what she had been able to achieve in the past years. She had performed her job in accordance with her now-deceased parents' wishes and as a result, Mahodayapur was the strongest kingdom in this part of Nabhi-varsh today.

Her brother Vishwarath, nay Vishwamitra as he was called now, had renounced the kingdom and retired to the eastern forests of Kamarupa, away from the political games of northern part of the country that they colloquially referred to as Aryavarta, and she didn't blame him for it. She herself had felt tempted to leave everything and move on to the next phase of life prescribed by the scriptures—Vanprasth, living as a renunciate in the forest, but her son Yamdagni, the principal advisor to the king, would have none of it.

Vishwamitra had been fond of military conquests. However, when she became the regent, Satyavati had realized that Mahodayapur would prosper more through peacetime alliances that would allow the neighbouring kingdoms to think of it as an ally rather than an overbearing big brother. She had helped strengthen trade relations with the mountain kingdoms right up to Gandhar while simultaneously promoting the use of river transport for the rapid delivery of goods from far-off places.

River Gomati, which formed the eastern boundary of the kingdom and separated it from the dense Naimish forest, had been notorious for its frequent floods even in her father's time. But Satyavati had reined it in by means of embankments and subsidiary channels that distributed surplus floodwater to the arid regions of Mahodayapur, giving the river the sobriquet of Kaushiki in honour of her clan father Kusha. With all these accomplishments under her belt, she thought, it was time to let others do their job now.

Closing her eyes, she replayed the events of that fateful evening, when Ruchik had left her in a huff after learning that she and her mother had switched the potions. Even after all these years, she hadn't been able to forget him completely. A random piece of conversation, a stray fragrance wafting through the window or a vague resemblance with one of the court members had the power to remind her of him and break her concentration. She had tried her best to bury his memories though, focusing her attention on the huge responsibility that lay on her shoulders and gradually things had settled down.

Vishwamitra had attained the enviable position of a Brahmarishi by sheer force of will and now his eldest son, Deval, had been crowned king. It was on his coronation day that Satyavati had resolved to wash her hands off the affairs of the kingdom, deciding that she had done enough as queen regent and deserved a life of quiet and peace with the household.

Since her brother's sons were grown-up men now, she was hoping that her own son, who was the same age as Vishwamitra, would start a family soon. Oh, how she would love to have the Rani Mahal echo with the pitter-patter of tiny footsteps running around the halls and the sound of children's gibberish. She smiled involuntarily at the thought and decided to nudge Yamdagni and his wife towards family life. Putting the parchment down on the ornate teak table beside her bed, she clapped her hands twice.

Satyavati wasn't an arrogant woman but she didn't hesitate to use the power that her status accorded her. How else could she command respect from others? She had become a single mother as well as guardian to a young prince-in-waiting when her husband and then her brother left the kingdom, and both these positions made her vulnerable in a predominantly patriarchal society. Making bold decisions that benefited the kingdom, she had managed to gradually create an aura around her that commanded immense respect from her subjects.

Two maids came running into her chamber, bowed low and waited for her orders. She asked one of them to request Yamdagni to visit her as soon as he was done with his court duties for the day. Her son was the principal advisor to the king, and since the king in question was still a teenager, his duties didn't quite end there. That done, Satyavati sent the other maid to fetch her daughter-in-law, Renuka.

Renuka's arrival was announced shortly after and as she looked at her, Satyavati noticed again how beautiful her daughter-in-law was. The princess from the central kingdom of Mahur, had a milk-white complexion that contrasted her own son's dusky hue. She was slightly shorter than the average height of women of Mahodayapur but was extremely pretty, with green eyes and long silken hair. Her petite form was draped in a glossy mustard sari with a profusion of mango motifs embroidered on it in rich red silk. Her mischievous smile gave her the appearance of a teenager and Satyavati couldn't help but smile on seeing her honest face. She bade her to enter and watched as the young bride almost ran to her.

Touching her mother-in-law's feet, Renuka gushed, 'Pranam, Rajmata, it's such an honour to have you back in the Rani Mahal! I was dying a slow death in the monotonous humdrum of palace life with nothing but social calls and pretence. It will be fabulous to have your stimulating company now.'

Satyavati laughed at her candour and said light-heartedly, 'Well, I am not sure how stimulating my company would be for a young girl like you but yes, I'm glad to be back in the Rani Mahal myself. By the way, if you wish to spend time with me, you will have to do away with the formalities of title and call me Mother and help me in a matter of great importance for me.'

Renuka agreed to the suggestion happily, 'It would be my pleasure, nay good fortune, to address you as Mother, for all of Nabhi-varsh knows of your achievements and the prosperity that your guardianship has ushered in for the kingdom of Mahodayapur. I would love to learn from you and help you in any way possible!'

Satyavati saw the excitement on Renuka's face and patted her cheek affectionately, 'All right, now calm down, child, let's sit comfortably and I'll show you what I have been working on.'

Leading her to the table where the parchment lay, she asked her to take a look. The sentences, written in perfect Brahmi, detailed the earliest origins of the lunar dynasty that Satyavati and Yamdagni belonged to, and Renuka read them out loud, 'The history of the illustrious House of the Moon began with a scandal that shook Devalok.' She was surprised by what she read and said excitedly, 'Mother this sounds deliciously interesting!'

Satyavati gave a full-throated laugh. She found Renuka's forthrightness refreshing after the doublespeak of bureaucrats and courtiers that she had got used to. She urged her to carry on reading and the princess sat down on the plump couch besides the table and continued, 'In the beginning of time, Srishti-Karta Brahma created the four Kumars followed by the ten Manas-putras, born from his thoughts. Thereafter he created the Asurs, Devas and finally the first man Manu and his wife Shatarupa, whose granddaughter Anasuya was married to Rishi Atri, one of the original ten sons of Brahma. The two established an ashram at Chitrakoot and in due course of time Anasuya gave birth to three sons—the Avatar Dattatreya, Rishi Durvasa and, most important from our perspective, the handsome Chandrama, who was made the lord of the moon and became the scion of the lunar dynasty.'

Renuka was entranced by the story and asked her mother-in-law, 'As interesting as it is, Mother, I want to know what made you start writing this history.'

Satyavati explained, 'For thousands of years the history of various clans that inhabit our glorious nation has been passed on by word of mouth. However, I have a feeling that in times to come we will require more concrete evidence to support the stupendous achievements of our ancestors. I have therefore been trying to put down the history of Chandravansh in this manuscript. If it interests you, I would like you to assist me in this endeavour.'

The princess nodded eagerly, 'I would be honoured to help you with this task! Since I am a Suryavanshi, it would be good for me to know more about the dynasty I have married into as well.'

Satyavati was glad she would have assistance to accomplish this massive task and realized that Renuka's company would help keep the atmosphere light as well, 'Thank you, child, it would be a big help for me since I do not want this chronicle to be written by the court scribes who tend to exaggerate the achievements of the past and downplay its shortcomings. I want it to be a historically accurate manuscript from which future generations can learn their true history.'

A deep baritone broke into their discussion, 'Well, what is history but the variation of facts by the victorious and the self-sympathizing delusions of the defeated!'

The women turned around to see Yamdagni standing at the doorway with a wide smile on his handsome face. Renuka ran to her husband to hug him but stopped short when she remembered she was in the presence of her mother-in-law. Instead, she coyly took his hand and brought him into the chamber. Satyavati had noticed the impulsive action and smiled inwardly; she hadn't been fortunate enough to live a life of marital happiness but was content seeing her son and daughter-in-law revel in that bliss.

Yamdagni looked refined in the blue garments of a courtier with a matching turban on his head, and a single string of silver beads adorning his neck. He had Ruchik's grey-blue eyes but his face, with its aquiline nose and high forehead, resembled Satyavati's own. Rigorous practice of yoga kept him fit and he looked a lot younger than his thirty-five years.

He came forward to touch Satyavati's feet and said, 'I got your summons, Mother, and tried to come as soon as I could. Is something the matter?'

Satyavati shook her head and, instead of answering, took both of them by hand to the small shrine of Lakshmi–Narayan in the north-east corner of her room. Making them sit in front of the deities, she recited the 'Narayan-kavach', a protective charm, to safeguard her two loved ones. Finishing the recitation, she applied a little smudge of kohl on both their foreheads, 'May Shri Hari Vishnu protect my children from all physical, mental and spiritual misfortunes.'

Yamdagni wasn't a superstitious man but tolerated his mother's quirks without complaint. If it gave her heart comfort, what was the harm in letting her apply a black dot on his temple? Holding her hand in his, he said, 'Don't worry, Mother, with you by our side no one would dare look upon us with an evil eye. You are our very own personalized version of Goddess Durga!'

Satyavati made a mock expression of ferocity at him and turning to Renuka, asked her to wait while she went to her boudoir and brought back a necklace of rubies from her own collection. Her daughter-in-law's face glowed at seeing the beautiful piece of jewellery and Satyavati made her put it on.

'A Chandravanshi princess should dress the part,' she said and gave Renuka the matching earrings set in gold. 'These will go so well with the outfit you are wearing.'

Renuka put them on excitedly, looking at her husband for approval. Yamdagni smiled and nodded in appreciation. However, when Satyavati presented him with an intricately carved silver bracelet embedded with emeralds he complained, 'Your gifts are priceless, Mother, but you know I am not too fond of jewellery. These adornments befit the queen regent and her daughter-in-law much more than a commoner like me.'

Satyavati hushed him with an admonition, 'My dear son, no matter how much you act like a common courtier, not even you can stop me from gifting my personal collection to my own children. It wouldn't hurt to wear a little more than what you are comfortable with for the upcoming wedding in Mahishmati where our entire extended clan will be present, ready to pass judgement on each other.'

Yamdagni laughed at her statement and said with a wink, 'Don't worry, Mother, we'll take care to keep up appearances in front of the relatives and won't give you any reason to complain. The fact that it will take us away from Kanyakubja for a month certainly makes me happy for Renu has been begging me to take her some place out of Mahodayapur!'

'As you should,' Satyavati said giving him a light cuff on the ear. 'Our dear Renu will also get to meet her father there, so it would be a good holiday for all of us. By the way, to keep you abreast of what's happening in the Rani Mahal, I have asked her to help me with writing down the history of our dynasty and, now, I want to ask you to write its future.'

Yamdagni looked confused, so she elaborated with a sigh, 'My dear son, though you are so well versed with court gibberish, when it comes to understanding social innuendo you are extremely slow. No history can be complete without the future generations looking back upon it. So, before I finish this chronicle, let me make it very clear that I wish to see my own grandchildren playing around my feet!'

Renuka blushed and Satyavati took her hand in hers, 'I know you both have consciously delayed expanding your family because of Yama's court duties, but now that his cousin Deval has come of age and is capable of discharging his kingly responsibilities, it is time you both turned attention to your own household.'

The two nodded sheepishly and Satyavati smiled with relief. She had had a difficult journey beginning with her unexpected marriage to Ruchik, his unceremonious departure from her life and the unwanted responsibilities of regency, but at last she was free to spend the rest of her days the way she wanted to.

There was no room for sudden surprises in her life now.

Adhyaye 2

Far away from the pleasant weather of Kanyakubja and its cheerful royal family, a middle-aged hermit sat in the shelter of his cave.

He was generally in a deep meditative state at this hour, but today he sat observing a blizzard covering the landscape in snow, like a funeral shroud. The few standing conifers visible from his vantage point had already begun resembling huge stalagmites while the entrance to the cave was lined by long spikes of ice that reminded him of the fangs of a giant beast.

Maruts, the storm gods, seemed to be in a frisky mood today, uprooting and tossing small trees in the wind for their friend Vayu to play with. It would be at least another month before he could feel the warmth of Surya at this high altitude. Not that he craved it. His yogic powers provided complete control over his internal environment and he sat comfortably despite the freezing temperature outside.

He was a siddha, the wielder of mystical powers called siddhis that had been attained through years of severe penance fuelled by the anger he had felt at his wife's betrayal. It had been thirty-five samvatsars since he had walked out of the royal palace of Kanyakubja, leaving behind his wife and newborn son. His disillusionment with the world of men had been absolute and he had decided to distance himself from the realm of eternal lies and fraternal ties. Yet, lately, his thoughts had been meandering towards his family repeatedly.

Years of solitude had made his heart immune to the caprices of human emotion and the futility of filial bonds. Ironically, they had also opened his eyes to his own unfulfilled obligations towards the family he had left behind for that was a debt he had to clear if he wished for true salvation. He had come so far away from habitation to embark on a journey of self-discovery and now that he had attained mastery over the physical existence and even gained access to the Bow of Vishnu from Indra, he felt compelled to free himself of his karmic duties as well.

Over the decades spent in the cave, Ruchik's hair had grown matted and a thick grey beard framed his face giving him a wise, sagacious look. His dusky complexion had turned pale due to lack of sunlight and his skin glowed with the inner fire of tapas. He scratched his short nose absent-mindedly, while looking thoughtfully at the swirling snow and contemplating his return to the world of men. His mind was free from all attachment yet his conscience gnawed at his heart. With his understanding of the cycle of karma, he had realized that a householder's responsibility could not be shed by taking up the garb of an ascetic. A man who wished to pursue the path of austerity like he himself did shouldn't get married, for it became unfair to his family when he took up abstinence later. And if the importance of spiritual pursuit dawned on men in the later part of life, it behoved them to make proper arrangements for their family's well-being before departing on their journey.

Ruchik did not feel guilty on that account, for he had left Satyavati and their son in the familiar comforts of Kanyakubja with the entire royal family in attendance. Yet, he knew that though his anger at the time had been justified, abandoning Satyavati, who had loved him with all her heart at the time when she had needed him the most was definitely not. She had taken his desertion to heart, steeling herself to look after the kingdom instead, pushing her own grief to the back of her mind. And she had taken care of Kanyakubja and her own family exceptionally well, Ruchik reflected with considerable pride.

But he knew there were practical things he had missed being a part of. He hadn't been there to hold her hand and provide support while she looked after their only child. He wasn't able to witness with his own eyes the first steps that his son took on his own or be the first one to hear his unintelligible words, or watch him read his first complete sentence with joy. He would never be able to retrieve these moments however hard he tried, but through his yogic powers, he had become aware of his son's unsaid questions about the absence of his father and his anger at Ruchik for forsaking him on the very day of his birth. Ruchik longed for an opportunity to tell Yamdagni how proud he was of all that he had achieved and the way he had taken over the responsibilities of managing the kingdom. For even from his remote perch in the Himalayas, he had followed Yamdagni's progress diligently, starting with the early palace life to the arduous routine of Dattatreya's ashram along with his friend and uncle Vishwarath. As they grew he had observed with satisfaction the camaraderie between the two boys who were connected by the bond of magic he himself had created through the potion that had been shared between their mothers. He had witnessed Vishwarath break the shackles of his Kshatriya upbringing as the potion's magic began taking hold and watched him attain the title of Brahmarishi Vishwamitra.

His own son had taken on the onus of managing the kingdom with great equanimity and had been mentoring Vishwamitra's son after the Brahmarishi had left the world of the men to follow his own journey. The effect of Ruchik's potion would soon become visible in Yamdagni's wife as well for the magic had been staggered by one generation. Ruchik knew his grandson would equal, if not surpass, Vishwamitra in his achievements and would need his mentorship to fulfil his destiny.

Rishi Dattatreya, Yamdagni's guru, had blessed Satyavati to become the grandmother of an avatar. That powerful benediction would surely manifest in the child that would be born to Yamdagni. Ruchik had to make sure that this boon came to fruition in a manner that was beneficial to mankind. He wished to impart to his grandson all that he had learned about the mysteries of the universe, the workings of the material world and the dharma of a man towards his society. He wanted to give him a proper foundation so that he could face his future with more preparation than he might otherwise get.

There was another reason for his thinking of heading back towards Kanyakubja. As his mystical capabilities had grown, he had become more attuned to the intricate world around him and had observed disturbing vibrations coming out of the central heartlands. Even though the rest of the country seemed to be flourishing, there was a large area in the middle of Nabhi-varsh that was giving off a dark aura. The area was a dense forest inhabited by wild animals and a few primitive tribes, so he had ignored it for some time. Now, however, with his own family on its way to Mahishmati, he couldn't rid his mind of the nagging doubt that something was amiss.

Focusing his yogic vision on the huge Chandravanshi boats that were gracefully floating southwards on the River

Charmanvati, more commonly known as the Chambal, he saw his son and daughter-in-law trying on outfits for the wedding while Satyavati sat in her room meticulously writing something on a parchment.

The vessels would conduct the royal passengers to the point of origin of the river from where they would be continuing the trip by road in the royal chariots sent by the king of Mahishmati. Ruchik realized that he would have to time his visit to coincide with their return to Kanyakubja. He would keep a watchful eye on them till they safely returned and confront them only when they were back in the comfort of their home.

It would be a challenging journey for him—not in physical terms for he could arrive at Kanyakubja with the speed of thought thanks to his siddhis. The difficult part would be to finally come face-to-face with the family he had left behind. He didn't know how his wife would react to his return or how his son would deal with this stranger who claimed to be his father; but he knew he had to make amends before he left this body.

True redemption could only be achieved when one accepted the future consequences of one's past mistakes and did whatever was required to fulfil one's obligations. No matter how far one travelled, one had to come back home at the end of the journey.

It was time for Ruchik as well to head back to Kanyakubja and face his demons.

Adhyaye 3

Situated on the banks of the gentle Narmada, the city of Mahishmati was celebrating the marriage of its Yadav prince Arjun with the Naga princess Manorama.

The city was ancient, having been settled long ago in the mists of time when Asurs from the lower lokas had managed to subdue the indigenous human population. It had been the capital of Mahish-Asur, the tyrannical Minotaur, who had established dominion over the region and obtained the boon of invincibility against the males of any species. Mercifully, the gods devised a way to circumvent the boon by combining their energies, and giving form to Goddess Durga, a female force. After a fierce battle, in which the goddess vanquished the demon, she returned the city to the humans.

Currently, it served as the capital of Haiheya Yadavs, who had tamed the tribal populations, and carved out the Chandravanshi kingdom of Avanti. Kirtivirya, the king of the land, watched in satisfaction as his son Arjun and his bride took the customary seven rounds around the holy fire. Queen Padmini, Kirtivirya's wife, had undertaken special fasting during Ekadashi in a leap year and their son had been the result of her severe austerities. Kulguru Garga Muni had even predicted that the boy had the birth chart of a future Chakravarti or universal monarch!

Kirtivirya turned to look at his wife who sat next to him, proudly watching her son step into the next phase of his life. Arjun had inherited her almond eyes, orange-tinged hair, round face and softly contoured nose that sat above thin lips, and Kirtivirya's own robust skin tone, broad forehead and high cheekbones.

The Haiheyas were a proud martial clan. They had become the rulers of Mahishmati after many brutal wars involving the primitive yet ferocious tribal clans of the region that claimed their descent from the Asurs. A few of their leaders were also attending the wedding as guests. Though their outward appearance was no different from that of other men, Kirtivirya knew their religious beliefs were poles apart and involved the dark arts, voodoo, frequent animal—and sometimes, even human—sacrifices! Thankfully, the banks of the Narmada had been rid of the barbarians by his ancestors but even today one or the other clan would attack the border towns and kidnap young children to be used as sacrificial offerings. Kirtivirya had made it his personal agenda to end their nuisance once and for all and, with the help of his son, had managed to push them to the land beyond the River Tapti.

Even today, various species of semi-divine beings thrived on earth in harmony with the humans—the Yakshas around Indrakeel in the Himalayas; Centaurs around the North Pole; Kinnars along Lake Mansarovar; the notorious Vanars of Kishkindha; the Gandharvs of the central forests; and Asur tribes suspected to survive in small pockets inside Dandak-Aranya, the forest that extended southwards up to the River Krishna.

Kirtivirya's thoughts returned to the present as the ceremony got over and the newly-weds walked towards him and Padmini to seek their blessings. Urging his son and daughter-in-law to make sure they individually met each of the invited guests, the king started to mingle with the visiting dignitaries while Queen Padmini saw to the dinner arrangements. The innovative cooks of Avanti had prepared a special menu for the occasion which included delicacies like grilled mahseer fish with mushroom sauce, smoked peacock dressed with its plumes, venison cooked in honey, belly of porcupine and roasted slices of wild boar. For vegetarians there were crisp mixed-grain chapattis, panch-mel lentils, chickpea and cashew gravy, cottage cheese dumplings, various kinds of curries, mango–capsicum salad and assorted sweetmeats. A delectable collection of fruit wines was being passed around and everyone seemed to be in a relaxed state. Once the Vedic chanting stopped, an orchestra of flautists, drummers and veena maestros began playing an uplifting rhythm that put everyone in a further good mood.

Moving along the assembled gathering, Kirtivirya spotted Satyavati, the queen regent of Mahodayapur, engaged in an animated conversation with the matriarch of Vidarbha and the princess of Nishadh. A young couple stood behind them politely and he recognized the girl as the daughter of King Prasenjeet of Mahur which was a protectorate of Avanti.

He requested the guests from Kanyakubja for an audience which they gladly complied with. Introductions were made and Kirtivirya expressed his gratitude to all of them for coming so far for the wedding, 'My lady, we are blessed to have you and your family here to grace the wedding of our son. I am sure Arjun would be honoured to receive your benediction as well and glad to meet his elder cousin who has been creating a name for himself in the spiritual circles of Aryavarta. I also welcome beloved Renuka, your daughter-in-law, whose father is a dear friend of mine.'

As Satyavati and Renuka smiled in acknowledgement, Yamdagni replied, 'My lord, the good fortune is ours, for who doesn't know of the great deeds that you and my brother have achieved! You are extending the beacon of civilization deeper into the heartland and showing the forest clans a better way to live. That is a truly commendable feat and not only Aryavarta but all of Nabhi-varsh admires your bravery.'

Kirtivirya gave a slight nod in acknowledgement and said, 'Well, my son, not everyone believes in our cause and many complain we are wiping out the ancient way of life of the forest dwellers. But the presence of the princess of Nishadh is evidence of our good relations with forest tribes. My agenda is only against those who follow inhuman practices. I firmly believe that the primitive way of life of the Asur followers needs to be changed so that even they can benefit from the advancements our culture can provide.'

Satyavati added her view to the discussion, 'You do have a point, Maharaj. I have personally seen how barbaric these nomadic tribes can be. I remember an attack on Kanyakubja from across the Hindu Kush, when I was but a young girl, that was fortunately thwarted by my father and his allies. These men live like nomads, pillaging cities, destroying citadels, maiming cattle, raping women and killing everyone who doesn't subscribe to their beliefs. Surely, it is in the benefit of entire humanity that they be shown a more humane way of life!'

The king nodded, 'I sure hope so, my lady. If I may be candid with you, this wedding itself is an effort in that direction. The Nagas thriving in these forests have a rich and ancient history and their culture is derived from the serpent kings of yore whom they still worship. They follow a different way of life than the Asurs and in order to lead them away from the dark traditions and bring them closer to us, I decided to seal an alliance with the Naga king Karkotak by getting our children married. This will also help consolidate our position and provide aid against the barbarians.'

Satyavati and Yamdagni lauded his efforts and after requesting the three to bless the newly-weds, the hosts gracefully took their leave to meet other guests. The visitors from Kanyakubja, exhausted after meeting so many distant relatives in one night, made their way towards the couches that had been thoughtfully placed around fire kilns that provided warmth.

When they had made themselves comfortable, Renuka turned to Satyavati, 'Mother, how exactly are we related to the Haiheya Yadavs? I know they are also Chandravanshis but I don't understand the relation between the royal family of Kanyakubja and the Yadavs completely.'

Satyavati, the soon-to-be chronicler of dynasties, smiled and said, 'Your confusion is well warranted for we are not related to the Yadavs by any direct familial ties. It is because of the distant connection Yamdagni's father has with Kirtivirya's family that I refer to them as cousins. Rishi Ruchik's elder stepsister Devyani was married to the Chandravanshi king Yayati and the Yadavs are her descendants.'

Even though Satyavati had answered the question in a neutral tone, Yamdagni's face became red at the mention of his father and he looked away. Renuka sensed his discomfort and changed the question, 'Oh, all right, but tell me, Mother, why have these tribal clans been allowed to retain their barbaric lifestyle even in this age of advancement? When the northern, southern, eastern and western kingdoms of Nabhi-varsh are well civilized, how then, do these central forests remain in the grip of Asurs even today?'

Satyavati wrapped her shawl tightly around the shoulders against the mildly chilly wind and began narrating, 'Well, my child, this is not a new phenomenon; in fact it harks back to the beginning of time with the birth of the solar dynasty. Like the good storyteller that I hope to be one day, I'll begin with the background before plunging into the actual story, provided you have the patience to withstand my monologue.'

Yamdagni grinned and Renuka nodded encouragingly, so she continued, 'You know that Vaivasvat Manu, the son of Surya Dev is the Manu for the current age. He was blessed with nine sons and the eldest of these, the god-fearing Ikshvaku was the progenitor of the branch of the Suryavansh that rules from Ayodhya. However, as is so often observed in royal families, one of Ikshvaku's sons, Danda, lost the proverbial path and developed a fascination for the dark arts.

'Because of his interest in what was forbidden in the scriptures, Ikshvaku banished Danda from the kingdom. Consequently, Danda took refuge in the densely forested central regions, where, unfortunately, he came in contact with the Asur tribes and got the opportunity to learn the dark arts directly from their guru, Shukracharya, who was more than willing to spread that knowledge among humans!'

Yamdagni and Renuka listened attentively while Satyavati carried on, 'As soon as he had mastered the craft, Danda started practising it on the forest tribes to control their minds and very soon founded his own kingdom, with its capital at Janasthan.'

Satyavati shook her head sadly and said, 'Poor King Ikshvaku could never have imagined that exiling his son would turn out to be so counterproductive. He requested the help of his grandfather Surya to set things straight who thought of an innovative way to teach his bratty great-grandson a lesson. Like any other spot on earth, Janasthan fell right under the Sun once every day and Surya, who ruled that star, decided to burn the place to ground by focusing its rays on the location every time it passed below his line of vision.

'But Danda's mind was so consumed by his newly acquired powers that when he heard of his father taking Lord Surya's help, he decided to destroy the Sun himself, forgetting that the deity of that star was his own great-grandfather. Using dark magic, he created a huge reflecting surface that would bounce the Sun's rays right back on itself and destroy Surya's chariot. Seeing his hubris, Surya decided to finish off the arrogant prince once and for all and sent out a flare that rotated the mirror around, converging the heat on the precise spot where Danda stood, vaporizing him and his city in an instant!'

'Incredible!' Yamdagni said with amazement. 'That would have been a sight to behold.'

Satyavati agreed with a sombre nod, 'It must have been, but the darkness didn't stop with Danda's death. His spirit permeated the forest around, turning it into a breeding ground for Asurs and a hostile environment for his father's men. That is the reason the Suryavanshis have never been able to breach this forest and it's a matter of pride for Chandravanshis that Kirtivirya and Arjun have taken the onus and managed to spread the light of civilization in this region.'

They were interrupted by the arrival of Renuka's father and they spent the next prehar catching up and sharing the latest news from their two kingdoms. While Satyavati and Renuka were busy with his father-in-law Yamdagni got up to take a short walk, his thoughts on his distantly related cousin. Arjun seemed to be a confident young man and Yamdagni was sure the alliance with the Nagas would help the Haiheyas strengthen their position in the region dramatically. The Naga king was also mingling with the guests though he did not seem as happy as Kirtivirya had been.

Yamdagni didn't know what the reason could be but he knew it was a good thing that the ambitious prince of Avanti would have his hands full with the barbarians on their southern border; that would keep Mahodayapur and its protectorates out of his line of sight.

Adhyaye 4

Renuka's room was a spacious chamber on the fifth floor of the Rani Mahal, overlooking the manicured front garden and its colourful fountains. Beautiful filigree cupolas housed potted plants, and ornamental lamps hung from the ceiling. The marble floor was inlaid with precious jewels, and silken drapes in varying shades of peach and cream dressed the windows. This was where Renuka spent a lot of her time, playing with her pet parrots, painting landscapes and chatting with other royal women who came to visit her.

They had come back from Mahishmati the previous night and she had been helping Satyavati settle down after the rigours of the long journey. She returned from her mother-in-law's quarters carrying the manuscript they had been working on, to find her husband waiting for her. Yamdagni lay sprawled on the bed diagonally, with a thick shawl covering his athletic frame, amidst all the jewellery that his wife had left about while unpacking.

'What's wrong?' she asked with concern. 'Are you not feeling well?' The days had turned cooler and evenings were especially chilly. Had he caught a cold on the journey back, she wondered.

Yamdagni shook his head. 'I'm perfectly fine; just relishing the cold northerly winds while waiting for you to join and give me warmth,' he said with a wink. 'What's so interesting in my mother's chamber that occupies your entire day, my beloved wife? I hope one of those handsome, brawny, security guards hasn't caught your fancy.'

Renuka laughed at the suggestion and replied with a twinkle in her eye, 'My dear husband, it's the scandalous history of *your* dynasty that has caught my fancy more than the thought of starting a scandal of my own.'

Brandishing the manuscript in front of his eyes she declared, 'Mahamantri Yamdagni, I cannot believe you kept all these titillating stories hidden from me! Let me read to you what Mother dictated today.' She flopped on to the bed by his side and started reading, 'Chandra, the youngest son of Atri and Anasuya, was extremely handsome and his good looks caught the fancy of not one or two but twenty-seven of Daksha's daughters.'

'He sounds like some really good eye candy!' she said with a grin.

Yamdagni knew what was coming next. Even the company of twenty-seven beautiful wives couldn't stop his glorious ancestor from eloping with Tara, the wife of Brihaspati, guru of the Devas. Apparently not just Daksha's daughters but even the star goddess couldn't resist his charms, he thought with a twinge of envy.

Meanwhile Renuka was happily chattering. 'Tara refused to go back to her husband and gave birth to a boy as beautiful as the moon himself. Brihaspati learnt of the birth of a child to his wife and wanted to claim it as his own but Chandra refused to part with the baby. The Devas intervened, which resulted in a messy situation with everyone pointing fingers at everyone else. Finally Brahma decided to mediate and ordered Tara to go back to Brihaspati, leaving the child with Chandra.

'And the gossip doesn't end here,' Renuka continued excitedly. 'This child, Budh, married Ila, the granddaughter of Surya and that is how the lunar dynasty began. What is even more interesting is that Ila was born a man and later transformed into a woman after she was cursed by Shiva! To my regret while you Chandravanshis have been living an exciting life full of debauchery, we Suryavanshis have been stuck following the rules and leading boring lives. Based on this information, *I* should be the one asking where *you* spend your entire day, my dear husband, not the other way round!' she declared with a triumphant grin.

Yamdagni gave a good laugh at this comeback and raised his hands in defeat. 'I give up! I can successfully argue about protocol and propriety with the best minds in court all day long, but even I can't afford to have a war of words with this Suryavanshi princess who happens to be my superior in intellect.'

Renuka put down the manuscript and got up to put aside the jewels she had left scattered, while Yamdagni looked on in adoration. Pointing to the ruby necklace Satyavati had given her, he said in jest, 'Renu, don't you think the central ruby in this particular piece is a different shade than the others and the earrings are a trifle different in size?'

Renuka jumped up on hearing this and after carefully scrutinizing the set, decided to put it on again. Looking at her reflection, she made a face at him in the mirror. 'Don't you go putting doubts in my head, dear husband! I trust my mother-in-law and her taste in jewellery more than your powers of observation. These ornaments are flawless and I cannot forget the look of pure jealousy in the eyes of the princess of Nishadh when she saw them!'

Her husband broke into a chuckle and said, 'Honestly, I don't understand what you women find attractive in these lumps of rock. If not cut and polished in a particular way, they would just be dull stones that no one would look at twice!'

Renuka set her latest acquisition down carefully before turning to face him with a serious look, 'But don't you see? That is exactly why they are beautiful! The skill with which these dull, lustreless lumps of rock are transformed into gems of such splendour is what makes them so special and wearing them is indeed an honour. I salute the craftsmen who have worked so hard on each of these stones, then set them in a finely detailed ensemble and created such a masterpiece. It is a valuable addition to my collection of emeralds and sapphires gifted by my father on my wedding.

'Tell me,' she asked her husband, 'why do you like collecting coins of different shapes and sizes? It's just money, is it not? So what makes one coin different from another? Isn't it the craftsmanship that makes them all different and thus treasurable?'

Not for the first time Yamdagni silently thanked King Prasenjeet for granting him his daughter. Their match had been ordained by Rishi Agastya, the famous seer, who had been passing through the kingdom of Mahur and, based on his reading of Renu's birth charts, he had advised the king to propose the match to Satyavati.

Acknowledging defeat once again and, pulling her close to him, Yamdagni said, 'Yes, my dear, as usual you are correct in your assessment while I lag behind in appreciating your thoughts. Understanding a woman is said to be one of the most difficult tasks in the world, but I am willing to attempt it for you. How about we rectify the situation by letting me spend some more time getting to know you better starting from say, right now?'

Renuka laughed merrily and cupped his face in her hands, 'And how do you propose to do that?'

He gave her a light peck on the cheek and said, 'How about starting with this?'

She blushed and said, 'Not a bad beginning, certainly,' and kissed him back.

Their affectionate embrace was interrupted by a polite knock on the door that both of them tried to ignore for as long as they could. However, the knocking became more insistent and Yamdagni had no option but to break the embrace. At Renuka's look of petulance, he momentarily held his ears in a gesture of remorse and walked towards the burnished wood doors of his room. He opened the latch to find a manservant standing on the threshold with his head bowed, 'Apologies, Mahamantri, for disturbing you after court but a guest has appeared at the royal inn and requests immediate audience with you.'

Yamdagni's brow creased in thought and he asked, 'Do you know the identity of this guest, Pramod?' He knew the names of most of his helpers and made sure he addressed them accordingly for these people were not mere servants doing the bidding of the royal household but attendants and confidantes whose loyalty to their masters was complete and absolute.

The attendant shook his head and replied, 'No, sir, I have never seen the guest before. He is dressed in the garb of an ascetic and has a fierce mane of hair. When I inquired for his introduction, he asked me to rush to you instead, stating that he has returned to the kingdom after thirty-five samvatsars and did not wish to be kept waiting any longer.'

Yamdagni was surprised. Who could this man be, returning to Kanyakubja after such a long time? Asking the attendant to respectfully bring the guest to the meeting room, he turned to Renuka who had heard the entire exchange, 'It seems some old general from my grandfather's time may have returned after spending time as a mendicant outside the kingdom. Uncle Vishwamitra wasn't too keen on retaining the old guard when he came to power and some of them had chosen to leave the city rather than live their lives in ignominy. I think it might be one of them returning home in need of help.'

His wife nodded slowly, 'Yes, that could be possible but thirty-five years ago your uncle and you were mere babies! Just to be safe, could you take a few attendants along when you go to meet him? I don't know why, but I have an uneasy feeling about this person.'

Yamdagni laughed off her concern, 'What danger could I have from a hermit, my dear? That too in my own home! I am merely the advisor to the king, not the king himself.'

Renuka replied thoughtfully, 'That may be precisely why you could be more dangerous than the king. With mother's retirement, the real power of his decisions rests in the hands of his principal advisor, you. If worse comes to worst, Deval still has two younger brothers to succeed him but I have only one husband!'

Yamdagni embraced her tightly and left the room, accompanied by two attendants. Little did he know that his wife's premonition was not due any physical danger to his life, but a portent of the emotional upheaval that he was about to face.

Adhyaye 5

After reaching Kanyakubja, Ruchik had hung around the marketplace, soaking up the sights and sounds of the city. It wasn't nostalgia that had prompted him to do so—since he had never been a city lover, choosing to live in the forest even after he was married—but the desire to get a sense of what the citizens thought about their royal family. And wandering around the gardens and bazaars, homes and offices, art establishments and arms factories, taverns and whorehouses allowed him a glimpse of the city in all its avatars, something that wouldn't have been possible had he gone directly to the palace. The ambling around had also given him an opportunity to think about the best way to approach his wife and son who clearly enjoyed a lot of appreciation from the people.

He hadn't wanted to face Satyavati right away for that would have required more courage than he currently possessed, so he had decided to meet Yamdagni, his son, first, hoping that as a grown man he would understand Ruchik's point of view better. When he heard the bells in the royal court signal the end of the day's session, he slowly made his way towards the royal inn and announced his wish to see the Mahamantri. After a brief delay he had been led to the palace where Yamdagni lived and shown into the meeting room where he now sat, nervously preparing his introduction. However accomplished a man may be in his professional endeavours, when it comes to family, especially one that he abandoned, there is no perfect way to behave when he finally comes face-to-face with them.

Yamdagni stepped into the room where the tall visitor sat facing the window, his gaze transfixed on the sky by some birds flying back home. He announced his arrival by clearing his throat and, folding his hands, addressed the hermit with the polite honorific used for people one didn't really know well, 'Namaskar, Mahanubhav!'

Ruchik turned and set eyes on his son for the first time in thirty-five years. The last time he had seen Yamdagni was on the day of his birth, that fateful day so many moons ago when he lay by his mother's side swaddled in bundles of soft muslin. The man who stood before him looked like an exact replica of his father-in-law, King Kadhi, except for the grey eyes and wavy hair, that were his own. His mouth refused to form the words his mind had so diligently practised and to cover his discomfort he blurted out a non-committal blessing for a long life, 'Ayushmaan bhava, putra.'

Yamdagni took in the fierce head of hair and the mark of Shiva on the guest's forehead along with his powerful aura. But the stranger's eyes, the same colour as his own, seemed troubled by something. Asking him to sit down on the chairs kept in the room, he requested one of the attendants to get water and fresh fruits for the guest while the other provided additional cushions to make his seat more comfortable.

Hoping to put the sadhu at ease, Yamdagni asked, 'Pardon my ignorance, Rishivar, but I do not know how to address you. I have been given to understand that you have returned to the city after many decades. Would you be kind enough to share your introduction and tell me what help you hope to receive from me?'

Ruchik had regained control over his mind by now and replied in an equable tone, 'Mahamantri Yamdagni, I left this city thirty-five years ago, the same day that you were born and my introduction will make the purpose of my return clearer. I am Ruchik, the son of Maharishi Chyavan and grandson of Maharishi Bhrigu, the great Manas-putra of Brahma.'

Yamdagni's thoughts were in a whirl as he processed the stranger's words. He swallowed hard and holding his breath asked, 'You are Rishi Ruchik, the son of Maharishi Chyavan, the husband of Devi Satyavati, the erstwhile queen regent of this kingdom?'

Ruchik nodded slowly. There seemed no better way to break it to his son than directly. 'Yes, I am Ruchik, the great-grandson of Srishti-Karta Brahma, husband of your mother Satyavati and the fire that has given birth to your flame,' he said softly.

The whispered answer however hit Yamdagni as if someone had punched him in the face. His knuckles turned white clutching the chair he sat on. As he tried to form a coherent reply, words tumbled out of his mouth, 'Why in the name of the Holy Trinity have you come back? Why after so many years?'

Though Ruchik had been dreading this question, he said with conviction, 'I have come to set right the wrongs done by me in my past. I have come here today to ask for your understanding and acceptance.'

'Acceptance! That too for the man who left me within moments of my birth?' Yamdagni asked incredulously. A cold draught entered the window and he shivered from the combined effect of the chilly wind and his own emotional turmoil.

Ruchik looked at the trembling lips and shaking hands of the man before him and knew he had upset his son to a degree he had not been prepared for. 'I am not talking about acceptance of our biological relationship,' he said in a calm tone, 'or the fact that I left you on the day of your birth. I wish for your acceptance of the circumstances that compelled me to leave and your understanding, for you are the only symbol of the love your mother and I shared.'

Yamdagni glared at the hermit with barely restrained anger, 'Forgive me, Maharishi, for I am still not that advanced spiritually that I can ignore the hurt one feels when a parent snaps all ties so unceremoniously. And I am certainly not magnanimous enough to accept that act as anything short of the heartless betrayal of a woman's love and a child's expectations!'

Ruchik began to say something but Yamdagni cut him off, venting all his pent-up emotion, 'I grew up watching Vishwamitra receive the guidance and love of both his parents while my mother became both mother *and father* for me! For a long time I didn't even know that my grandparents were *not* my own parents; it was only when I left for gurukul that my mother shared the story of your departure. I spent the years in the ashram hoping that you would return one day and admit that you had made a mistake, and reclaim your love for us but that day never came!'

Tears were streaming from his eyes and Yamdagni struggled to control his emotions. 'You come here today not begging for *forgiveness* but demanding *acceptance*! Today, when my mother has finally got respite from years of being bound by duty and is looking forward to living a life free from trouble? Today, when I myself am looking forward to becoming a father and starting my own family? Who gave you the right to intrude in our lives now and disrupt them with your sudden arrival?' He looked at Ruchik with eyes full of anger and said, 'There shall be no acceptance for you till you express repentance to my mother. Go seek her pardon, O learned sage, and then we'll see where you and I stand.'

With this final declaration, Yamdagni turned around and stormed out of the room, punching the wooden door on his way out. The resultant pain he felt in his hand was nothing compared to the mental agony he was going through. How dare this man, who had never bothered to find out how he was or what he was doing, demand acceptance! Instead of walking back to his room he turned towards his mother's chamber to warn her of Ruchik's arrival and spare her the shock of meeting him unexpectedly. He would not get the opportunity to catch her off-guard and obtain forgiveness so easily!

Adhyaye 6

Satyavati was still overseeing her unpacking when Yamdagni burst into the room. He was panting lightly and quickly gestured to the maids to leave the room. As soon as they were alone, she asked with concern, 'Yama, what's the matter? Is everything all right?'

Yamdagni led her to a comfortable chair and made her sit before he answered her question. Taking her hands in his, he knelt beside her and said softly, 'Mother, things are not quite all right, our very lives as we know them are about to change. Before I explain further, let me make it clear that not for a single moment of my life have I regretted the absence of a father for you more than compensated for it with your love and devotion.'

He looked at the ground as he finished and a tiny tendril of suspicion started creeping in Satyavati's mind. 'I appreciate that, son, but why are you suddenly saying all this today? What has happened? Why are our lives about to change?'

'A rishi who has spent the last thirty-five years in the Himalayas has come to visit us, Mother. He left Kanyakubja on the day I was born and has returned only today.'

As her heart beat faster and breathing came to a virtual

standstill, Satyavati could not believe what her son was trying to tell her. 'Yama, stop talking in riddles and tell me clearly who this rishi is!' she demanded.

'It is my father,' Yamdagni answered. 'I met him moments ago and poured out the vitriol that has been simmering inside me all my life. I asked him to beg your forgiveness before even thinking of a reconciliation with me!' He paused, giving Satyavati a chance to absorb his words, and then said, 'He might be on his way to this chamber even as we speak and I thought it best to warn you and spare you the shock that I received on seeing him. I will support you in whatever you decide but do remember that you are and will always remain both my mother *and* father as long as I live.'

Satyavati saw the torment her son was going through—he was clearly shaken by the sudden arrival of his father. Patting his head, she said, 'Thank you for the warning, my child, for I wouldn't have known how to react had he appeared in front of me all of a sudden.'

Even as she gave him confidence her own defences were breaking down. Tears sprang involuntarily from her eyes and started making their silent journey down her cheeks. She averted her gaze and continued, 'Even though meeting him might shatter whatever's left of my heart, my mind is asking me to listen to what he has to say. We are together in this, you and I, and we shall take whatever decision needs to be taken jointly. If either of us doesn't feel comfortable having him here we'll ask him to leave Kanyakubja and just let us be.'

Watching his mother exhibit so much restraint, Yamdagni reined in his own anger and nodded in acquiescence just as the visitor was announced by the maids. He got up and walked towards the bed and Satyavati took a deep breath and stiffened herself to brave what would surely turn into an ugly discussion. She asked that the guest be shown in.

Moments later, as Ruchik walked into the chamber with hesitant steps she saw the face of her husband for the first time in thirty-five years. Walls that she had built for years to protect her heart came crumbling down as she got a glimpse of his visage and unfurled a chain of memories in her mind. Memories of the time they had spent together, starting with their first quarrel where she had berated him for asking for her hand against her wishes and the way he had pacified her anger and promised to take care of her every future wish. True to his word, Ruchik had taken care of her every single desire and let her pay more attention to her parents rather than his own needs, going so far as to prepare the magic potion that would beget an heir for her father's kingdom. And yet, she couldn't forget the fact that he had left her the very day she had given birth to his child and hadn't bothered about her in more than three decades.

Ruchik took in Satyavati's greying hair, the fine lines on her face and the crow's feet around her doe eyes, but all he saw was the lovely girl he had lost his heart to all those years ago. After a moment's indecision, he asked softly, 'How are you, Satyavati?'

Satyavati gripped her son's arm, not trusting her heart to reply equitably, and Ruchik, seeing the reaction, said gently, 'I know it is a shock for you and Mahamantri to see me here today but I could not keep myself away from you any more. Three-and-a-half decades I have lived alone in the caverns of the great white mountains but there hasn't been a single day when I haven't watched over you both through my yogic vision.'

'Lies!' Yamdagni snarled. 'Mere words to compensate for your absence for all these years! When you didn't think twice before leaving us why do you spend so much time trying to justify your presence here now?'

Satyavati patted his hand and spoke, pleased with the measured tone of her voice. 'Yama, let him speak. Let us give the learned rishi a fair opportunity to tell us the story he has been fabricating for over thirty years.'

Ruchik looked at her with a pained expression and said, 'You have every right not to believe anything I say, but Shiva knows I never stopped looking after your interests. I have watched you deal with all that life has thrown at you with such strength that my heart burst with pride even from so far away. I know what you will say, that *I* should have been here to take care of the two of you, to face those challenges with you. But the sad truth is that I wasn't and that's something we will all have to accept and put behind us if we want to move on.'

When his audience didn't respond he continued, 'The anger I felt at your betrayal fuelled my mission for a long time but over the years I have lost the will to attain salvation knowing that I left my duties towards you unfulfilled. I accept full responsibility for the hardships you have faced because of my absence and I'm here to beg for your forgiveness. Whether you accept me back or not is secondary but I sincerely hope you can find it in your hearts to forgive this repentant old man who stands before you.'

Holding back the torrent of emotions that was threatening to engulf her, Satyavati said with an equanimity that belied the inner storm, 'Maharishi Ruchik, even if we were to forget the past how can you expect us to contemplate a future with *you*? Abandoning us wasn't the first time you acted without thinking of the consequences of your actions and it certainly wouldn't be the last!'

Ruchik understood her unspoken words: he had asked for Satyavati's hand in marriage without knowing her own wish in the matter and later abandoned her in a moment of anger; what guarantee did they have that if they accepted him into their lives today he wouldn't leave them again in a fit of rage in the future?

Satyavati pushed her point further, 'You left my son and me at a time when we were most vulnerable and now you come here seeking forgiveness without considering the effect your sudden appearance would have on us!'

'Satyavati,' Ruchik broke in softly, 'I am fully cognizant of the effect my arrival has had on both of you. But please know that it hasn't been an easy decision for me either. My very presence here today shows my honest desire to reconcile with my family; there is nothing else for me in this city.'

He looked at both of them earnestly and pleaded for the last time, 'I have no desire to be sucked into the quagmire of worldly affairs once again. I don't require financial assistance or protection or food for as a hermit I can subsist solely on the merit of my tapas. Yet, I have come here so that you can find peace in your heart and forgive me, and if not, at least we all can get some closure.

'I do not expect an immediate response from you. I shall wait outside the city for however long a period you require to think matters through. The decision of the queen regent and the mahamantri of Kanyakubja will be final and I shall respect it but I fervently hope that my wife and son will set aside their suspicion and try to understand the motivation behind my return.' With that Ruchik turned around and strode out of the chamber.

As the door shut behind the departing figure of her husband Satyavati was reminded of the first time he had left. She had lost him then due to her own mistake but if she let him go today it would be just to spite him and get even. She looked at Yamdagni and saw a softening in his features as if Ruchik's words had made an impression on him. There was no denying the fact that Ruchik *had* left them to pursue his own spiritual ambition, but it wasn't as if he had forsaken them in the middle of the forest with no one to look after them. He had also forgiven her transgression and promised to remedy the effect of the potion on her own son and shifted it from Yamdagni to his yet-to-be-born child, thereby lightening the burden of her guilt. And in all honesty, it was this very benediction that had helped her brother Vishwamitra strive to become a Brahmarishi. Life was giving her another chance—was it too late for her to atone for her mistake and secure the fulfilment that Yamdagni had subconsciously craved all his life?

If Ruchik *had* followed the events in their lives, it meant that he still cared for them. What other reason could he have for coming back today and facing their anger? It would have been much easier for him to never return, to disappear from their lives completely instead. Yet, he had not done that.

The one question that was swirling in her mind now was: Could one really stay away from their loved ones for an entire lifetime?

Adhyaye 7

Ruchik felt equally shaken by the encounter with his family. There were thoughts he hadn't been able to articulate and feelings he couldn't express in front of them since he had spent the last three decades cultivating a self-image of invincibility, trying to protect himself from the reactions of those who thought of him as a deserter. But he hoped in his heart that they would sense the sincerity in his words and find the courage to gradually let go of their anger and grant him forgiveness.

He promised himself he would not enter Kanyakubja again till he was actually welcomed. Selecting a tall banyan outside the city gates, he built a small hut below it with a wave of his hand where he could spend the night and think about his future course of action. He had another reason for re-entering their lives that he had not mentioned yet.

He had a bad premonition about the times ahead of them for his perception of the Asurik forces had been building from the moment he had come closer to the Dandak forest. He could feel the dark, negative vibes emanating from the forests further south and he would need to check on them now that he was here.

His magic had been extremely potent even all those years ago when he had created a thousand horses white as the moon to fulfil Kadhi's condition for letting him marry Satyavati. They had helped catapult Kadhi's Kshatriya son into the exclusive league of Brahmarishis and he knew that the second part of his prophecy, which was yet to be fulfilled, could unravel the very fabric of society. For now, he needed to figure how the developments in the central heartland could affect his yet-to-be-born grandchild.

He closed his eyes to meditate and cleanse his self of all the negative emotions that had accumulated in the royal palace. Once that was done, he started to focus his energies on Dandak-Aranya, the wild untamed land where the dark spirit of Danda still pervaded.

Within moments his mind was transported to the forest and he could see a group of tribal folk roasting deer for dinner. Inside another hut, a mixed group of men and women was busy in a frenzied orgy. Fleeting over other banal sights of a sleepy hamlet, his gaze fixed on a tribal dressed in a dark, hooded robe kneeling in front of a huge idol of Goddess Kali.

The man, if you could call him that, was a seven-foot giant with scaly skin of a greenish hue. His ears were slightly pointed and as he turned to look around, Ruchik saw keen yellow eyes that resembled those of a predator rather than a normal human. But the creature's most fascinating feature was its short fleshy tail! Ruchik wondered what species the creature belonged to, for though it was a biped, he did not seem to have evolved from primates like humans had. This plateau region of Nabhi-varsh was much more ancient than the northern kingdoms and Ruchik knew there was a time when massive reptiles had ruled the area. Even today, one could find gigantic fossilized eggs of the monsters known as Sharabhs, and there was talk of some of them still roaming deep inside the forests.

Since the existence of such terrible lizards couldn't be kept hidden for long, Ruchik doubted the veracity of the claims; but for some reason, this creature reminded him of them and he concluded that it must have evolved from a reptilian ancestor. Sifting through the various species in his mind he hit on an identity that matched with that of the creature—it was an Urag, a species that had emerged from cross-breeding the Nagas with the Asurs.

Ruchik watched in amazement as the Urag took out a sharp dagger from his robe, and in a sudden movement, chopped off a finger from his right hand! The creature's face contorted in pain as greenish ichor oozed from the severed joint, which he poured at the feet of the idol as an offering. The bleeding stopped soon after and Ruchik observed that the creature was already showing the emergence of a rudimentary finger where moments ago there had been a wound. This regenerative quality was a hallmark of reptilian blood and he was more than sure now that this creature was actually of Asurik origin.

Ruchik had heard of many ancient tribes that practised self-mutilation, yet seeing it happen with his own eyes was a different experience. The creature looked at his regrowing digit with satisfaction and rapidly moved through the forest to join another one of his kind, presumably for their daily discussion. Most of their conversation revolved around how to maintain the secrecy of what they were doing.

What could these creatures be planning that requires so much secrecy, Ruchik wondered. He decided to widen his sensory field to probe their surroundings and see if there were other creatures like this one. Sure enough, three more of his kind were performing a similar ritual at the other three cardinal points of the forest. He was surprised that these beings had escaped notice of astute rishis like Kanav whose ashrams were situated close to the Narmada. He decided to check with them once morning arrived.

Ruchik had never felt too comfortable around reptilian races and found it hard to trust them. He knew it wasn't just an individual quirk, and the revulsion most humans felt towards reptiles stemmed from an evolutionary instinct that had lodged itself firmly in the human brain. Reptiles were the most persistent predators of early mammals and their ruthless hunting had actually helped shape the development of primates, resulting in the selection of traits that helped avoid these predators. For one, the enlarged visual centre that humans possessed was a modification to readily detect a predator camouflaged among the vegetation and it had become the primary sensory organ for humans and primates thanks to the reptiles. No wonder then that the image of a serpent still evoked awe and fear in men and women.

He followed their conversation to figure out their agenda but all that he could glean from his eavesdropping was that some covert activity was being planned in Mahishmati, the seeds for which had already been sown on the day of the prince's wedding. Ruchik's brow creased with concern for it could very well be a plot to assassinate the king of Avanti who was waging an all-out war against the barbarians.

Snapping out of the trance Ruchik decided to keep track of the activities of the Urags for the next few days and try to find out whatever else he could. He also hoped his wife and son would come to a positive conclusion by morning for he would need their help to warn Kirtivirya and Crown Prince Arjun. For a second he debated whether he should have come to Kanyakubja at all! His family certainly didn't approve of his unannounced arrival and his exploration seemed to be getting him involved in something really sinister. But he was already here and turning back and leaving things the way they were was out of the question.

The only way now was forward.

Adhyaye 8

The forest of Dandak was the largest in Nabhi-varsh and stretched for thousands of miles southwards,

At its northern perimeter was Lake Payoshni, a frequent haunt of black panthers and cheetahs. Its western boundary was the Sahyadri range while its eastern limit was set by the Mahendra Mountains. The Godavari and Krishna rivers ran through its width providing nourishment to the numerous species of plants, animals and aquatics thriving in the forest. However, no kingdom, except that of the Vanars in Kishkindha was able to survive in its dense hostile environment.

Janasthan, the erstwhile capital of Danda's kingdom was a lifeless mound of rock on the western edge of the forest and extended for miles as Saptashring or the seven peaks. The peaks in question were a result of solidified heaps of ash that had accumulated when the kingdom had been burnt down by an angry Surya. The vegetation in Janasthan consisted mainly of thorns, brambles and carnivorous plants that would gobble up unsuspecting animals that were foolish enough to wander into the area.

The Urag that Ruchik had seen in his vision was on his way

to one of the peaks with another man, looking at the overhead Sun gratefully. Winter was never too severe in this part of the country, which was just as well, since he and his cold-blooded brethren needed the warmth of the Sun every now and then. The two were visiting the cavern carved in the side of the hill that now housed the last genuine surviving Asurs in Nabhi-varsh and their leader.

As they climbed upwards, the stench around the area became unbearable and the Urag twitched his tail to get rid of the flies. Piles of animal carcasses in various stages of putrefaction littered the hillside—leftovers of the meals the residents of the cave had partaken. The entrance to the cave was halfway up the hill and was guarded by two Urags who greeted the newcomers enthusiastically and showed them into the dimly lit passageway that led into the cavern.

Inside was a maze that had many dead ends and extended throughout the width of the hill. What nature had created, the Asur engineers had enhanced with their architectural skill. The heart of the mountain was the central hall that branched into numerous smaller caves visible from the entrance where the two guests now stood. The man who had accompanied the Urag was tall, dark and well built with somewhat flattened features. His tongue quickly darted in and out like that of a serpent and he looked around in wonder.

The Asurs had found an ingenious way to thrive comfortably by scooping out the interior of the mountain and inhabiting it, rather than living in dwellings on the outside that would have been visible to anyone. The cavern was lit by blazing torches that fit into the innumerable sockets that lined the walls and lent an eerie glow to the atmosphere. The walls themselves were decorated with the skulls and bones of a myriad variety of animals and birds. The most prominent display, however, was the entire preserved skeleton of a gigantic lizard at the far end of the circular hall! The man marvelled at its size and the teeth that were bigger than most swords he had seen. Beneath the monstrosity stood a throne, currently occupied by Marich, the eldest son of the fabled Asur architect and engineer Maiy who was recognized as the best architect in fourteen lokas. No wonder, the man thought, that the Asurs had been able to create such an innovative safe haven for themselves right in the heart of Nabhi-varsh. Three black panthers sat around the throne and as the guests moved forward, two of them growled at them. The man was a master of magic and knew the animals in front of him couldn't harm him but Marich patted the animals' heads to calm them down. Greeting the new arrivals in a loud sibilant voice, he said, 'Ah, so you are finally here! Welcome home, friend Shambhar, I see you have brought a guest with you today.'

The Urag bowed and said expansively, 'Lord Marich, it is always a pleasure to visit this pleasant Asur oasis in the middle of the human forest. As you had requested, I have sought the company of Nagraj Karkotak and convinced him to visit you to discuss a proposal that may be mutually beneficial.'

Marich smiled with satisfaction and said, 'Good work, my friend. This is the perfect time to strengthen our forces and prepare for the attack that is bound to come sooner or later.'

Karkotak looked at Marich appraisingly: the Asur was an impressive specimen of his kind and easily towered over him by a foot. His skin was the tinge of copper, but with fine golden scales that gave him a freckled appearance. His eyes blazed with a yellow fire but the most magnificent portion of his anatomy were the antlers that protruded from the two sides of his head, branching gloriously like the limbs of a tree and ending in razor-sharp points.

'Welcome to our humble abode, Lord Karkotak,' the Asur said. 'You may be wondering why we chose to make our existence known to the outside world by requesting your presence here but the very fact that you are here shows that I place utmost faith in you. Before we begin our discussions, which I am certain will be of immense interest to you, let us first raise a toast and hope for a fruitful partnership between us natural allies.'

Scantily clad Asur women appeared with trays bearing overflowing tumblers of frothing liquor and the motley gathering grabbed their drinks with gusto raising them high. Karkotak bowed graciously and raising his own tumbler said, 'Asurs and Nagas have shared a close bond for centuries, Lord Marich, and I trust your word. Though once I've partaken of your excellent liquor, I hope you shall divulge the purpose for this invitation as well.'

Marich gulped down his drink in one swig and gestured to Karkotak to follow him into an auxiliary chamber behind the giant reptilian skeleton. Karkotak had never been in an Asur palace before and walked around the massive tail gingerly. Hell, he hadn't even known they still existed in Nabhi-varsh! As he entered the chamber, he was momentarily stumped by its grandeur. Unlike the gory outer assembly hall, this room was decorated with glittering jewels of various hues that bounced light off its cavernous walls in a veritable rainbow of colours. Soft sensuous music filled the room and he saw three gorgeous Asur women lounging on the couch. One of them locked eyes with him and he felt as if he would be hypnotized just by staring into them.

She gestured to him with her fingers and he felt compelled to move in her direction but Marich broke his trance with a bellow of laughter, 'Veera, don't distract our guest right now, there will be time enough for him to do whatever you ask of him later. Be a dear and let us discuss a few things first.'

The siren slid off the couch with a seductive smile at Karkotak. Marich guided him towards the seat saying, 'Don't feel embarrassed, even I find it hard at times to resist the lure of our lovely ladies though I am constantly surrounded by them. Make yourself comfortable and tell me, my friend, how are things in Mahishmati and how is your lovely daughter?'

Karkotak was beginning to get a sense of where the conversation was headed and replied candidly, 'My daughter is happy as a newly-wed should be, but why don't we skip the pleasantries, Lord Marich, and come to the real reason why you have invited me here. I was completely unaware of your presence here till our mutual friend Shambhar revealed it a month after the wedding, so I am assuming that I have become important only *after* my alliance with the Haiheya Yadavs.'

Marich smiled, showing off his fangs, and decided to respond with equal candour, 'Since we are being honest let me tell you, Naga king, that I know for a fact you were not very forthcoming when your daughter's hand was sought for the Yadav prince. Much before our King Mahish established his kingdom on the banks of the Narmada, this land was inhabited by Naga tribes and after his demise, your people, who consider themselves the original residents of the region, had wanted to start your own civilization. Pity, that was not meant to be and you were displaced by the Chandravanshis who possess superior technology and more ambition than you ever had.'

Karkotak looked at the Asur with indignation at the

comparison but Marich continued regardless, 'New cities coming up along the river brought an increased influx of outsiders and the Nagas were slowly reduced to a minority in Avanti. Your people had no choice but to move east of the river and could establish yourself only with the support of the Suryavanshi kings.'

Marich knew he was right. The Nagas were grateful to the Suryavanshis for helping them in their time of need and resented the Chandravanshis for occupying the land that originally belonged to them. In fact, Karkotak had wanted his daughter to marry a Suryavanshi prince but Kirtivirya's proposal had been hard to refuse. The Asur spies had identified the Naga king's weakness and now Marich knew the key to his heart.

He smiled again and said, 'As you mentioned, Asur tribes have remained hidden for quite some time, content to live on our own, gorging on the plentiful prey available in the forest and an occasional Urag or human foolish enough to cross our path. You ask why we choose to reveal our presence now. The answer lies in Kirtivirya's agenda against the Asurik way of life. You see, it presents a bit of a problem for us since sooner or later, his army will march into the forest and even with all the spells we have been putting around the perimeter with the help of the Urags it will be difficult to stop him.

'How you come into the picture will be clear to you in a minute. Mahishmati, for all its garb of civilization does have an underbelly and I have managed to rake up the resentment against the king and his son in certain less privileged sections of society.'

He leaned in closer now and said with a hiss, 'Your daughter's marriage to Kirtivirya's son has opened up a new door for both of us. Nagas and Asurs have both evolved from reptiles—we are different branches of the same family. I am sure we shall find some common ground and successfully work out a mutually beneficial arrangement.'

Adhyaye 9

Yamdagni had been waging a war with himself, trying to assess the situation that stared him in the face.

From where he stood, he didn't see any particular merit in his father's actions. He could never imagine himself leaving his wife however grave the insult to his pride. Yet, he realized he couldn't judge his father by his own standards; Ruchik was from an older generation. Personally he couldn't care less for Ruchik's homecoming (or so he liked to believe), but what about his mother? Wouldn't it be good for her to have her husband back after all these years? He knew she hadn't forgotten him as was evident from her reaction on seeing him again. It was only because of the infinite kindness of her heart that she did not wish to drown her dear ones in her sorrow and had never talked about her loneliness with him.

He had asked for Renuka's advice since she, being a woman, was likely to be more appreciative of Satyavati's predicament. Not surprisingly, his wife advised him to at least consider letting Ruchik back into their lives for the sake of his mother's happiness. Besides, having a learned rishi like him to guide the new king would only help the kingdom prosper.

Satyavati had come to the same conclusion but for a slightly different reason. More than the king, she realized her own son would benefit from Ruchik's guidance. It was difficult to forgive but perhaps they could give time a chance to heal things enough for them to have a civil relationship with Ruchik. Once both of them had made up their minds, Yamdagni asked the difficult question: 'Who will go outside the city to invite him into the palace? Should one or both of us go or should we just send a messenger?'

Satyavati shook her head, 'No, sending a messenger will be taken as a deliberate insult and it is against the Chandravanshi way of greeting a learned rishi. Under the current circumstances, I believe our beloved Renu would be the best suited for this job!'

Yamdagni looked at her surprised but then the logic of what she proposed hit him, 'That is brilliant, Mother!'

He turned to look at Renuka who sat between them, 'If you agree my dear, it would take care of a lot of complications. Your honest exuberance would act as the perfect ice-breaker and it would also spare both of us the unwanted agony of begging him to come back to the city!'

Satyavati smiled at the last sentence and said softly, 'Yama, I know you don't want him back in our lives any more than I do but as we agreed, it would be in the best interests of the kingdom to welcome Maharishi Ruchik back into the royal household. He will have his own quarters to reside in and you would be well within your rights to refuse him an audience if he ever wished to meet you. As would I. But let's honour the Chandravanshi spirit of sportsmanship and give him a fair chance to prove his sincerity.'

Yamdagni nodded silently.

Renuka was more than happy to oblige. 'Yama, I would be more than happy to act as your messenger and welcome my respected father-in-law home. Having grown up in a large family in my father's home, I couldn't help but feel there was something missing here. But now with the return of Rishi Ruchik, I see this family becoming whole once again.'

Yamdagni beamed with pride upon hearing Renuka's words and planted a soft kiss on her forehead, 'You know we men make jokes about our wives and laugh at the servitude we have to endure but believe me when I say this'—he pointed to himself—'this is one man who doesn't for a moment regret having chosen you as his wife! I really don't know what I would do without you in my life.'

Renuka's eyes misted over and she said hastily, 'Very well, now you, smooth talker, leave us and let Mother and me prepare for the welcome of the eldest member of this family! I'll arrange for the royal chariot and an entourage of well-wishers to greet and invite him formally into the city and then ask the cooks to prepare a special meal for the occasion. Can you arrange comfortable accommodation for his residence and most importantly announce his arrival to the city? Oh, there's so much work to do!'

Yamdagni smiled at her enthusiasm and clapped his hands to summon his attendants, asking them to help the two ladies with whatever arrangements needed to be made. Bowing to them like one of the attendants himself, he left to share the news with the teenage King Deval before making the announcement in the royal court of Kanyakubja.

The news of Maharishi Ruchik's return was applauded by the entire council and by early afternoon a welcome delegation had been dispatched to escort him into the city. Ruchik arrived in the court accompanied by Renuka by the end of the prehar. As per protocol, he was welcomed by the king who washed his feet and offered him a seat next to his own onyx elephant throne while the council showered flowers on them.

A wave of nostalgia washed over Ruchik as he recalled the very first time he had come to this assembly to ask for the hand of the princess of the kingdom. King Kadhi had greeted him in a similar manner then as his grandson had done today. He still remembered how helpless he had felt when the king had demanded a thousand horses of a particular description for letting him marry the princess, and how he had managed to fulfil it with help from the lord of the oceans, Varun. He had returned to the court a second time with the horses, surprising not only Kadhi but the entire council.

Of course, that was a long time ago. The people occupying the chairs around him had changed since but the wholehearted welcome he had received from the citizens remained unchanged, Ruchik thought happily. Satyavati sat on the right of the throne in her erstwhile capacity as the queen regent, with Yamdagni to her right. Renuka sat beside her husband watching the proceedings happily.

Deval, who resembled his father Vishwamitra to a large extent in appearance as well as demeanour, addressed the gathering, 'Citizens of Mahodayapur, it is our great fortune that we have been given the opportunity to welcome such an accomplished sage into our court and receive his blessings. By the grace of Chandra Dev, he has agreed to fill the position of our kulguru which has been vacant since the passing away of Acharya Dhanu who guided my father and grandfather before me. I urge you to welcome him with folded palms and request him to sanctify our kingdom with his continual presence.'

The gathering burst into loud cries of 'Swasti, Swasti', wishing auspiciousness for the kingdom. Spring was in the air, the time for renewal and change.

Adhyaye 10

A brief summer had followed spring and life had gradually settled into a comfortable routine at Kanyakubja. The royal gardens were filled with a veritable riot of colours with orange-red gulmohar, yellow amaltas and purple jacaranda in full bloom and Yamdagni sat with his mother in the portico of her palace, taking in the view as he had done so many times as a child.

Peacocks perched majestically at one end and parakeets created a ruckus on the mango trees around it. The area was shaded from the sun by means of cane drapes and the latticed side walls supported fragrant creepers. They were waiting for Renuka who had said she had big news to share and had asked them to wait while she quickly visited the Gauri temple in the palace before meeting them here.

They sat there, watching the pre-monsoon clouds gather in the sky, discussing Deval's progress in handling the affairs of the kingdom and Ruchik's integration into the system. Satyavati asked, 'Yama, do you have any idea what Renuka wants to share with us?'

Yamdagni shook his head but replied, 'I am assuming it's some news from her side of the family . . . maybe another one of her cousins getting betrothed or married or even having a child!'

Satyavati smiled and said, 'Men can really be dense sometimes. That sort of news could be shared individually or through a messenger; why call both of us here together? I have a feeling it is something much more important than that and of a more personal nature.'

Yamdagni looked at her perplexed and was about to ask what she meant when Renuka burst into the veranda accompanied by her maids. Her face glowed with a faint flush and her lips curved in a shy smile. Looking at her glowing visage he finally comprehended what his mother was alluding to. 'I am going to become a father!' he blurted out with some incredulity.

Satyavati laughed seeing his expression while Renuka rushed into his arms. Sill feeling a little dazed, he cupped her face in his hands, seeking confirmation. She nodded shyly and his heart filled with pride. He clasped her to his chest, showering her with all the love he felt in his heart. After a brief moment they turned to touch his mother's feet who couldn't stop the tears of joy coursing down her cheeks.

'This is the happiest day of my life!' she said, 'From the day I surrendered the responsibilities of the royal court my only dream has been to see my grandchildren before I move to the next stage of life. I can't express in words the joy that my heart is filled with today!'

The soon-to-be father beamed with happiness and Renuka thanked her mother-in-law, saying, 'I won't let anyone talk about going away on this day! You have to put off the idea of Vanprasth at least until your grandchild can understand who you are!'

Satyavati laughed, 'Of course! I wouldn't want to go away without hearing the child snuggling in my arms calling me "Dadi" in his or her lilting voice and getting spoilt by me in return. Yama grew up away from me in Dattatreya's gurukul but I will make sure his child does not stay away from me for long!'

In their excitement they didn't hear the sound of approaching footsteps and were startled to hear Ruchik's voice break into their conversation, 'Many congratulations, daughter Renuka. I was meditating on the affairs of our kingdom when I spotted you running to the temple to receive the blessings of the goddess. May I suggest you maintain a slightly slower pace from now on?'

Ruchik's face split into an uncharacteristically broad smile and Satyavati nudged the couple to seek his blessings. Yamdagni didn't object. Had he been king, he would have forgiven all the criminals in the kingdom, he was that happy today. Ruchik advised them to get a thorough check-up done by the royal vaidyas and midwives. When the happy couple left, he turned to Satyavati. This was the first time since his arrival at court that he was meeting her face-to-face.

He had decided not to bother her directly and, when required, had only sent messages through couriers. But they couldn't avoid talking forever. She looked at him defiantly now, daring him to speak but the words that came from his mouth drowned her battling spirit.

'My lady,' Ruchik said, 'I know you do not desire a prolonged conversation with me but I am hoping that you will hear me out this once for it is important for the future of your grandchild. I do not wish to discuss the past but rather apprise you of what lies in the future for my boon comes to fulfilment with the birth of this child.'

Satyavati, who had been expecting another round of apologies, was surprised at his words. With all her time devoted to taking care of the kingdom and the royal household, she had almost forgotten that the second part of the boon was still pending! Making sure to maintain a formal note to her words, she asked, 'May I know, Rishivar, the implications of that boon on my grandchild? As I remember, this baby is destined to be born with Kshatriya traits but I don't foresee that being a problem in Kanyakubja.'

She couldn't resist taking a shot at him and let her residual bitterness show, 'Had I been living in my husband's hermitage in the middle of the forest it may have been a matter of concern but fortunately, that's not the case any more.'

Ruchik acknowledged her resentment with a tilt of his head, and said, 'My lady, I am glad you are living in the lap of luxury here and being taken care of by hundreds of attendants. I agree, it is an infinitely better situation for a Kshatriya child to grow up in rather than a hermit's ashram. Regardless, the child will have to be prepared to face the clouds gathering on the horizon. They are not just harbingers of rain but also a portent of the circumstances brewing in the heartland of the country. And they will hit Kanyakubja without warning.'

Satyavati was surprised on hearing this and sensed that there was something more on his mind, 'Do you allude to the events happening in the Narmada Valley? Kirtivirya and Arjun have been doing their best to keep the barbarians restricted to the forest. Do you see a threat to them which could have consequences for Kanyakubja?'

'Your political acumen has always astounded me, my lady,' Ruchik said. 'Yes, this is related to what's happening in Mahishmati even as we speak and from what I have been able to observe, the threat may not remain limited to the central kingdoms but extend to the entire Nabhi-varsh!'

Satyavati looked at him in alarm and asked, 'Rishivar, are

you sure? What you are saying can have serious repercussions on the future of our kingdoms!'

Ruchik replied with a hint of a smile, 'I hope, my lady, that you have not forgotten the extent of my yogic powers, and believe me when I say that even though on the surface everything seems to be calm, it is nothing but the proverbial lull before the storm. I had sensed the clouds gathering even before I arrived here but now my realization of the darkness fermenting in Dandak-Aranya has become much more acute.'

Satyavati was looking at him, incredulously. He explained, 'I have felt unholy vibrations rising from the Dandak forest, and Rishi Kanav who lives near the northern boundary of the forest has confirmed my suspicions. Before I can say anything more we need to investigate the state of affairs further. I intend to contact Rishi Agastya who is busy developing the Siddha system of medicine in the south and your own brother Vishwamitra in the east to see if we can limit the spread of this rot from all directions.

'On another matter,' he said, 'even though you don't yet consider me a part of this family, I feel an obligation to mention that Rishi Kanav's ashram is not very far from where your brother became a Brahmarishi, and he has been raising your niece, Shakuntala, since Menaka returned to heaven.'

Satyavati gave a start on hearing this. When her brother had renounced the kingdom and embarked on the journey of becoming a Brahmarishi, Indra, the king of demigods, had felt threatened and had sent the gorgeous Apsara Menaka to disrupt his penance. To say that she had been able to seduce her brother was an understatement for they had ended up living together for ten long years. When Vishwamitra had finally come to his senses, he had broken up with the celestial nymph and sent her away. But Satyavati had no idea that their dalliance had resulted in a child!

Ruchik could see the astonishment on her face and said softly, 'I'm sorry to break the news to you so abruptly but I thought it best to inform you since the child is related to you by blood.'

'I am glad you did,' Satyavati replied graciously, 'for as you can tell, I had no inkling about the existence of this child till this moment! I shall talk to Yama and immediately arrange for the child to be brought to Kanyakubja.'

'You are free to get in touch with Rishi Kanav but before you make such a request, do remember that he has been raising the child as his own and may not be amenable to parting with her. Given the current circumstances, I would suggest Yamdagni visit them first and then decide on a course of action.'

Satyavati saw the logic in Ruchik's suggestion and nodded in agreement. A few months ago she couldn't have imagined the return of her husband let alone learning that there was another child of her bloodline growing up so far away from her home! Whatever the outcome of these developments, she would have to find her peace taking each day as it came and being thankful to god that her family was finally complete.

Arjun

Adhyaye 11

The undulating river wound its way towards the sea on the west. Arjun, the prince of the land, sat on a small vantage point on top of the cliff, absorbed in his surroundings, listening to the Vedic chants of the evening aarti on the ghat, along with his bride who seemed equally mesmerized by the vista below.

Manorama was an exotic beauty: a tanned complexion, dark kohl-lined eyes, gloriously curled hair that fell to her waist in ringlets and a frame almost as tall as her husband's. She looked at him now, Kartavirya Arjun, the king-in-waiting, and smiled. His orange-tinged hair fell in a mop over his broad forehead that sported the mark of a crescent moon. She had tried in vain to keep it in place by combing them herself every day and now had even stopped trying. His brown almond eyes seemed relaxed and he had a bit of colour on his high cheekbones. Clearly he was happy. She leaned in and rested her head on his shoulder. Arjun kissed the top of her head and asked if she was tired.

'No, my dear husband, I am just absorbing the glorious sights of the river and its worshippers. I wonder though, of all the temples that dot the landscape, which one is the oldest?'

Arjun's handsome face broke into a smile, revealing a perfect set of teeth. He pointed to a temple in the distance whose towering spires and fluttering banners could be seen even from this far. 'That, my dear, is the Narmadeshwar Temple,' he said. 'It is dedicated to Lord Shiva and commemorates the birth of the river which is believed to have sprung from the perspiration of the Lord when his body burnt with the fire of tapas as he engaged in a severe penance on the Amarkandak hill. For that reason, the river is also known as Shankari by the people in this region.'

Manorama folded her hands to pay her respects to the divinity of the temple. Shiva was also the patron deity of the Nagas because of his association with serpents and his daughter Mansa, who was a snake goddess.

Arjun further elaborated, 'Like the Ganga in the north, Saraswati in the west, Brahmaputra in the east and Kaveri in the south, the Narmada is the lifeline for the central kingdoms. While the waters of other rivers are believed to be purifying, it is the pebbles from the Narmada river bed that are considered holy for each is shaped like a Shivalingam.'

Manorama nodded. 'The river is worshipped as a saviour by my people as well! According to our beliefs, about ten generations ago, the Nagas were attacked by the Gandharvs and a fierce battle ensued. At the time, Narmada, the daughter of Rishi Mekal and sworn sister to the Naga king, sought help from her husband, Purukutsa, the Suryavanshi ruler of Ayodhya, and helped throw the Gandharvs out. It was in her honour that the Nagas named the river thus and since then, we have venerated her as a saviour. Even today, we believe that invoking her name provides protection from all sorts of poisons.'

Arjun listened to her story attentively and said, 'So then you and I belong to very similar religious traditions. You know, the more time I spend with you, the more I begin to appreciate my father's decision to set this match for us despite my initial reservations about an arranged marriage. I respect you as a person and have come to love you over time. I hope you don't have a cause to complain in Mahishmati, my dear.'

His wife shook her head and smiled, 'Not at all! I have been very happy in the capital and this trip has been even more special. I can't believe it has been six months already since we got married!'

Arjun smiled and took her hand. Together they set out towards the palace at the top of the hill reserved for the royal family. While walking there he said, 'Barring my parents, I have never spent so much time with anyone as I have spent with you in the past few months, princess, and I have cherished each moment. But the war against the barbarians is far from over and I will need to head out again soon. I hope you will become my strength and not my weakness in this crusade.'

Manorama looked into his eyes and promised, 'I shall support you in all your endeavours, especially this campaign against the Asur tribes. The armies of my father are also available at your service whenever you need them.'

Arjun was glad to hear that for the support of her clan could be just the push the Chandravanshis needed. Acknowledging the offer with a nod, he replied thoughtfully, 'I have a feeling I may soon require the help of your father, if not his army, since the Asurik influence has been steadily increasing in our realm. It's nothing that I can pinpoint yet, but I feel its subtle effects everywhere.

'The number of taverns, gambling dens and pleasure places is steadily increasing in the kingdom as is the number of people frequenting them. The crime rate is going up too, not alarmingly but unfortunately steadily. I have a feeling the barbarians are using underhanded tactics to weaken the kingdom from within, spreading dark magic like a substratum in our soil.'

Manorama thought for a moment and replied, 'Yes, it could be a sinister way to create discontent in the minds of our people.'

Arjun smiled at her use of 'our' for it showed her acceptance of his city and its people as her own, and clasped her hand firmly. They had reached the palace by then and were welcomed by the warm glow of brass lamps and the fragrance of rajnigandha flowers that decorated the hallways.

Reassuring him again Manorama said, 'I understand your concern, my love, but I assure you complete support from my family and tribe. Father doesn't think too highly of the barbarians himself and I am sure he will be glad to help you rid Avanti of the Asur menace as well. He is a master of Naga magic and an expert in toxicology and potions. If anyone can detect the presence of Asurik magic in our realm it is he. I'll personally request him to help you identify those who have put such snares on our people.'

Arjun gave the broadest smile she had ever seen and clasped her to his wide chest. Together they went to the royal chamber and lay down on the bed.

After some time Manorama began hesitantly, 'I know our kingdom is going from strength to strength but I have heard that Mahishmati had been once cursed by the gods. In the six months I have spent here, I have encountered whispers of it but no one has ever told me anything directly.'

Arjun grinned, 'Well, there is a reason for that! But enough stories for today, otherwise we'll be talking all night instead of doing something more productive!' He said with a wink.

Manorama hit him with a pillow and said petulantly, 'I really, really want to know!'

Arjun snatched the pillow from her and sighed, 'All right, listen. Do you know why my father arranged our match or why he himself married a princess from the eastern lands instead of someone from Avanti itself?'

She shook her head, so he replied, 'According to an old legend in our kingdom, when Mahishmati came under the Chandravanshis, it was ruled by a king named Neel whose daughter's beauty rivalled that of the Apsaras in Indra's court. So great was her fame that the fire god Agni fell in love with her and, she returned his feelings. Every night, Agni dev would take the form of a man and appear from the lamp in her chamber and they would stay together till dawn broke on the horizon. In time their chemistry became so sizzling that whenever the princess came close to any flame, it would blaze up with vigour and soon people began to notice this effect.'

Manorama listened in rapt attention for she loved romantic stories.

'A secret love affair between a mortal and a demigod had begun within the palace walls and both of them plunged into it throwing caution to the wind. However, one day the couple was discovered by the king as he arrived at his daughter's chamber unannounced. He was furious to see Agni and not knowing his true identity ordered that he be flogged for daring to enter the princess's bedchamber. Agni flared up at this affront and, resuming his true form, he cursed the king that the women of his kingdom would never follow the rules set by men and would be free to live unbound to a single man.

'Since then, polyandry has been the norm in our kingdom and is deeply entrenched in the psyche of the populace. In time, Agni dev's broken heart was mended by Svaha but his curse, even though liberating the women of Mahishmati, created a problem for the ruling class. As kings, we can't support polyandry since that complicates the issue of inheritance.

'A man may marry many women yet all the offspring would bear his name but if a woman has more than one husband, who decides the paternity of the child? The custom has therefore never been followed by the ruling class while all our subjects practise it. Ironic isn't it, since it's the other way round in most other kingdoms where the ruling class exercises no such self-imposed restrictions!'

As Manorama reached for another cushion to hit him with, he added hastily, 'Not that I would want to belong to more than one wife since I am quite enamoured with a certain exotic Naga princess!'

'Good you accepted that,' she said laughing. 'You better not even dream of marrying another woman else I'll invoke my inner serpent goddess and poison those who compete for your affection!'

Arjun smiled. 'I have heard about the famed vengeance of Nagas and I officially declare my undying love for you which no other woman can lay claim to. And now, let me prove to you the truth of my words,' he said and blew out the lamps.

Adhyaye 12

The Asur leader Marich's original plan had been to foment trouble in Mahishmati by inciting the sections of society that had something to grumble about. In every country or society, there exist a few who are unhappy with the way things are and the kingdom of Avanti was no different.

There were people who resented their kings for their privileged lives, ethnic minorities that felt threatened by the strong culture of the majority, disgruntled employees who didn't like the efficiency demanded from them by the king, criminals who had spent time in jail and now hated everything official, wealthy businessmen who resented having their daughters' marriage proposals for the prince turned down—the list was endless.

Marich had initiated this long-term plan quite early when he had realized that Kirtivirya was not going to let them be, but thanks to the treaty he had made with Karkotak, their fortune could turn around sooner than he had expected. He had invited the Naga king to the cavern, shared his plan with him and let the Asur girls seduce him into agreement. He had also promised to spare no expense in providing any kind of help that would be required as well as taught Karkotak some

Asurik magic that might prove useful to him in supporting this mission.

When Karkotak thought about it, it made perfect sense to help the Asurs who had enough resources to support him. The one reason the Chandravanshis had managed to expand so fast was the use of superior weapons. But his knowledge of Asurik dark magic would certainly help balance the equation. It could help him create what he hoped would be a defining moment in history, the resurgence of a grand Naga kingdom right in the middle of Nabhi-varsh.

Marich wished to make Arjun a pawn in Karkotak's hands and manipulate his regard for his in-laws to draw his attention away from the Dandak forest. Fortunately, Arjun had himself given the Naga king an opening by requesting him to help weed out the Asurik influence spreading in his kingdom. He had been amazed at the young man's perceptiveness about what the Asurs were trying to do and agreed to help, with one suggestion—a look-north instead of look-south policy that would allow the Asurs to remain hidden for a few more generations at least.

'Think about it, my son,' he had said, 'your father's plans will definitely expand your boundaries but what will you get out of the forest-dwelling tribes? They don't have any riches to share nor is the land cultivable; you will just gain additional responsibility without any return on your efforts. Glory lies in annexing the prosperous and fertile kingdoms of the Ganga and Saraswati rather than the forests of the Narmada that can be tamed later. If you focus your energies on conquering the north, not only will you obtain more valuable bounty but also be one step closer to fulfilling your destiny of becoming a Chakravarti Samrat as was prophesied at the time of your birth.'

Arjun had replied, 'I appreciate your thoughts, my lord, but

I will have to discuss this with my father. As far as I understand his philosophy, this campaign against the tribals is not an expansionist idea. Rather, it is a by-product of his endeavour to rid the world of all barbaric practices including the ones they follow. In that light I think looking north wouldn't make sense.'

Karkotak nodded, then added, 'I hope you realize that I only say this for your benefit since nothing would give me greater pleasure than to see you don the mantle of a universal monarch and see my daughter, your wife, being called the queen of a Chakravarti Samrat.'

They sat now in the guest chamber of the royal palace of Mahishmati, a seven-storey structure made of sandstone and supported by a thousand intricately carved pillars. Manorama, who had been giving them privacy to discuss politics, sat in the veranda looking resplendent, her tall frame wrapped in a saffron sari. She waved at them as they looked up at her after the discussion ended and smiled when Arjun gestured to her to come and join them.

As she gracefully walked into the room Karkotak patted her head and said, 'Sorry to have kept you waiting, my child, but I did not wish to bore you with the political discussions we were having. I have agreed to help Arjun in his mission and I am glad you invited me to visit. It feels good to see you glowing with health and so happy. Clearly, my son-in-law has been taking good care of you.'

Manorama blushed and said, 'I'm afraid he has spoilt me completely!'

'Well, that is my right,' Arjun said lightly. 'After all, I just want my princess happy.'

Karkotak smiled, delighted to see Arjun showering so much attention on his daughter and decided that he would not let his plans for the resurgence of the Nagas affect Manorama's happiness. The three of them walked towards the royal dining hall where they were joined by the king and the queen and Karkotak made sure he didn't mention the discussions he had with Arjun in front of Kirtivirya.

The conversation at dinner centred on the alliance of their two clans.

'You know we Chandravanshis have been quite open to the mixing of races as people call it from the time of our founding forefathers. If you care to remember, our founding father Chandrama's son Budh had married Ila, a Suryavanshi princess, and their son Pururava managed to woo no less than Urvashi, one of the most ravishing Apsaras from Indra's court! Their sons Ayu, Shrutayu, Shatayu, Ayutayu, Vishwavasu and Amavasu carved new kingdoms out of the wilderness and spread our lineage far and wide. Maharaj Ayu's eldest son Nahush was even made the Indra for a brief time period due to his good karma and he married Viraja from the clan of Pitris who are heavenly deities older than the Adityas. And that's not the end of it, what most people find surprising is that Yayati, the son of this man who was made the leader of Devas, was married to an Asur princess Devyani as well as Daitya guru Shukracharya's daughter!'

'Wow, that must have been a difficult marriage to solemnize!' Manorama said for Asurs hardly ever intermarried with other races, preferring to take them as harem slaves instead.

Kirtivirya nodded and continued enlightening his audience proudly, 'Maharaj Yayati can be considered the original forefather of most Arya nations in the world today. With his two wives, he sired the five clans we know as the Panch-Manav—Druhyus, who moved westwards beyond the boundaries of Nabhi-varsh; Anus who established the north-western kingdoms of fire worshippers; Purus who settled the region between the Saraswati and the Ganga; Turvasus who crossed the Vindhyas and populated the south-eastern lands, and us Yadus or Yadavs who have established ourselves in the south-western part of Nabhi-varsh.'

Karkotak's lips curved into a fake smile of appreciation for he knew that history generally neglected to mention those who were less fortunate such as his own tribe. While Kirtivirya prided himself on the mixed genealogy of his dynasty, there were many acts like that of Yayati sleeping with Sharmishtha, the Asur princess, when he was already married to their guru's daughter Devyani that never found mention in polite conversation. The fact that Pururava had to literally beg Indra to let him be with the nymph Urvashi was also seldom mentioned. Compared to these mixed breeds, the Nagas were a far superior race, the purity of their lineage indisputable, coming down as it was, unbroken, right from the legendary kings Takshak and Vasuki. Thousands of years of evolution may have changed their form but they would never sleep with the enemy like these Chandravanshi mongrels.

After dinner, when Karkotak took their leave, Arjun accompanied him to the chariot and said, 'Father, thank you for agreeing to help me and your valuable advice today. The idea of northward expansion does hold merit but it would be difficult to convince my father for the northern plains are ruled by our own cousins, some of whom even attended my wedding. I doubt I will get the opportunity to act on your advice until I become the king.'

Karkotak nodded silently and mounted his chariot promising to return the week after to begin touring the kingdom with his son-in-law to identify and weed out Asurik influence if any. An idea was forming in his head, one that could avenge the marginalization of Nagas in the politics of Nabhi-varsh as well as help hasten his son-in-law's ascension to power.

Kirtivirya, the blabbermouth, would have to be taken out of the equation soon.

Adhyaye 13

About the same time as Arjun started his tour of Avanti with Karkotak, Yamdagni arrived at Rishi Kanav's ashram.

Satyavati had told him about the existence of Vishwamitra's daughter and she, Deval and Yamdagni had debated for months about how best to deal with the situation. They had tried to contact Vishwamitra but he was not reachable, lost in the forests of Kamarupa. Deval's adherence to Chandravanshi values made him feel that the right place for the child, his half-sister, was in Kanyakubja, regardless of what the rishi raising her had to say about it. Satyavati agreed with him in principle but felt that Rishi Kanav, who had raised the child and given her a new life, had an equal say in the matter and deserved to be heard before a final decision was made. Yamdagni had taken the suggestions of both into consideration and decided that the best way forward would be for him to check on the child's progress and discuss the possibility of her moving to Kanyakubja with Rishi Kanav in person. Besides, there was the threat Ruchik had perceived in the forests beyond and he had told Yamdagni that a meeting with Rishi Kanav could help them better gauge it's exact nature.

As he neared the ashram Yamdagni could make out the outline of a tall fence and observed large heaps of firewood lying around. From within the hermitage he could hear ritual chants and see the holy fire of a yagnya rising high.

A few young hermits dressed in coarse homespun jute cloth walked past. Yamdagni hailed them and introduced himself; he told them he wished to consult Rishi Kanav on an important matter. They took him inside, asking him to wait while the rishis finished the yagnya they were performing. Sitting in one corner of the campus, he noticed hermits of all ages, from young acolytes to middle-aged ones engrossed in their duties. As he waited for the learned Brahmin to arrive, he counted eighteen sanctums all along the perimeter symbolizing the seventeen vowels of the Sanskrit alphabet and one for the divine word Om. The first of the seventeen was a shrine to Srishti-Karta Brahma, followed by one to Lord Shiva and then Shri Hari Vishnu. The other sanctums undoubtedly followed the standard template of most ashrams and would be dedicated to Indra, Surya, his own ancestor Chandra, the Aditya Bhaag, lord of riches Kuber, fate gods Dhata and Vidhata, followed by Vayu and Varun. The next shrine was for Gayatri—the presiding deity of knowledge who had been perceived by his friend and uncle Vishwamitra when he had discovered the Gayatri Mantra and revealed its power by using it to become a Brahmarishi. The sanctum after that housed the eight elemental gods or Vasus, and was followed by shrines to Sheshnag, Garud, Kartikeya, and finally Yamraj, the presiding deity of all hells and a guardian of men's Karma.

Yamdagni knew that Kanav, who had added many mantras to the Rig Veda, was no ordinary rishi but when he finally came face-to-face with him, his honest smile immediately put him at ease. The rishi was a fair-complexioned man of average height and build, with genial features and a flowing beard that covered the lower half of his face. His long greying hair was tied in a knot behind his head and instead of the usual ochre or saffron robes of an ascetic, he was dressed in pure white.

With folded hands, Kanav said, 'Welcome to my humble abode, Mahamantri of Mahodayapur. I hope I didn't keep you waiting for too long and that my students took good care of you while I was occupied.'

Yamdagni thanked him pleasantly and replied, 'It is indeed my honour to meet one of the authors of the Rig Veda in person, and an even bigger privilege to be able to converse with a dharma-gyata like you!'

'Mahamantri,' the rishi said humbly, 'I can no more claim authorship of these verses than the bees around the ashram can claim motherhood over the jackfruits hanging outside. Just as the tiny insects carry pollen from one flower to the other giving birth to a seed, similarly rishis like Vasishth, your own uncle Vishwamitra and I act as a conduit between the other world and this one to transmit the knowledge of the universe to the humans. We are mere messengers of the divine word that is revealed to us when in a deep meditative state and hold no authority over it.'

Yamdagni was impressed with his humility and said, 'Rishivar, you are a very knowledgeable man and perhaps understand the reason of my current visit better than I can explain it myself. The queen regent and King Deval send their deepest regards. They are appreciative of your attachment to your adoptive child. However, they also wish for my cousin to receive an upbringing befitting a princess in Kanyakubja. I wished to seek your opinion on this matter personally before the king himself came to put forth his request.'

Rishi Kanav looked at his guest intently and replied, 'I understand your concern, Mahamantri. Please convey my regards to King Deval and the queen regent as well. However, I need them to understand that after the demise of my wife who passed away last winter, I am the only person the child has known as family. Abandoned by both her father and mother, the ashram's pet Shakunts found her and alerted me to her presence and that is why I named her Shakuntala. In fact, once I found out her celestial origins, I contacted Brahmarishi Vishwamitra as well and took his permission to continue looking after his daughter for him. My late wife was very fond of her and separating her from the only family she knows and taking her so far away from all that is familiar to her would be counterproductive.'

Yamdagni's face fell on hearing this, and realized that if Vishwamitra had given Kanav his permission to raise the child there was nothing he or Deval could do about it. But the rishi was not done yet. 'Listen to what I have to say, son. Rather than take her away from the denizens of this ashram who have all helped raise her, I would advise your mother and cousin to visit her here and help her get acquainted with her real lineage. Once she grows up, she can decide for herself where she wants to live. I hope this arrangement will be acceptable to the king for we all ultimately want what's best for her.'

Yamdagni realized it was a reasonable suggestion. Had the rishi not taken her in, Shakuntala would surely have perished in the forest with all the wild beasts roaming around. He could also understand that the rishi, who no longer had a family of his own, found the company of that small child endearing and naturally felt protective towards her. He decided not to take the one person that mattered most to the rishi away from him and said, 'I am grateful to you for taking in the child whose actual responsibility lies on us and indeed our family is deeply indebted to you for this generosity. I know now the reason that my uncle Vishwamitra did not inform us of her existence since he knew she would be well taken care of in your ashram. I shall convey your view to the king and my mother and together we can take care of my cousin's every need.'

Rishi Kanav acknowledged the compliment with a silent nod and Yamdagni said, 'Now that this delicate issue is out of the way, I wish to ask for your help on another matter that is equally important. My father has been in touch with you regarding the developments in Dandak-Aranya and I just wished to know your opinion as your proximity to the region may have helped you gain better insight to the situation.'

The learned rishi nodded sombrely and gestured to Yamdagni to make himself comfortable; what he had to share would take considerable time.

Adhyaye 14

Manorama looked at the approaching flag of her husband's returning army with mixed feelings. She was happy he was back but the circumstances that had forced him to cut the trip short were solemn.

Kirtivirya had been taken violently ill and the royal vaidyas had diagnosed it as the effect of a rare poison. His condition was worsening by the minute, and the queen, who had not moved away from her husband's side since his symptoms began, had sent out the missive to summon the prince immediately.

Arjun galloped into the palace courtyard, his face lined with worry. He swiftly dismounted from his steed and rushed into the palace, with Karkotak trailing behind. Manorama's heart went out to him and even though she had just returned to her own room, she ran down the stairs and headed to the king's chamber as well. Queen Padmini sat by the bed just as she had seen her earlier while a variety of vaidyas, attendants and maids surrounded the ailing king. Manorama held Arjun's hand as he rushed to his father's side, hoping he wasn't too late in returning.

Kirtivirya's handsome face was twisted in a grimace as he battled the pain that was wreaking havoc inside him. His broad forehead was lined with fine drops of sweat and there were purple bruises all over his body. Silent tears flowed from his bloodshot eyes for he could not bear the pain but was too proud to openly cry.

Arjun couldn't believe the change in his father's appearance and the realization that he may be on his deathbed hit him hard. The queen looked completely devoid of hope. Even the chief vaidya shook his head in dismay. Kneeling down beside him, he took his father's hand whispering words of comfort, 'Father, I'm here now, don't worry, everything will be fine.'

He had been out for just about two months and the mission had been quite successful in terms of quashing minor rebellions along the border, giving the citizens a sense of security and allowing them the chance to directly interact with their prince. He had told them Kirtivirya's grand plans and shared with them the dream of a glorious future under the able guidance of their chosen king. Yet now, that king lay writhing in pain, his own future uncertain.

The son whispered a silent prayer to the gods to help his father win this fight.

There was a sudden commotion and everyone turned to look at the source. Karkotak was rushing into the room accompanied by a helper who was urging people to make way. The Naga king hurried towards Kirtivirya and sat down taking his head in his lap, gesturing to the helper to pass him the small bag he was carrying. He quickly sifted through its components, selected a small vial and poured its contents into the twisted mouth of the king. Within seconds the expression on Kirtivirya's face changed and Arjun watched in amazement as his father's body relaxed and colour returned to his cheeks!

The entire gathering gave a collective sigh of relief for the king looked visibly better. Arjun looked at his father-in-law in wonder. Karkotak just shrugged simply and said, 'No one can cure the effects of a toxin as well as a Naga. Praise be to Mother Narmada and the numerous herbs growing beside her life-giving banks that can cure any kind of poisoning!'

Kirtivirya's eyelids fluttered and he managed to open them slightly though he was still too weak to say anything or get up. Queen Padmini grasped his hand and wept tears of joy as the gloom in the chamber was replaced with a feeling of excitement and hope. Arjun rushed to Karkotak and fell down at his feet. Thanking him profusely, he said, 'Father, by your quick actions, you have saved not only the life of my father but also the future of Avanti. I don't have the words to express the gratitude that's brimming over in my heart. How can we ever repay this act of kindness? What you pulled off today is nothing short of a miracle!'

Karkotak replied with a warm smile, 'My dear child, I haven't done anything that a decent human being wouldn't do for another. Besides, Kirtivirya is not just anybody; he's a dear friend and my daughter's father-in-law. I am glad my knowledge of toxins and their antidotes proved useful today.'

'We are certainly lucky to have you here,' Queen Padmini gushed with relief. 'I can't thank you enough for saving my husband's life! Arjun, Manorama, please make sure the good news reaches everyone in the kingdom and the efforts of brother-in-law Karkotak find worthy mention. We shall have a grand celebration tomorrow and you, my lord, shall be our guest of honour till such time as my husband can thank you properly himself.'

Karkotak bowed graciously and after talking briefly to the vaidyas, took their leave to go and wash the dust of the journey. As he entered the guest chamber he couldn't help rewarding himself with a smile of satisfaction. The elaborate plan he had concocted before leaving with Arjun had worked to perfection. Admittedly, his first thoughts had been to do away with Kirtivirya completely but he realized that the prince was quite attached to his father and his death may affect him deeply and might even alter his behaviour towards Manorama. Since he did not want his daughter to suffer in any way because of his impulsive actions, he decided to improvise the plan. Instead of killing the king in one stroke, he decided to put his knowledge of venoms to good use. He secured the employment of one of his trusted servants in Mahishmati's royal kitchens where, for months, the man had been mixing small amounts of extremely potent venom into the food that was served to the king, giving the toxin time to build up in his body. There was no guarantee that the king would get his daily dose of poison for he occasionally missed a meal, or had it at his queen's palace which had necessitated the prolonged planning. It also saved the trouble of killing someone else accidentally since consuming a single dose of the toxin wasn't harmful.

Then had begun the patient wait for the news of king's poisoning. Karkotak had utilized the time to gain his son-in-law's confidence. He had genuinely helped him quash small rebellions in the border areas and accurately identified Asur followers using the knowledge of the same magic that Marich had shared with him. He had explained his plan to the Asur leader, informing him that he should be prepared to face some casualties if he wanted rapid results.

They had almost finished their journey when the missive finally came. He had been a little worried since once the poison took effect the antidote had to be administered within a specific time frame but, thankfully, they had managed to reach just in time.

His diabolical plan to poison Kirtivirya little by little till he reached the brink of death and get him back from the edge had worked to perfection and now he had gained the favour of both the king as well as the prince. Kirtivirya would take months to recover completely and it was very likely that he would transfer the crown to his son as soon as possible. The moment that happened, Karkotak would begin the process of influencing Avanti's policy in a way that favoured the resurgence of the Nagas. History would remember him as the king who revived their glorious past.

Adhyaye 15

Ruchik read the message from Yamdagni grimly.

Yamdagni had spent a month in Rishi Kanav's ashram and besides confirming what he had suspected, had made two startling discoveries. One, the Urags had been in touch with the Naga king and had set in motion a plan to overthrow the Haiheya Yadavs, and second, but more alarming, these two clans were not alone in this!

The entire plan had been hatched with aid from an external agency, and through some explorations into the forest with the rishi's young disciples, Yamdagni had discovered that the Urags would disappear for days, heading southward, and a few less careful tribals had told them stories of a hidden coven of Asurs. Rishi Kanav had proven to be of big help and had gifted him two inexhaustible quivers full of deadly arrows that could wreak havoc on any Asur army. Ruchik was glad to know that combined with the Bow of Vishnu that was in his possession, the force would be deadly.

At the other end of the palace, Satyavati was reading a similar courier which briefly outlined the above scenario but also talked about Shakuntala. The old rishi had allowed the family to meet the child and had invited the queen regent for a visit. Shakuntala still believed Kanav was her biological father and it was up to them to tackle the difficult task of breaking the truth to her. Satyavati knew it would be tough but it had to be done; Chandravanshis didn't believe in neglecting their responsibilities however challenging.

She gave orders to start packing for her trip and informed Renuka to prepare for the journey as well since she would have to be taken to her father's place in Mahur for the last trimester of her pregnancy. They would spend some time with Shakuntala, and then head to Mahur with Yamdagni.

Her thoughts were interrupted by the announcement of Ruchik's arrival. Since the day he had informed her about Shakuntala's existence, the rift between them had begun to mend and she had started seeking his advice on occasion. In Yamdagni's absence, the rishi had also become an important guide for Deval and she wanted to talk to him about the political game being played by the Nagas.

Ruchik entered her chamber and inquired, 'I trust you have gone through the contents of Yamdagni's message, my lady?'

'Yes, Rishivar,' Satyavati replied, offering him a seat. 'My primary concern was the welfare of my brother's daughter, but Yamdagni assures me she couldn't be in better hands. He has passed on Rishi Kanav's invitation and I intend to head there as soon as possible with Renuka while it is still safe for her to travel.'

Ruchik nodded in agreement and commented, 'That seems like the best thing to do under the circumstances. I would also like to know what you think of the situation developing in Avanti. No one in Nabhi-varsh knows about the existence of Asurs for sure, but Yamdagni's investigations certainly point to their involvement.'

'Yes, that does add a twist to the situation,' Satyavati said thoughtfully. 'I myself wanted to talk to you about their involvement since it may have political ramifications for not just Avanti, but other kingdoms as well. Including ours. I wonder how these Asurs have managed to remain concealed till now!'

Ruchik knew her question highlighted the failure of the intelligence-gathering mechanisms of all the Arya kingdoms surrounding Dandak-Aranya and said sombrely, 'It is no secret that Asurs are masters of dark magic. Yamdagni himself encountered a number of concealing spells used by them to keep their location a secret. I have a suspicion that they are being funded by an external benefactor, possibly the precocious teenage lord of Lanka who is rumoured to be quite ambitious.'

Satyavati had heard of the Asur her husband was talking about who was born of Brahma's grandson Vishrav and the Rakshas princess Kaikesi. Part Rakshas–part rishi, Ravan seemed to have imbibed the best of both worlds. His mastery of the scriptures was flawless as was his knowledge of the dark arts. Even though still a boy he had managed to overthrow his elder half-brother Kuber from the throne of Lanka and appropriate his riches, including the flying plane Pushpak.

'I wonder how they managed to convince Karkotak to join them?' Ruchik continued. 'The Nagas are not known to have a favourable opinion about the Asurs or the Urags, but then there are no permanent enemies in politics and the three clans seem to be hand-in-glove this time. I feel that Arjun, who has been crowned king now, should be warned about the situation.'

Satyavati hadn't thought about this aspect and concurred with his assessment. 'I think I can visit them in the upcoming trip. We haven't visited the Haiheyas since Arjun's wedding and I should check on his father's condition as well. Would you like to accompany us since Kirtivirya is related to you by familial ties?'

Ruchik nodded and replied, 'I'd be honoured. If you don't mind, I would like to accompany you to both the places to get a first-hand view of the situation as well as provide you protection.'

Satyavati couldn't help but smile to herself. 'Yes, that would be acceptable I think. Let me be honest and acknowledge that over the past few months your presence has helped the kingdom in many ways and the royal family is grateful to you.'

The rishi bowed gracefully and left the room with a smile. It was good that their interactions were becoming smoother over time. Even if their previous relationship could not be revived, they might yet become good friends.

Perhaps they could still forget the bitterness of the past and create a new future together.

Adhyaye 16

Mahishmati was celebrating the coronation of its new king when the four travellers reached the capital. They had visited Rishi Kanav's ashram and the plan now was to meet the ailing Kirtivirya, spend some time with Arjun and see for themselves what the ground reality was before heading to Mahur.

The Haiheyas welcomed them with genuine affection. Ruchik now sat with Kirtivirya and his wife in their private chamber while Satyavati, Yamdagni and Renuka talked with Arjun who looked resplendent in his regal finery.

'I speak for all of us when I say that we truly believe your ascension to the throne will usher in a new age for the Chandravanshis,' Satyavati said, congratulating him on his coronation. 'Kirtivirya has ruled wisely and impressively managed to curb the growth of the barbarians during his reign and I'm sure you will carry on his work with equal aplomb.'

Arjun accepted the compliment gratefully. 'My lady, I know you have nothing but good wishes for me. Avanti is lucky to have allies like you in the north. It is kind of you to visit my father and I truly appreciate the presence of your entire family here, especially since my lovely sister-in-law should be resting in her condition,' he said, smiling at Renuka.

Renuka responded with a warm smile of her own. 'As a matter of fact, brother, I was getting tired sitting at home and needed a change of scenery desperately! Besides, I have to be at my parent's place for the delivery and Mahishmati conveniently happens to be on the way so it isn't a problem at all.'

Arjun asked Manorama to help make Renuka more comfortable in the guest chamber. When the two women had departed, he turned to Yamdagni. 'How was your visit to Rishi Kanav's ashram? There was a delicate matter to be handled there if I am not mistaken?'

Yamdagni replied with a grin, 'Well, I see nothing escapes the notice of the king of Avanti! The visit had mixed results and I hope you understand why we do not wish to make the matter public till we can convince the child, Shakuntala to accompany us back to Kanyakubja. She has decided to stay on with her adoptive father for now and we have to be content with taking care of her needs from a distance.'

'You need not worry in this regard, brother,' Arjun said graciously, 'for the child is as much family to me as she is to you and I hope you succeed in convincing her to move with you soon.'

'That is really kind of you,' Yamdagni said.

Satyavati added, 'We also want to know if you require any help in the management of your father's condition. We have easy access to Himalayan herbs through our trade relations that may be useful for him.'

'That would indeed be helpful,' Arjun replied. 'Even though the vaidyas are doing a fabulous job they do often require certain herbs that are difficult to find in this region. The Nagas have been very helpful as has my father-in-law who is extremely resourceful in procuring these, but I would like to stop abusing his generosity so selfishly.'

Satyavati exchanged a look with Yamdagni and said, 'I have heard that Nagraj Karkotak played a pivotal role in saving your father. I wonder what kind of drug it was that had such a rapid and miraculous effect. It was fortunate that the Naga king had just the right antidote available as well!'

'Well, it wasn't just luck,' Arjun responded with good humour, 'since my father-in-law, being a Naga, is an expert at recognizing the effects of all sorts of poisons and keeps a collection of herbs that can act as antidotes. It was only his keen observance of my father's symptoms that gave him a clue as to what would work and thankfully he was right.'

Almost as if on cue, Karkotak's arrival was announced in the chamber, and when he walked in, his dark presence filled the entire room. His somewhat flattened features and tongue darting in and out reminded Satyavati of a king cobra, the most poisonous serpent south of the Himalayas and she gave an involuntary shudder. There was something sinister about this man.

The Naga king's keen eyes appraised all of them even as they got up to greet him with folded hands and he reciprocated. 'It is my good fortune to meet the queen regent of Mahodayapur for the second time. The first time I met you at my daughter's wedding I wasn't aware of your exalted reputation but in the time I have spent here, I have realized that you are somewhat of a legend and a role model for many Chandravanshi women.'

Satyavati bowed her head slightly and said, 'You are much too kind, my lord. I'm not the first and I certainly won't be the last woman to set new standards in our society. There are indeed many women all over the Chandravanshi kingdoms who are doing a lot of good work even today. I wanted to meet you and thank you in person for saving the life of the king with your quick action. However distantly we may be related, a Chandravanshi never forgets a favour done to one of our kinsmen and I shall be glad to help you with anything that the Naga tribes may require.'

Karkotak couldn't keep the pride out of his voice when he said, 'Thank you, my lady, for your gracious offer, but the Nagas are a strong race and do not require any external help. Together with the Haiheyas, we soon hope to emerge as a strong self-reliant nation rivalling the likes of Mahodayapur.'

Satyavati looked at Arjun for a reaction to this comparison with Mahodayapur but he seemed to accept Karkotak's statement without even a frown. She immediately understood that the Naga king's influence on him was more pronounced than they had assumed. She decided to put the upstart in his place with some well-chosen words and said, 'Well, it's only family that can help each other and I am sure you will get enough assistance from the Haiheyas to help you stand on your own feet since the Nagas haven't really seen the best days in the past.'

She saw Karkotak bristle at the statement but continued with a smile, 'Mahodayapur has good trading relations with the Himalayan kingdoms of Nepa, Kashyap-mir and Gandhar; it is a protectorate of Kausambi, Dharmaranya and Girivraj, all three of which are sister kingdoms, and also enjoys robust relations with the kingdoms of Matsya, Kashi, Mahur and Madra through family ties. If ever your fledgling clan requires any aid from us, please don't hesitate to ask.'

Karkotak gave her a look of pure venom as he realized what she was trying to do. Deciding to save his retorts for a later time he made a silent promise to himself: He would punish this woman for this veiled insult to his clan and wipe that smug smile off her face.

Adhyaye 17

The royal family of Mahodayapur had barely spent a week in Mahur when a plague gripped the city.

It started with the death of a few livestock animals, and over the next week progressed to the human population as well. King Prasenjeet, worried about the effect of the airborne infection on his daughter and her unborn child, urged his son-in-law to take them back to Kanyakubja for their own safety. Renuka was still able to travel and he would make sure their return journey was comfortable enough for her not to experience any shocks.

Yamdagni consulted with his parents who agreed. Ruchik had a feeling that this plague had something to do with their meeting with Karkotak, as did Satyavati. She remembered the look of hatred Karkotak had given her as they had taken their leave but had never imagined he would stoop so low!

Three weeks after they had arrived, they were on the way back, floating along the Chambal in a huge vessel provided by King Prasenjeet for their safe return while two smaller-sized boats trailed behind them. The wide, expansive rain-fed river flowed majestically in a northern direction for the first part of its journey and then took a gradual north-eastern turn to join the mighty Ganga. Unlike the Himalayan river however, the

Chambal was more tranquil, its banks lined by dense forests of unparalleled beauty.

As they drifted slowly down the river, Satyavati and Ruchik rested inside while Yamdagni and Renuka strolled on the deck, taking in the sylvan surroundings that were home to tigers, cheetahs, lions, bison, black bucks, antelope and a myriad other creatures. Forests of teak, sal, khair, vijayasar and dhaora trees dominated the landscape and golden kadamb and white kulu flowers provided contrast to the many-hued greens.

Yamdagni pointed out the saja trees that provided a home to millions of silkworms that were used to obtain the famous tassar silk, and immediately regretted it when he was beseeched for a new sari. Women, he thought belatedly, could never have enough of clothes and jewellery! He promised to fulfil her wish and brought her attention from the trees to the amazing riverine fauna. The clear waters made it possible to look into the depths of the river and observe the antics of a variety of freshwater turtles, smooth-coated otters and magnificent river dolphins while twenty-foot-long gharials basked in the sun on the sandbanks.

Renuka was by far the most enthusiastic animal lover he had met in his life. She genuinely believed in the interrelatedness of all species and shared with Yamdagni the story of how Rishi Kashyap, a grandson of Srishti-Karta Brahma, created the major species of life with help of his wives. His eldest wife Aditi had given birth to the current Indra—Shakra, and his eleven brothers while his second wife Diti gave rise to Daityas, a class of Asurs.

The third wife, Danu, became the mother of Danavs or the giants while Kadru and Surasa helped create the Nagas. Khaga gave birth to Yakshas, Muni to Apsaras, Krodha to vampires and Arishta to Gandharvs. His other wives proved to be more creative and Ira produced vegetation while Vinta created the birds. Surabhi gave rise to the cattle, Sarama issued forth the carnivores and Timi gave rise to the aquatics. In short, most species of life present on the planet were related to each other through their father Kashyap.

Yamdagni had heard the legend of Rishi Kashyap before and knew that he was acknowledged as the Prajapati or lord of creation, an epithet otherwise reserved for Brahma. His logical mind knew that the wives of this legendary rishi, who was counted amongst the Seven Great Seers or Saptarishis, had not literally given birth to all these species of life but had probably used genetic engineering or somehow helped them gain a foothold during the long process of evolution.

As he wondered with awe about the long lifespans of Brahma's sons and grandsons, he saw a shoal of ducks glide gracefully along the banks and shrugging off his heavy thoughts, he turned his attention back to Renuka. Noticing the other exotic birds around he pointed out to her the white-and-orange skimmers, black-bellied terns, Sarus cranes and storks though her fancy was caught by the paradise flycatcher that the locals knew as Dudhraj. She squealed in delight when one of them came to perch on the ship's rails not far from them but was sad that it didn't stay there for long. They had been floating down the river for three prehars now and the evening was turning darker.

The attendants on the ship had just started lighting the lamps when the ship shook all of a sudden and they had to hold on to the balustrades to stay upright. The two looked at each other and then ran inside to where the elders were just as an attendant came running to the upper deck with a worried announcement, 'The ship has hit a massive boulder and there seems to be a breach in the hull. The captain has advised us to abandon the ship. Please follow me as we deploy rope ladders and lower the backup boats!'

Renuka looked stunned.

'How could that happen!' she exclaimed. 'My father's ships are specially lined with a double coating of wood mixed with metal. Mere river boulders can't breach their contours. Are you sure it is unsalvageable? Do we have to really abandon ship?'

Even as she asked this the ship shook again. Yamdagni didn't want any harm to come to his wife and unborn child, and so decided not to argue and followed the attendant. They could hear shouts coming from the lower deck where water had already started filling in. Even the rowers were abandoning their positions in a hurry.

The four of them tottered towards the edge to climb down the dangling rope ladder to the two boats that had been trailing them. Yamdagni first helped Renuka on the ladder, lowering her carefully into the boat waiting below and heaved a sigh of relief when her feet touched the bottom. He followed the same procedure with his mother and father before stepping over the edge himself.

As he began climbing down with the boat's captain, he heard a huge groan coming out of the ship. The massive vessel was breaking right down in the middle due to the uneven load of water filling its cavernous bottom. He hurried down, urging the others still on the ship to follow him but it was too late for them. The vessel broke with a loud crack and the two men lurched, lost their grip on the ladder and plunged into the dark waters.

Renuka shrieked in fear as she saw her husband sink into the deep river and almost jumped from the boat herself but was restrained by her in-laws. Yamdagni tried to swim towards the boat they were on while the captain and attendants struck out towards the other boat even as long dark shapes stealthily started to surround them from all sides. Yamdagni shouted for help. The gharials that had seemed so benign from the safety of the upper deck suddenly posed the greatest danger to his life and he frantically swam towards the boat, fighting the flow of the river that was dragging him away.

All of a sudden, he saw a huge ball of fire shoot out from the staff that Ruchik had been carrying since Mahishmati. It filled the area with light and seemed to drive away the gharials. Planting it in the middle of the boat, Ruchik himself jumped into the river, towing his son to the safety of the boat just as the gharial closed its massive jaws around the empty space where Yamdagni's leg had been moments ago!

Others were not so lucky for the boat they were trying to get into was turned over by the gharials. More than a hundred interdigitated teeth sank into those still in water, filling the pristine river with warm human blood. The royal family watched in mute horror as the men who were responsible for taking them to Kanyakubja were dragged into the depths of the river.

The adrenaline rush that their bodies felt helped them row against the current and negotiate the boat around the debris that littered the river. They dared not head to the banks for no one knew what dangers lurked in the shadows, waiting to pounce on them. While the women gradually slipped into fitful sleep, the men decided to keep rowing till the first light of dawn flushed the eastern horizon beyond the thick trees.

It would be a long night of struggle for the royal family of Kanyakubja.

Adhyaye 18

Karkotak was fuming; not only had he failed in his mission but he had also inadvertently alerted Ruchik to his intention of hurting them!

To hide one clandestine act, you sometimes have to perform a hundred more and Karkotak's cycle of endless subterfuge had begun when he had to personally stab the servant who had done his bidding and poisoned Kirtivirya. He had justified the man's death as a necessary sacrifice but now, to keep the secret of his attack on the Chandravanshis safe, he had to make sure they met a similar fate.

He had known Satyavati's visit had nothing to do with Kirtivirya's health the moment he was told of their arrival. She had cleverly disguised her desire to snoop around as a family visit by bringing her children along. The Asurik magic he had learned from Marich helped him detect guile and deceit easily and he could see the treachery written all over her pretty face. He also knew that Ruchik was a shrewd man, one who could easily find out about his complicity in the events happening in Mahishmati.

He had first tried to kill the Chandravanshis by spreading a dangerous virus in Mahur but they managed to escape unharmed. Rallying from his disappointment, Karkotak planned to attack them on their homeward journey. He had selected the location carefully and planned the attack at a time when there would be few other boats plying on the river. He had used Asurik magic to create a boulder in the middle of the river and it had ripped the metal-lined wooden hull of the ship to shreds. As he had hoped, the ship had begun to sink immediately but the family had still managed to climb into one of the trailing boats. Cursing himself for forgetting to destroy those simultaneously, he had then controlled the minds of the otherwise harmless gharials along the banks and incited them into attacking the survivors. Those crew members who had not drowned instantly had been swallowed by the unlikely predators and Yamdagni and his family would have met a similar fate had Ruchik not intervened.

Karkotak had followed them along the riverbank until dawn broke but it seemed that Ruchik had sensed his presence, so he decided it would be safer to retreat and wait for the opportune moment to present itself. He was back in Mahishmati now, ruing his luck while the kingdom prepared for the festival of Dev Deepavali.

The Festival of Lights of the Gods was the biggest occasion for Shaivites—second only to Shivratri—and was celebrated on the auspicious full-moon night of the month of Kartik known as Kartik Purnima. The steps of all the ghats on the Narmada river front were lit with tens of thousands of earthen lamps in honour of its presiding goddess who was closely associated with Shiva. The gods themselves were believed to descend to earth to bathe in the holy river on this day. Scores of tiny lamps floated on the river, offered by devotees to symbolically share the light of enlightenment with the numerous riverine creatures.

The entire kingdom was decked up like a newly-wed bride, each and every building and marketplace illuminated. Lamps were placed under the sacred tulsi, fig, banyan and amla trees. This year, the festival had even more significance since the moon god was in his favourite zodiac house of Rohini. It was said that any philanthropic act performed on this day returned benefits equivalent to that of ten yagnyas and the denizens of Avanti were busy accumulating good karma.

Karkotak hated the pomp and glory of Chandravanshi festivals. He slipped quietly into his chamber to freshen up before meeting the king who would undoubtedly be looking for him. Taking a quick shower to rid himself of the dust and vegetation that clung to him, he presented himself in the royal chambers.

Arjun looked every inch a ruler, with a tall silver crown, emerald and sapphire necklaces and a peacock-blue ceremonial robe worthy of the occasion. Thick bracelets of turquoise and aquamarine graced his wrists and he held in his hand a ceremonial dagger whose sheath was studded with smaller semi-precious gems. He looked at the Naga king and exclaimed in relief, 'Father, where had you disappeared? My servants combed the entire city but couldn't find any trace of you!'

Karkotak smiled at the expression on his face and bowed his head, 'I am sorry for the inconvenience caused, my king, but I had to take care of a matter in my own kingdom which I didn't want to bother you with. I apologize for the delay in returning but I see I have arrived well in time for the ceremony.'

Arjun's face took on a concerned look. 'I hope things are under control now, Father. I am sorry my reliance on you forces you to neglect your duties towards your own people but then you are the only one I can look to now for guidance.'

Karkotak looked at the young man who had proved to be a willing apprentice and, in more ways than one, become the son he never had. This boy trusted him blindly, which was what he wanted but he felt guilty manipulating him to secure the future of his own tribe and that of the Urags and Asurs. Till now, he had not done any such thing that could arouse his suspicion but sooner or later he would have to take over Arjun's mind completely if he wanted his own dream to achieve fruition.

As Arjun turned to leave, the Naga king voiced the doubt nagging his mind, 'Tell me, my king, how much faith do you place in your cousins from the north?'

Arjun looked surprised, 'Well, I have no reason to not have faith in them! Why do you ask, Father?'

Karkotak did not want his protégé to mistrust him because of any unwise comments, so he replied in a non-committal tone, 'Well, do you know Rishi Ruchik was exploring the city while you were in conversation with his wife and children here? I bumped into him while entering the palace and got a feeling that he didn't really want to be noticed.'

'Oh,' Arjun exclaimed, 'I did not know that but I am sure he must have stepped out to take in the sights and sounds of the city after meeting my parents. If there was any cause for suspicion I am sure your excellent spies would inform us just as they did about their visit to Rishi Kanav's ashram.'

Karkotak nodded thoughtfully. 'Yes, maybe you are right, but it wouldn't do us any harm not to take whatever they say on face value.' Their conversation was broken by Manorama entering the room looking absolutely stunning. Her tall dusky frame was draped in a cyan silk sari embroidered generously with silver thread and pearls. She wore a headpiece of diamonds and emeralds with a matching necklace and earrings. Diamond bracelets hugged her slender wrists, and she looked like a vision from Swarg as she came to stand next to her husband.

Karkotak blessed the couple as they touched his feet and asked them to proceed to the river front while he followed with Kirtivirya and Padmini. Moments after they left the palace, a visitor was announced for him and Karkotak stopped when he heard that the guest was a senior rishi. He urged his in-laws to go ahead while he took care of the visitor and hastened to the meeting room with his heart thudding in his chest.

Ruchik had spent the night pondering on the events that had occurred and was convinced it had been a deliberate attempt on their life. For one, the royal boats of Mahur were doubly protected at the bottom, so a breach in the hull was unexpected. Moreover, they'd been sailing on deep waters navigated by many traders every day, so the possibility of bumping into a massive boulder was remote. Most astonishingly, the gharials that had attacked them were known fish eaters who didn't attack humans and definitely did not prey at night, yet a whole bunch of them had devoured the attendants right before their eyes!

Quite unsurprisingly, he had sensed the presence of powerful dark magic along the riverbank and his sixth sense told him of Karkotak's involvement in it. He knew the safest thing to do at that time was to wait till morning, for night was when the Asurik powers were strongest. He hadn't forgotten the miasma that had spread in Mahur taking hundreds of lives and once his family had been taken to a place of safety, Ruchik vowed to teach the Naga king a lesson. He had decided to confront Karkotak before going to Arjun and had arrived in Mahishmati with that agenda. As he waited, Karkotak entered the meeting room and asked the attendants to leave. Once they were alone, he turned to Ruchik and asked in a sinister tone. 'What treacherous mission brings you to Mahishmati now, hermit?'

Ruchik had been thinking of how to approach the subject of Karkotak's involvement to elicit the truth but the direct question brought a smile to his face. Clearly the Naga king was not afraid of admitting his role in what had happened, so he decided to answer candidly himself, 'I came here to see your face when you accept your heinous deeds, Naga, and to see your reaction when I expose you to the king you have been fooling all this while.'

Karkotak's tongue flicked in and out and his face twisted into an expression of pure hatred. More than ever the Naga king reminded Ruchik of a cobra raising its hood to strike and he immediately chanted an incantation to envelop himself in a protective shield. He was just in time for he felt a curse soaked in dark magic hit the shield with massive force.

Addressing the Naga with a wry look, he said, 'I haven't even blamed you for trying to kill us yet and you are already charging at me? You can sputter like a cornered serpent all you want but your black magic is useless in the face of the pure power of Brahman Shakti. It is in your best interests to stop this foolishness and accept that your days of manipulating Arjun are over.'

'Don't you dare talk to me in that tone, you arrogant rishi,' Karkotak blurted in rage. 'I am equally if not more powerful than you with my knowledge of Asurik magic! I will keep doing what is in the best interests of my clan, and no one can stop me!'

The declaration did not surprise Ruchik and he countered, 'No dark magic can match the sublime potency of Vedic mantras. The former is steeped in the tamasik mode of ignorance while the mantras come from the enlightened satvik power of Brahman.'

The Naga king hissed in response and reached for the dagger in his belt but Ruchik countered with a mantra that froze his hand in mid-air. Karkotak struggled to get the weapon out and hurl it at the rishi but his hand seemed to have lost all motor power! Without a moment's hesitation he used his left hand to seize the dagger and threw it at the rishi but Ruchik easily deflected it with his staff which now glowed with the same golden light that Karkotak had seen that night at the river.

Ruchik shook his head at the desperate attempts of the Naga king and said, 'You know what I was doing in the city the other day when you bumped into me at the palace gates? I had come to collect this staff which was sent to me by Rishi Agastya in order to counter any Asurik attack on my being and I am glad I got it just in time to foil your plans the other night. Your days are numbered, Karkotak, and this nefarious plan you and your brethren have hatched in the darkness of Dandak-Aranya will never see the light of day.'

Karkotak fumed hearing this; the old rishis had decided to join hands and that would indeed make fulfilling his desire more difficult. He desperately needed to free himself of Ruchik's restraining mantras for he could not let him destroy all that he had been working for in one stroke. Summoning all his dark powers and garnering his inner strength, he grabbed the nearest vase with his free hand and threw it at the rishi's head but again it was easily countered by the staff. Realizing that he had to stop Ruchik from meeting Arjun at any cost, he dashed towards the hallway, making the mistake of turning his back to the rishi. Ruchik didn't hesitate twice and let loose a volley of shots from his staff that nearly ripped Karkotak's right arm off.

The Naga king stumbled into the hallway shouting for help. As the soldiers outside rushed in to apprehend the intruder who had hurt the man whom their king regarded like his own father, Ruchik disappeared from the scene in a flash of light!

Adhyaye 19

Meanwhile, at the ghat, Arjun was relishing the atmosphere of celebration. The air was filled with the hypnotic sounds of Vedic hymns, the rhythmic beating of drums and the deep sonorous tones of conch shells. The fragrance of jasmine flowers used for decoration and the burning sandalwood incense made the atmosphere heady. Citizens of Avanti, dressed in their finest, were jostling with each other to catch a glimpse of their new king and queen and the banks of the Narmada seemed to throb with the colours of the rainbow reflected in their finery.

Arjun was relishing the experience, soaking in the atmosphere when suddenly, without preamble, everything came to a standstill. Gone were the sounds of chants and drumbeats, the swishing movements of the braziers held by the priests and the gentle lapping of the waves on the riverbank. The crowds thronging the banks seemed frozen in their revelry and even the floating diyas and fluttering flags seemed to have come to an abrupt stop!

Arjun looked around in bewilderment and was stunned to see every living being except him frozen in time. Manorama was still looking at him with a fond expression while others were locked in various postures—some were showering flower petals in the air, many were offering diyas to the river and others were arrested in mid-conversation. His soldiers wore the same stoic expression of disinterest, their eyes alert to spot any unexpected movement yet their gaze was unblinking and blank. The thought that this could be an attack orchestrated through Asurik magic occurred to him, and he tensed in anticipation. Before he had time to react though, he perceived some movement and the next minute found himself face-to-face with Ruchik.

'What's happening, Rishivar?' he asked in confusion. 'Why are only the two of us capable of movement and, more importantly, how are you in Mahishmati when you should be just about reaching Kanyakubja by now?'

Ruchik replied in a calm tone, 'My king, the vessel we were travelling on was attacked on our way back. My family and I were lucky to have escaped with our lives and have found temporary protection in Janapav, near the source of the River Chambal. Unfortunately, the same cannot be said of our attendants and crew, many of whom were swallowed by the river and the gharials swarming its banks. The incident took place in the widest part of the river and the vicious attack by the animals in the middle of the night was quite suspicious. It suggests some manner of external manipulation by someone currently in Mahishmati, that too using magic of a forbidden kind.'

Arjun was still trying to make sense of all that he was hearing. He realized that Ruchik had used his yogic powers to stop time momentarily but he did not understand why he had chosen to tell him all this in such a bizarre fashion! 'I have no reason to doubt what you say, Rishivar, and am glad all of you are safe but what how is the attack connected to Mahishmati?'

Ruchik didn't want to beat around the bush. So he said, 'My

king, this may come as a shock to you but I believe your father-in-law is the man who orchestrated that *accident*.'

Arjun couldn't believe what he was hearing. The man who had saved his own father's life and guided him in weeding out the Asurik influence from his kingdom was trying to kill Ruchik and his family using the same dark magic? It was impossible! 'You must be mistaken, Rishivar, for what enmity would the Naga king have with Mahodayapur when his own daughter is married to a Chandravanshi?'

Ruchik had known this would be the toughest part, convincing the young king of the villainy of the man he had learned to admire. So he simply said, 'Believe me, son, I felt the presence of the Naga king in the forest and, instead of carrying on to Kanyakubja, I decided to come here and confront him. What happened afterwards has just corroborated my conclusion. Rather than tell you what transpired, let me just *show* it to you right here!'

Ruchik waved his hand majestically and a sheet of water rose from the river, creating a screen in front of the king. He chanted a mantra and the events that had taken place in the palace just a few moments ago appeared on the screen of water, with a slightly muffled sound. Arjun was shocked to see how Karkotak had reacted to Ruchik's questioning and realized something was definitely amiss with the whole scenario. However, it was difficult to believe something that sinister of someone you deeply respect, and Ruchik understood the young king's reluctance.

'I am afraid that I will now have to show you something that might be more difficult for you to bear,' he said and, accessing the very ether around them, showed Arjun glimpses from the past few months of Karkotak approaching the cook in Mahishmati's kitchen, bribing him to do his bidding, the cook poisoning Kirtivirya's food in undetectable quantities, the old king falling grievously ill, his magical revival by Karkotak and, finally, the Naga king's stabbing of the cook.

Arjun's face was ashen as the realization that he had been tricked all along dawned on him. He became conscious of the subtle influence Karkotak had been wielding on his decision making but to what effect? All of a sudden, he was filled with loathing for the man and fell at the feet of the rishi who stood in front of him, begging forgiveness for his father-in-law's actions.

Ruchik told him not to worry and decided to share some of his own powers with Arjun to make him strong enough to fight the influence of Karkotak's magic. The Naga king would certainly not hesitate to attack his own son-in-law if it meant saving his own skin.

Bathing the king in a golden-blue aura, he said, 'The time is fast changing and Asurik influences are gaining a foothold in Nabhi-varsh. I have contacted Brahmarishi Vasishth to seek his guidance and he has confirmed that the troubles in Mahishmati are being fomented by the Asur leader Marich and his hidden coven in Dandak-Aranya. Srishti-Karta Brahma himself has urged him to go back to Ayodhya and once again take up the seat of the Suryavanshi kulguru, a position he had renounced earlier. The kings of Aryavarta would certainly need his help to counter the oncoming Asur onslaught.'

Arjun looked at the rishi dumbfounded for he had not known the Asurik influence was gathering so much momentum even after his own campaigns to rout it from his kingdom. He cursed himself for not being able to identify its effect on his own family and felt completely dejected.

Ruchik addressed him in soft yet firm tones, 'Arjun

Kartavirya, do not forget you are the son of a great king who almost single-handedly pushed the barbarians beyond the banks of the Tapti. You don't need the support of a Naga to achieve your goals nor the guidance of any senior member of your family. Your mother performed severe austerities to be blessed with you and destiny has a lot in store for you. My responsibility lies in ensuring that you know of this treachery and I am sure you can deal with any adverse situation that fate decides to throw at you. Being the king, how you deal with the current circumstances is entirely your decision but I ought to mention something here. Nagraj Karkotak's motive for this subterfuge was paradoxically noble for he wanted to better the lot of his own people by bringing about the ruin of Chandravanshis. Of course I do not condone any of his actions but I feel you should keep the thought in your mind before deciding on any future course of action.'

He gestured then with his hand and the screen of water fell back into the river, creating a loud splash even as movement returned all around them. Out of the corner of his eye he saw the limping figure of Karkotak approaching the royal enclosure and decided to let Arjun deal with the situation without his intervention. He only said, 'You are the king of Avanti, the scion of Haiheya Yadavs and the light of civilization in this part of the world. Do what you think is best for your people.'

Adhyaye 20

The view from the top of the Janapav hill laid open a vista of a yellow-orange forest, bounded by the Vindhyas on the south and east, and the Aravallis in the north-west. If he peered over the edge, he could even see the winding course of the Chambal and hear the faint gurgle of the river.

The events of that fateful night had left a deep impression on Yamdagni's mind and he had begun to feel differently about his father. Ruchik and Yamdagni had taken turns rowing the boat against the massive flow of the Chambal and didn't rest till they were assured of safety. They had stopped at the sandy bank as dawn arrived and then ventured inland. Ruchik had cleared a path through the thick vegetation using his staff and he had taken them to the nearest hill where they could gain a vantage point and be safe from predators and other attackers.

As the weary travellers finally found some respite, Ruchik had used magical incantations to create a sandstone enclosure, inside which they could all sleep and recover from the stress of the previous night. Yamdagni collected water from a nearby pond and had helped his father secure the perimeter using powerful mantras. Over the past months his feelings of animosity towards Ruchik had gradually given way to apathy but the way the old man had risked his own life to save his had made the younger man think about him in a new light.

Stranded from the nearest city by a thousand miles, he realized how important family was especially in these deserted parts where nature ruled supreme. Humans had managed to modify their environment to the extent that they could survive in almost any corner of the world but without the benefit of science and technological advances, man was nothing but a weak mammal poorly equipped to survive his surroundings.

As Ruchik came back from Mahishmati, Yamdagni decided to make amends for his past rude behaviour, 'Maharishi, I have been reluctant to let go of my feelings of ill will towards you all this time despite what you have done for Mahodayapur and our family. You were the one who informed us of the existence of Shakuntala as well as the threat looming in Dandak-Aranya. You have been guiding cousin Deval for Mahodayapur's governance, have helped take care of Mother and Renu on this trip, and quite literally snatched me from the jaws of the messengers of Yamdev that appeared suddenly that night. I don't know how to express my gratitude for your intervention at the risk of your own life!'

Ruchik replied with a smile, 'Let bygones be bygones, my son, and thank the Holy Trinity that we are all safe and together. It is not easy for any child to grow up without a parent and I would probably have reacted in a similar fashion had our positions been reversed. I'm sure you would not have hesitated to save my life had I been the one in the water.'

Yamdagni's eyes misted and swallowing the last vestiges of his pride he said, 'If you give me permission, I would like to address you as "father" from now on. I hope you find me worthy of being called your son.'

Ruchik's eyes filled with tears of happiness. He got up to

embrace his son who had finally let go of all the anger that had made him judge his father for most of his adult life. He was glad that their relationship had taken a positive turn. It was important for them to work together, especially since the prophesied child was to be born in a matter of months.

His encounter with Karkotak had made him worry about the future and he shared his thoughts with Yamdagni, 'Son, the poison that is spreading through Dandak-Aranya has extended its tentacles deep into Mahishmati. I know Arjun would deal with it with a firm hand but I need to make sure it doesn't sneak into the northern kingdoms. I have decided to stay back here while arranging for the return of our family.'

Yamdagni looked at the determination on his father's face and after a pause said, 'If you say we are family how can you send us back to safety while you fight this menace alone? I wish to be with you to help in this mission and take it to its conclusion.'

'I appreciate that, my son, but I do not wish to keep you away from your family the way I did, especially since the path ahead is full of danger. Brahmarishi Vasishth has informed me that Ravan, though not powerful enough to openly challenge the kings of Nabhi-varsh yet, has been gathering support from various Asur tribes and his uncle Marich is responsible for the current situation in Mahishmati.'

'Even more reason for me to stay with you,' Yamdagni declared with determination. 'Now that I know all this, you can't possibly expect me to let you venture into this quagmire alone, however powerful you may be. I *am* a Bhargav, a descendant of the great Maharishis Bhrigu and Chyavan just as you and you *did* give me life not once but twice. It is my turn to return the favour and protect you now!'

Ruchik looked at his son with pride and the two men locked

hands in a pact of solidarity. Just then, a soft voice from behind them proclaimed, 'Then I shall accompany you too!'

They turned around to see Renuka standing at the doorway of their new dwelling place with a determined expression on her face. Satyavati, who stood beside her, was nodding in agreement. 'As shall I! I did not abdicate the duties of regency to live as a sanyasin all by myself! Wherever my family goes, I go too.'

Ruchik smiled at the show of solidarity by his family and said, 'So be it then! May the gods be with all of us.'

Yamdagni

Adhyaye 21

The house of Kanyakubja had been informed of the family's decision to continue staying at Janapav for the time being and Deval had sent helpers and maids to make their stay more comfortable. However, Yamdagni had sent them all back, retaining only a maid and a midwife to help Renuka who was almost ten lunar months into her pregnancy. Now that they were in the forest, all of them wished to live the simple lives of forest dwellers. The region, being densely forested, sustained Nishadhs, tribes who were on good terms with both Avanti and Mahodayapur and since Yamdagni and Renuka knew them from Arjun's wedding, they gladly helped the family settle down. King Prasenjeet had also rushed to meet his daughter as soon as he had been informed of the mishap and agreed with their plan to stay where they were for the safety of the soon-to-be-born child. He had however forced upon them a few more maids till the time Renuka gave birth and that fateful day had finally arrived. Yamdagni and Ruchik sat outside their dwelling now while the midwife and maids tended to Renuka who was in labour. Suddenly the telltale cries of a baby rent the air and the men's sombre faces broke into a grin.

Satyavati came running out and announced the arrival of

the baby to Yamdagni, 'My son! You have finally been blessed by the gods and become a father!'

Yamdagni's blue-grey eyes twinkled with tears of happiness and his face was flushed with excitement. He followed her inside just as the midwife finished cleaning the wailing baby and wrapped it in soft muslin while Ruchik waited outside. Renuka was lying spent on the bed and Satyavati brought the baby to Yamdagni. As the little brat set eyes on his father for the first time, he burst into a toothless grin and Yamdagni couldn't help but smile himself noticing the ruddy complexion and the hazel eyes that seemed to dance with joy.

The usual fussing around the baby and mother followed and, finally, the boy received the blessings of his grandfather. As Ruchik sat down with Yamdagni preparing the birth chart of the baby, he couldn't help remembering doing the same for his own son many winters ago. 'Yama, when I had prepared your birth chart I had seen the very same planetary conjunctions that I see now in your child's and this is the corroboration that your destiny has indeed been passed on to your child.'

Yamdagni said, 'I know that the switch in destiny was inevitable, Father, but I don't know what exactly it implies for my son's future.'

Ruchik gazed at the birth chart he had been preparing and replied thoughtfully, 'The planets predict a lot of upheaval caused by your son's birth but can't predict what exact role this baby would play in the grand scheme of things yet. His future actions and the decisions he makes can modify his destiny to some extent but the birth chart clearly reflects the dichotomy of his Brahmin and Kshatriya nature. He may also have to go through massive emotional upheaval and take decisions that might prove to be difficult.'

'What kind of decisions, Father?' Yamdagni asked, worried for his newborn child's future, but Ruchik replied in a reassuring tone, 'Decisions as momentous as the ones taken by your uncle Vishwamitra that could change the course of our history. Don't worry, I believe this child will bring great joy to our lives and in anticipation of that happy future, we should call him Raam—the reservoir of joy.'

Yamdagni turned to look at the tiny baby sleeping in the arms of Renuka as she hugged him close to her chest and whispered, 'Raam . . . that's a beautiful name.'

Renuka and Satyavati liked it too and the name was finalized. As the two men went out of the room to give the mother and baby some time to rest, Yamdagni asked, 'Father, do you think the challenges in my child's life could have anything to do with the affairs of Mahishmati?'

Ruchik nodded and said, 'It is more than likely, my son.' He had replayed that night of Kartik Purnima in his mind many times over when he had confronted Karkotak and then revealed his treachery to Arjun. 'I stood there that full-moon night watching Arjun, the innocent boy turn into a hardened man in front of my very eyes. I knew he wouldn't take the life of the Naga king because of the pain that would cause his wife. But he could not forgive the attack on his own father and would have to banish Karkotak from the kingdom. Since then he has followed a brutal campaign against the Nagas, Urags and Asur supporters and I wouldn't be surprised if in the process he wipes out their entire race from the planet!'

Yamdagni nodded in understanding, 'I feel sorry for their species, but what do you think would be the final outcome of his campaign?'

'Well,' his father replied, 'in a broad sense I can say that

Arjun would become a Chakravarti and rule wisely but the exact sequence of events leading to that is hard to predict even for me. A lot of factors including the individual karma of each of the kings who would be forced to make the choice of either facing him in battle or surrendering peacefully would come into play and I don't know how things would stand by the time Raam has grown up.'

Yamdagni thought about this for a while, then said, 'Not that I doubt Arjun's abilities and the prophecies of his birth, but don't you think he would need support from a higher authority to achieve his goal? The Asurik influence might prove to be difficult to counter and he needs someone like you to guide him.'

Ruchik smiled and answered in a matter-of-fact way, 'My role in his awakening is over and now it is your erstwhile guru, the Avatar Dattatreya who can help him with whatever he requires. He possesses the powers of the Creator, Preserver and Destroyer and if he blesses Arjun with those, it could give the lad a mastery over all elements and help him achieve his goals much faster.'

'Guru Dattatreya?' Yamdagni asked incredulously, 'Why would he bless him? I think we were the last students to study from him after the twins Yoginath and Eknath! Arjun would be extremely lucky to even get his darshan in the first place. I myself haven't seen him since the time Vishwamitra and I returned to Kanyakubja!'

Ruchik laughed at that and said, 'Well, you obviously aren't updated on the whereabouts of your guru. The Avatar is currently in Mahur, that happens to be his birthplace as well as your sasural, and you may yet get the chance to meet him again . . . and so could Arjun.'

Adhyaye 22

Kartavirya Arjun sat with Garga Muni in the latter's spartan chambers, listening to the story of Dattatreya's miraculous birth. The kulguru was an accomplished sage, being the grandson of Brihaspati, the preceptor of the gods and had taken a vow of silence or *maunvrat*, hence was referred to as a Muni and not Maharishi. He would never speak unless spoken to first. so Arjun had to request him for all the details to know the complete story.

'The legend of Datta guru begins with Rishi Atri,' the kulguru, told him in measured tones. 'As you know, Rishi Atri is the father of Chandra, the progenitor of your race, as well as the short-tempered Rishi Durvasa. It is said that he once developed an unusual desire to obtain the Supreme Lord as his son.'

'But how is that possible, Gurudev?' Arjun asked, perplexed. 'God is the Supreme Father of all living beings, the One from whom all of us have emerged. How can anyone obtain Him as his child?'

Garga Muni gave a throaty chuckle, 'Kartavirya, the Supreme Lord is above all relationships. But, He can present Himself in any form for His devotees. The wise sages say it is possible to have six types of relationships with the Lord—parent, sibling, friend, lover, master—or even as a child. Consequently, one can worship the Lord in a paternal, fraternal, friendly, amorous, devotional—or even protective—manner and He very gracefully obliges His devotees and appears in those forms because of His love for us.'

'That is interesting! So has it happened before as well?' Arjun asked excitedly.

The kulguru appreciated the curiosity of his king and so explained patiently, 'The Supreme Lord is Unborn but still He appears in such avatars for the benefit of the righteous. There are some instances where He has appeared as a child to his devotees. First was his incarnation as Prishnigarbha, born to Prajapati Sutapa. Another was as Adinath Rishabhdev, born to Nabhi, the emperor from whom this country derives its name Nabhi-varsh. In this very Manvantar, we have the example of Kashyap, the progenitor of numerous species of living beings and his wife Aditi, mother of the Devas, who had prayed to the Lord to obtain Him as a son. The Lord obliged her by incarnating as the Vaman and took the three lokas back from the Asur Mahabali bringing his brother Indra and other Adityas back to Swarg!'

'I knew that Shri Hari Vishnu appeared in the dwarf form as an incarnation, but hadn't thought about the consequent relationship with Rishi Kashyap and Mother Aditi. So then, this account of Him appearing as a child of Rishi Atri would be the fourth such instance?' Arjun inquired.

The guru nodded. 'Yes, but I'm sure it won't be the last even though one needs to be a devotee of the highest order to obtain the Lord as a child. Now coming back to Atri and his desire, the rishi started focusing on the composite form of the Lord as Brahma, Vishnu and Rudra. Pleased with the rishi's unwavering devotion and honest heart, the Lord blessed him by appearing as his third child who possessed all the qualities of the Holy Trinity. Since the Trimurti had gifted a portion of themselves to the great sage, the child was called Datta—that which is given—and since the receiver was Atri, his complete name became Datta-Atreya!'

Hearing this fascinating story, Arjun's desire to meet the Avatar grew stronger. He knew obtaining the blessings of this composite incarnation of the Holy Trinity would help him fulfil the prophecy of his becoming a universal monarch. He took his leave from the kulguru and rushed to Mahur, without wasting any time, managing to secure an audience with the help of King Prasenjeet.

Dattatreya looked like a younger, fairer version of Lord Shiva with his three eyes, long dreadlocks and the trident that lay by his side, but he bore the saffron robes and V-shaped marks of a Vaishnav sadhu. He was surrounded by devotees who were thronging Mahur to receive his blessings and it had been a task to secure a personal meeting even with the king's help. Now, as he kneeled in front of the Lord who was looking at him with kind eyes, Arjun couldn't find the words to explain what his heart was feeling, drowning as he was in the positive vibrations emanating from the spiritual master.

Folding his hands he started with an invocation, 'Guru Brahma, Guru Vishnu, Guru Devo Maheshwara, Guru Sakshat Parambrahma, Tasmai Shri Gurve Namahaa!'

Overwhelmed with his powerful aura, he bowed low to touch his head to the Lord's feet. The Avatar put his left hand on Arjun's head and said in a voice that was like the rumbling of clouds, 'Don't be intimidated, my child, I have come back to the land of my birth just to fulfil the wishes of my devotees before renouncing this world.'

Arjun gathered the nerve to look up and dared to speak. 'My Lord, I can't believe I am in the presence of the most exalted spiritual guru of this world! You have written the Avadhut Gita for those who wish to follow the Gyan Yog and taught Hatha Yog for others, but I feel myself drowning in Bhakti, the third yog. Having seen you with my own eyes, I have no desires left at this moment.'

'I can see inside your heart and feel the honesty of your words.' the Avatar said with a smile. 'But to fulfil your karma on this planet, you have to ask me for the boon you had come here for. Look at me and without any fear put forth your request.'

Emboldened by these words, Arjun folded his hands and said, 'I had come here, my lord, to seek your blessings for the campaign my father had begun and one I intend to complete. I wish to create a kingdom extending to the farthest corners of the world that allows equal rights to all its citizens. There shall be no evil in this global kingdom and no internecine wars for land, cattle or wealth. Each man, woman and child will live a life of dignity and no Asurik influences will be permitted to find root there.'

Dattatreya contemplated what had been asked and replied cryptically, 'All humans are a mix of good and evil and it is only through their mixed karma that they can repay the debt owed to each other as well as other life forms. You wish to create a utopian worldwide realm, but knowing what I do of human nature, let me tell you that such an existence is not only difficult but also extremely boring, for then life would become predictable and monotonous. What would be the challenge in that?'

'I don't understand, my lord,' Arjun asked perplexed with his words. 'Are you saying that human beings should not live in such a setting?'

'I wish for it to happen as much as you do,' the Avatar replied, 'for that would release everyone from the basic worries of food, shelter and security, and let them focus on spiritual advancement. However, each individual soul gathers good as well as bad karma during its many births, and these can be repaid only by performing more karma to neutralize the previous ones. When a butcher kills the goat for its meat, his act of violence against the animal, which was till then happily living a life of blissful ignorance, can only be repaid by reversing their roles in a future birth.

'Such needless violence does not exist in the golden age of Satyug but as the proportion of people indulging in adharmik practices keeps increasing, this settlement of previous accounts can only happen in subsequent yugs. In other words, the yugs keep changing so that the repayments can continue till the Kaliyug comes to its end and we are back in the golden age of peace and harmony. So while I wish you all the luck in your efforts to create a world full of equality, I cannot grant you the boon of turning it into a utopian society just yet, for this is the Tretayug and two more eons need to pass for the cycle to return to Satyug.'

Arjun understood what the Avatar was saying and rephrased his request, 'If that is the case, my lord, I shall request you for something simpler. Please grant me the strength and wisdom required for creating such a society so that I can at least make efforts in that direction. Even if I fail at it, it won't be for lack of trying.'

Dattatreya was impressed by Arjun's devotion to the cause of spreading dharma and said magnanimously, 'I hereby grant your wish to rule the globe according to the principles of dharma! To help you in this noble task, I bless you with the possession of a yantra that can ride on any terrain and take you to the farthest corners of this world. You will be able to visit countries never explored before by your kinsmen and understand the requirements of various people inhabiting this planet. No one shall be able to match you in valour and those who dare to challenge you shall ultimately have to bow down to your might.'

Arjun was ecstatic for such a valuable input would definitely help him in his endeavour. The Lord however put a caveat to the boon, 'Since you wish to remove all Asurik maya from this world I also grant you the benediction that only a man who is more devoted than you to the cause of creating an egalitarian society may be able to defeat you. No one steeped in Asurik sorcery shall be able to halt your progress.'

Adhyaye 23

Yamdagni got the opportunity to meet his erstwhile mentor when he and Renuka came to stay at Mahur. His father-in-law insisted on giving the newborn all the comforts worthy of a prince and they had no option but to spend some months in the capital of Matripur.

He had studied under Dattatreya's guidance with Vishwamitra in the early part of their lives but had lost touch thereafter since the spiritual master had headed to the Himalayas for an unbroken penance till now. No one knew why he had returned to civilization after all these years but Yamdagni considered his arrival a godsend. He had been deeply influenced by his guru's teachings and now, wishing to secure the same education that he had received for his son, he decided to take Raam with him to visit the Avatar. When Dattatreya saw his erstwhile student he couldn't resist a smile for he was genuinely fond of him and Vishwamitra. On seeing the plump, happy boy sitting in his father's lap his smile widened even more!

He placed his hand on Raam's head and chanted a short mantra of blessing that would help him follow the right path always. Turning to Yamdagni he said, 'Long before you were sent to my ashram to study, I had been invited by your grandfather

Kadhi to bless you and your uncle. And now, I do the same for your son!'

Yamdagni beamed with pride and said, 'Gurudev, your blessings helped transform Vishwamitra into a Brahmarishi and me into a skilful advisor. It is my dearest wish that my son train under you as well!'

Dattatreya shook his head solemnly and said, 'It was my karma to instruct you and Vishwamitra before heading to the abode of my *isht dev* Shiva-Shankar, just as it was my destiny to meet you once again, here at my birthplace. But now, I must head to other lands to share the wisdom of the scriptures with their people. I have returned to my birthplace for a final farewell and intend to renounce everything and become an Avadhut to roam free without calling any country my own. I have faith in you though and am sure you and Maharishi Ruchik shall make this boy into a fine member of the Bhargav clan!'

Yamdagni was saddened by this but understood the reasons for his guru's refusal. He was lucky to have secured Dattatreya's blessings for his child and would have to be content with that.

The guru continued, 'Your father had renounced the world of men and taken sanyas very early but he returned to honour his unfulfilled commitments. Taking cue from his life, I wish for you to follow the path of Karma Yog too since you have a family to take care of. There is a potential threat to dharma looming on the horizon, and I see your son playing a big part in restoring normalcy to this world.'

Yamdagni promised to follow his directive. Thereafter, he asked the guru about his benediction to Kartavirya Arjun, 'Gurudev, I am aware that you have blessed my distant cousin with the power to defeat anyone who doesn't follow dharma and the means to ensure it physically as well in the form of the yantra that allows him to travel to distant lands. Do you think that would be sufficient to establish a kingdom of righteousness in the country?'

Dattatreya smiled at the question and responded with one of his own, 'Do you doubt Arjun's capabilities, Yama?'

Yamdagni laughed and replied, 'No, not at all! In fact I am certain that if someone can establish a rule of dharma it would be Arjun for he possesses the physical strength, personal charisma as well as devotion to dharma needed to succeed in such a task. My only concern is that Karkotak's betrayal and the attempt on Kirtivirya's life might cloud his judgement regarding his treatment of the Asurik tribes.'

The guru nodded in understanding, so Yamdagni continued, 'Arjun has already launched a campaign to push the tribals further beyond the Godavari, and I feel sorry for the species that may now be on the verge of extinction because of his campaign. The Urags, for instance. Arjun will hunt them down and decimate their population. Don't you think it would be an extreme step?'

Dattatreya replied in a sombre tone, 'Yes, and perhaps his troubled mental state could push him to perform such extreme acts of violence, but my boon doesn't make him invincible! I have blessed him with ability to defeat anyone who is not following dharma, but if he encounters someone who is following all the prescribed rules and still decides to attack, he will certainly be defeated. *That* is my safeguard against his desire for revenge getting out of hand and dictating his actions.'

Yamdagni realized that Arjun's victory was conditional to his abiding by dharma at all times and marvelled at his guru's ingenuity that had amazed him even when in school. The Avatar sighed. 'I feel sad for all loss of life, be it plant, animal, human or Urag but this material world thrives on one organism living off the other, be it in the form of food or labour or slaves or soldiers. With Arjun's dominion spreading across the country though, the numerous ambushes and internecine wars between various kingdoms will come to an end and there will be greater peace than before, thereby saving more lives in the future.'

Raam, sitting in Yamdagni's lap was listening to Dattatreya attentively, as if he could understand everything, and the guru smiled seeing his expression. The child responded with his own toothless version, revealing pink gums, and the Avatar burst out laughing. 'Yama, this boy of yours can understand everything! Even if he cannot share his thoughts yet, I am sure he can grasp the import of our words. Be very careful about what you say around him as he grows into a toddler.'

Yamdagni nodded his head obediently, not knowing whether the guru was jesting or if he was serious, but he realized that it was a good advice to follow, especially around a young impressionable child. As the Sun god's chariot began its journey towards the western horizon, he took leave of the Avatar and returned with Raam to his wife's side sharing the conversation he had had with Dattatreya. Though disappointed about his renunciation, Renuka was glad her son could at least receive the blessings of the Avatar.

As she fell asleep with the baby by her side, Yamdagni realized his accountability towards his son was greater than that of any other father. It was *his* destiny that had been passed to his son and whatever happened, he would have to make sure he trained his boy rigorously to prepare him for any future eventuality.

Adhyaye 24

After pushing the tribals living near the River Tapti to beyond the Godavari, Arjun turned his attention to the east, conquering the kingdom of Kalinga. Then he turned southwards subduing Talinga, Andhraka and Kuling till he reached the banks of the River Krishna, effectively surrounding Dandak-Aranya from the north, east and south. Now only the western coast remained.

The Asurs had gone underground but the Nagas and Urags had been routed and forced to flee to distant lands. After having been banished from Arjun's kingdom, which now extended to the deep south, Karkotak had no option but to move further down towards the tip of the Indian peninsula and find refuge in the forests that were home to small pockets of ancient tribes.

Ruchik had been observing his activities from Janapav using his yogic vision and as he watched him again now, he sighed thinking of the troublesome Naga. During the course of evolution, the mammalian brain had developed through three distinct phases that now co-habited inside the human skull. The overall behaviour of a species was dictated by the most dominant of the three—primates were governed by the most recent of these, the neocortex or 'new brain', which also happened to be the most dominant part in a human, while the midbrain governed the actions of most other mammals.

The most primitive though was the reptilian or the hindbrain. It was important since it controlled body's vital functions, such as heart rate, breathing, temperature and balance. But it was also responsible for instinctual behaviour such as aggression, supremacy, territoriality, and the fight for survival. This was the dominant part in Naga tribes and the reason Karkotak reacted like a wounded snake whenever cornered.

Arjun had not even let him meet Manorama before leaving. Karkotak hated him for putting the distance between father and daughter. In the Naga king's mind, he wasn't the one at fault and the Haiheya king had been extremely ungrateful after all that Karkotak had done to help consolidate his empire. However, he would not rest till he found a way to avenge his humiliation.

Having found shelter with the tribals, he used his knowledge of Asur magic to create a dwelling for himself near the edge of the forest that abounded in life forms ranging from elephants and sloth bear to tigers, antelopes and pangolins. The overhead canopies were filled with birds, lion-tailed macaques, flying squirrels and herds of grey langurs. Karkotak found their noises annoying, to say the least, and burned with a desire to return to his own city.

He had dug out a secret alcove in a nearby hill where he could get away from all the noises of the forest and meditate. The small recess was camouflaged by multiple tree branches that Karkotak pushed aside to enter. One of the walls possessed a small shrine; he sat in front of it in the lotus position, chanting hymns till dusk enveloped the forest in its embrace.

Usually this was when he headed back to his dwelling but today he got the feeling that something momentous was about to happen. As he finished chanting and leaned against the wall of the small cave, a rumbling began from the very heart of the hill and seemed to get stronger with each passing moment.

The walls shuddered and the forest, which had gone silent just a few moments ago, was suddenly filled with the sounds of animals fleeing in terror. Karkotak opened his eyes and smiled. After losing touch with the Urags as well as the Asurs and being stranded at the other end of the forest, he had been praying to the new Asur king and the rumble told him that his prayers had been answered.

When he stepped out of his small cavern to greet the guest he had been waiting for all these past months, he saw that the forest was bathed in a blinding light. It felt as if a large meteor was about to crash into the forest but he knew it was the portent of the arrival of something even more ingenious—an aircraft designed for Kuber, the erstwhile lord of Lanka, which now served his stepbrother Ravan.

The Pushpak Viman settled down on the forest floor, flattening trees and shrubs alike. It had a sleek triangular shape and the power of its engine could be gauged from the deep hum that was causing massive reverberations even when the aircraft was stationary. Its gleaming exterior reflected the scant light of dusk, multiplying it manifold so that the region seemed to be experiencing an artificial dawn.

Karkotak, who had not seen the aircraft in action before, now marvelled at the technology that Vishwakarma, the divine architect of Devas, had used to create it. Before he could think more about it though, a hitherto concealed door opened, revealing steps for the craft's occupant to descend and the Naga king caught his first glimpse of the new Asur leader.

Ravan was an Asur of mixed descent—his father Vishrav,

was one of the grandsons of Srishti-Karta Brahma, and his mother, Kaikesi, was the daughter of the Rakshas king Sumali. He seemed to have inherited the physical features of both his parents, retaining the sturdy well-built frame of his mother's clan and pleasant looks of his father. It was hard to believe that the boy was a mere teenager for he stood seven feet tall with a physique that an ordinary man could only hope to obtain after years of training.

His features were sharp with a faint moustache starting to appear on the upper lip and he was dressed in regal finery that could put Indra to shame. Karkotak could not help but feel impressed by his appearance and he rushed forward to greet the visitor. 'I can't believe my prayers have been answered! I have been craving an audience with you, Asur lord, and not having any other way to contact you resorted to praying to you myself!'

Ravan listened to him with a smirk and replied haughtily, 'You have been pestering me for many months now and your use of Asurik maya to send me messages has finally worked. So rise, Naga, and make the best use of this opportunity I have given you. Tell me what you want.'

'My lord, you are the only saviour I have,' Karkotak said, falling down at Ravan's feet, 'and the lone person in this world capable of avenging the attack on my tribe, decimation of the Urags and the consequences of Kartavirya Arjun's campaign faced by your own tribesmen holed up in the Dandak-Aranya. I seek your support to punish this carnage caused by the Chandravanshi king who has taken a vow to wipe all Asurik races from the face of this earth.'

Ravan had been briefed about the effect Arjun's campaign had had on his maternal uncle's tribe in Janasthan. He hadn't bothered to help Marich though because he was not too fond of his people who lived like rodents buried deep in their glorified hill. No wonder they had to retreat to their burrows as soon as someone found out their location.

'You think a mere man can challenge the might of the Asurs?' he asked dismissively. 'This Chandravanshi you seem to be so afraid of survived this time only because he did not face the considerable forces at my disposal. I can wipe him out with one stroke of my sword.'

Karkotak continued to plead passionately, 'My lord, you are right, he is just a man but he has been blessed by two rishis— Ruchik and Dattatreya—and now possesses immense power as well as a yantra to travel all over the globe! He may not be a match for the prodigious strength of the Asurs now but what about the future? The boons he has received have made him unconquerable. You must nip this threat in the bud!'

Ravan heard his argument impassively. 'You earthlings are so attached to this tiny planet but my vision is not limited to it. Arjun's campaign has actually helped me; giving shelter to the Asur tribes running away from Nabhi-varsh has earned me their gratitude and loyalty. For years the various clans have been fighting with each other, forgetting their glorious ancestors who came from the beautiful planets of Patal waiting, for a leader like Mahish-Asur to reorganize them.

'My own uncle Marich and his men have lived in the forest, hiding like vermin, but I am going to change everything now. I, Ravan, part rishi and part Rakshas shall unite all the tribes and create a force that even the Devas will fear! Go and seek shelter with my uncle, Naga, and I shall keep an eye on this man's activities. The Asurs are meant to rule this world and I, Ravan, son of Vishrav and Kaikesi, shall establish an Asur empire that spreads outwards from the earth to the three worlds.'

Karkotak sighed and nodded in acquiescence. In the absence of any other way to avenge himself he would have to go along with Ravan's plan. Who knows, staying in Janasthan, he might just get an opportunity to convince Marich to get rid of Arjun himself even if Ravan didn't keep his promise.

As the vision faded, Ruchik, who had been witnessing the exchange between the two from his ashram, opened his eyes and shook his head with dismay. Instead of resolving, the situation was only getting more complicated!

Adhyaye 25

Notwithstanding the developments in the south, life in Janapav had settled into a comfortable routine.

Happy in each other's company, and content with the regular supplies being sent by both Deval and Prasenjeet, the erstwhile residents of Mahodayapur had dismissed the idea of returning completely, sending all the maids and attendants back to their respective kingdoms. And since Yamdagni and Renuka had begun teaching the boys and girls of the Nishadh settlement, their parents gratefully paid them back in goods and food items.

Their own dwelling had expanded and turned into a proper home, surrounded by jackfruit, lemon, guava and bilva trees that had been planted and nurtured by Renuka. She had turned into a horticulture expert, planting a variety of flowering and fruit trees around the hill and Ruchik had used his powers to speed up their growth. Numerous flowering creepers graced these, giving nourishment to swarms of bees and sunbirds while the humans of the dwelling survived on tubers and vegetables growing in patches all around.

Raam was almost five years old now. His day began early when he accompanied his father to the river for prayers, followed by a full prehar of martial exercises that Yamdagni had learned from Dattatreya as his student. By the end of the session they would be famished, so he would plunge into the river to clean himself up before returning to the ashram where his grandmother would serve him sumptuous food.

The second prehar of the day would be occupied by theoretical sessions imparted by Ruchik who would share with him the knowledge of language, mathematics, astrology, science, philosophy, morality and history. Raam was most fascinated by the stories of good guys triumphing over the bad ones. The legends of Shri Hari Vishnu's incarnations and Lord Shiva's martial feats filled him with wonder and he dreamed of becoming a hero like them some day, saving the world from terrible monsters and demons. Ruchik also shared with him the stories of his own family members. Ruchik's Druid father Chyavan had created the potion of immortality called Chyavanprash, and his grandfather Bhrigu was the one who had taught the art of fire-sacrifice or yagnya to mortals. The tales encouraged him to put more efforts than his fellow students and become worthy of his lineage.

As he recited and memorized the shlokas, Renuka would sit and watch him with pride. Her son was growing into a fine lad with a toned body, sharp mind and a healthy appetite for knowledge. He was tall for his age, like his father had been, but had her milky complexion and mischievous eyes. His evenings were spent playing with tribal boys in the vicinity and he had become quite popular in their group, being the son of their teacher. By sundown, the entire family had spent several hours in pursuit of knowledge and would sit together to offer evening prayers and then discuss their individual experiences of the day.

As they huddled around the sandhya fire, pouring the last oblations into it as the last of the sun's golden rays retreated from their ashram, Ruchik said with a sigh, 'You know, living in the far-off mountains, I thought I was living a life of contentment being on my own, but I have to admit, these past years spent with my family have been so enriching that I feel more content performing these rituals with all of you than I ever did alone.'

Satyavati and Renuka smiled, while Yamdagni commented, 'Living here as a single unit with you as our head has been a good experience for us as well. Your guidance has helped me progress on my own spiritual journey and by the looks of it, Renu and Mother seem to be happy too!'

Satyavati nodded. 'The comforts of palace life hold no charm for me without my children to share them with. Truth be told, I am glad to be away from all the worries of court politics, wondering who could be the next threat to Mahodayapur, and what plot the Asurs are hatching in Dandak-Aranya. I would trade all those in a moment for this life of simple needs and yet simpler fulfilments.'

Renuka too concurred. 'I was happy in Kanyakubja but it couldn't have been more than I am here! I can visit my father anytime I want and pursue my passion for studying the flora and fauna of this region while enjoying the loving care of my husband and in-laws. What more could a woman ask for?'

'But don't you miss your rubies and emeralds, my dear?' Yamdagni teased her and she retorted with a sweet smile, 'Only as much as you miss your coin collection, my dear husband. My jewellery was important to me because of its beauty and perfection, not because of its monetary value, and there is more than enough beauty around me in the thriving life forms here to make me forget those lifeless rocks!'

'You make me lose yet again in our verbal spat! It's true what they say, you should never argue with a woman.' Yamdagni smiled, and accepted defeat gracefully.

Ruchik turned to Raam, who had been listening to the friendly banter of his elders, and asked his grandson, 'What was the most important lesson for you today, child?'

Raam thought for a moment and replied, 'Pitamah, the most interesting thing I learned today, but one I don't yet completely understand is the theory of three *guna*s. It excites me to think of myself as not just one person but a mixture of three, just like the Supreme Brahman is manifested as Brahma, Vishnu and Mahesh! But how can anyone have so many facets to their personality? I mean people are either good or bad isn't it?'

The elders smiled and Ruchik explained patiently, 'My child, hardly anyone in this world is either pure goodness or evil and unlike the stories, in the real world, most heroes as well as villains are more a shade of grey. The three gunas that you mention—satvik, rajasik and tamasik—are not abstract concepts created by philosophers but the manifestations of our own desires in the three modes of goodness, passion and ignorance respectively. Don't you feel that all the activities you are a part of fall under these three?'

Raam looked thoughtful, so Satyavati prompted, 'Okay, let me help you understand these better. If you analyse the events of your entire day, beginning with the morning routine, martial practice, breakfast, theory session, lunch, playtime with friends and the final evening prayers, can you segregate your activities according to the three modes and classify them under each?'

Raam grasped the meaning of his grandmother's words and said, 'Yes, I think I can. My morning routine with father is satvik in nature, for even though it's violent, the intent is learning not to kill but to protect the self. After the heavy exercise, I practically devour the first meal of the day because your cooking is delicious, Grandmother, and because I am ravenous by then. Since I overindulge in it, I think it would fall under the second mode of passion.'

When he saw Satyavati nodding in encouragement, he continued, 'In the evening, while we were playing, my friend Alark cheated in the game and the rest of us bashed him up. I suppose that would fall in the mode of ignorance?'

'You got into a fight with the other boys?' Renuka asked in an alarmed tone, 'I hope you did not get hurt yourself!'

Raam gave a sheepish grin and shook his head.

Yamdagni thought it wise to intervene, 'Well, such fights and fisticuffs are a part of growing up but you should know, Raam, that a Brahmin doesn't raise his hand even against a person who has done wrong for the power of words is greater than that of violence.'

'But, Father,' the boy said, 'who would listen to what I have to say if they don't think I have the power to hurt them? After all, Kartavirya Arjun has become a Samrat not because of his smooth talk but the strength he received from lord Dattatreya's boon!'

Yamdagni heard his son's argument and realized that the Kshatriya trait from his father's potion was beginning to show itself. He replied in a way that would make the young boy understand the importance of non-violence early in life, 'You are right: one should be strong enough to ensure the other person heeds your word but more than that fear, it should be the strength of your words that should be able to convince them.'

Satyavati spoke. 'Look at me, child, I have spent a whole lifetime advising people on what course of action would be in the best interests of Mahodayapur. Do you think I would have been able to enforce anything if I had to depend on my physical prowess alone?' she finished, laughing.

Raam smiled but then countered, 'Even if you are not physically threatening to look at, wouldn't your position as the queen regent have assured you that power?'

Satyavati marvelled at the argument thrown at her and answered, 'That's a clever observation, Raam, but do you know how many people *I myself* had to listen to even when I held that position?'

As her grandson looked on dubiously, she explained, 'It's true that my position added weight to what I had to say but my decisions were not just mine. Rather they were based on advice from various others including the council of ministers, the Crown prince, prominent traders, women's emancipation groups, animal rights groups, teachers, students and many others! Had all these people tried to convince me of their words based on how strong their members were, the weakest groups would have been completely left out.'

Raam nodded thoughtfully; his elders' words were beginning to make sense.

'There's no harm in possessing the strength to deal with any eventuality,' Yamdagni added, driving the point home. 'In fact your morning martial practice is meant to ensure just that. What we are stressing is to use dialogue as the primary means of negotiation in *any* situation rather than using brute force. In the course of your life, you are bound to meet some people who love dominating others. *These* are the people who need to be shown your strength rather than any random person you may have a disagreement with. Those who are strong have the responsibility of protecting the weak to help create an environment where every voice can be heard.'

As the young boy imbibed this important lesson, Ruchik said the final words for the evening, 'Sometimes in life, you may have to take a stand that may not seem desirable or socially acceptable, but you must take it if you feel it can bring about a better society. Remember this, for it may be the one thought that helps you chart your destiny.'

Adhyaye 26

Karkotak was on all fours, crawling towards Marich's cave in a last-ditch attempt to save his life. Arjun's spies had been trailing him since he had left Mahishmati and, following their king's orders, had waited for him to make contact with the Asurs and lead them to their hidden coven.

The Naga king had almost reached the lifeless mounds and was panting for breath but he dared not stop since the Yadav soldiers were not too far behind. He hoped the cloak of invisibility the Asurs had cast on their hills would conceal him from Arjun's men, and fervently wished for the carnivorous plants around the hill to make a meal out of them. Clambering on to the lifeless mound as fast as he could, he rushed through the gates guarded by Asurs and realized that the Urags that had been guarding the den earlier had been replaced already.

He ran into the central chamber which lacked all the bustle of his previous visit and came face-to-face with the sole occupant of the hall. Marich sat on the throne alone with just the towering skeleton of the giant lizard and his panthers for company. He was visibly agitated—his golden-red skin was the colour of blood and his eyes blazed with a smouldering fire. He had been briefed

156

by his spies about the presence of the intruders whom Karkotak had led here, and had taken precautions to hide everyone else while he dealt with the Naga.

Karkotak ran to his feet and explained his position, 'My lord, Arjun wants to wipe our tribes off the face of the planet. I have come here to seek your protection on the suggestion of your nephew. Please help me for I am being hunted by his soldiers even at this moment!'

'Ahh! So that's why you have come here,' Marich said in a voice dripping with sarcasm. 'Do you think I take orders from my adolescent nephew? I am the lord of this coven and I decide who gets admittance and who stays out! Do you realize how impossible you have made it for us to stay hidden here by bringing along your darling son-in-law's minions? I entrusted you with one task, one simple task and you blew that up as well! How difficult was it to find a suitable candidate who could be used for our cause?'

'Don't say that, my lord,' Karkotak whined, 'I blindly did whatever you asked of me. I did not come here immediately after being banished to avoid any trouble to you and hence contacted your nephew instead.'

He knew his life depended on his ability to convince Marich to help him, and continued pleading, 'I did persuade Arjun to turn north instead of south and our plan was running like clockwork until Ruchik started snooping around! I have been loyal to you and have made sure that the Haiheyas don't know anything about your existence!'

Marich's eyes filled with rage as he said, 'You may not have told them anything directly but you have still managed to lead them here you fool! Arjun's hounds are on your scent already and won't quit sniffing till they have explored every nook and cranny on these mountains. Because of you my entire tribe is in danger now.'

'My lord, those human soldiers are no match for your prodigious strength,' Karkotak tried to reason. 'Like your guards, I too am your loyal servant and if I don't run to you in the time of crisis whom else can I go to?'

Marich couldn't believe this puny half-breed was challenging his word. He kicked him in the chest and sent Karkotak crashing into one of the pillars. 'You lowly serpent, how dare you compare yourself to my people? Your species is a shameful abomination that crawls on the ground and has nothing in common with us Asurs! An Asur would have died fighting them rather than lead them to his home, and I couldn't care less if the lot of you become extinct!'

Karkotak couldn't help give a vent to his anger and said, 'Well, if my tribe is derived from those who crawled yours is not much different! In the end we are both hiding inside a burrow dug into the earth.'

Marich roared at this insult and ordered his pets to lunge forward at the Naga. Karkotak sat cowering at the base of the pillar while the panthers surrounded him, growling viciously each time he tried to stand up. As he looked into the eyes of the ferocious predators he pleaded with the Asur leader, 'My lord, please forgive me for my words are just a result of my desperation. You can easily fool the soldiers outside by wrapping the hill with your powerful magic or send a few of your own guards to add them to the pile of carcasses outside! Please let me live and I shall yet be of use to you in the future.'

Marich snarled angrily, revealing his poisonous fangs, and said, 'Yes, Naga, I could easily take care of the human soldiers but that isn't what has angered me so! You scrambled here knowing well that you were being tailed and your disappearance inside the hill would give away our location! *That* is the reason you shall never receive my trust again. And without that credibility, you are just a worthless piece of meat that even my pets wouldn't eat.'

Terrified, the Naga king looked around for an escape but there was no way other than the one he had entered from, and that had already been secured by Marich's guards. There were many rooms that led out of the chamber and into the cavernous depths of the hollowed out mountain but he didn't know if any of those connected to the outside world. Scrambling to all fours, he leaped on to the stone walls using the Asurik magic he had learned and climbed it like a reptile. His limbs developed adhesion and he felt like a lizard grabbing on to the wall as he started rushing upwards.

The guards threw their spears at him but he evaded them and focused on going as high as he could, hoping to escape through the air vents that were too small for a burly Asur to pass through but large enough for him. He would take his chances with Arjun's men rather than these honourless and heartless beasts inside. As he felt the fresh forest air on his face he let out a sigh of relief realizing that he had almost made it. Just as he thought he was about to crawl out to safety, a dozen arrows lodged into his back, causing him to lose his grip and fall down into the maws of the very cavern he was fleeing from.

As he was pulled down by gravity, he realized with a heartbreak that there would be no escape for him now. He lay on the floor watching with wide eyes as Marich approached him with a scimitar in his hand. Its sharp blade glinted in the light of the torches lighting the cavern, and the Asur leader's magnificent face was twisted into a vicious snarl. The Naga's last thoughts were full of regret. The last true chance for the revival of his race would be lost with him. He had failed not only his daughter and son-in-law, who had loved him with all their heart, but also his entire tribe, which was facing the brunt of his bad karma. As the Asur leaped to his side with his blade raised high, he was hit by the belated realization : nothing good could ever come out of trusting an Asur.

Adhyaye 27

Arjun's campaign to establish a global empire was turning into a huge success.

Riding on his mechanical hovercraft that could easily accommodate most of his generals, he first toured the entire world to see which kingdoms required assistance and which could be left alone. His goal was to attack the belligerent nations with a well-prepared army and establish the dominion of Avanti over them while strengthening relations with those kingdoms that welcomed him in friendship.

The northern territories of Mahodayapur and its trade partners were left alone for they belonged to the family and their rulers readily took an oath of fealty to the new emperor. One by one all kingdoms south of the Himalayas swore allegiance to Kartavirya Arjun and he crossed the great white mountains to move northwards covering Kimpurush-varsh, the land of centaurs. He had only heard of these semi-divine beings living in the cold deserts beyond Himalayas but seeing them with his own eyes made the stories come alive.

Fortunately, the centaur tribes were devoted to dharma and readily recognized his dominion and Arjun breathed a sigh of relief as he ordered his armies to march towards Hari-varsh, the flatlands that extended northwards and where the women were fabled to be as beautiful as the Apsaras. He faced stiff resistance from the various warring tribes inhabiting the land but managed to subdue them without effort, finally reaching the northernmost Ilavrita-varsh, the location of Mount Meru, the axis-mundi of the world.

Arjun had heard numerous stories about the mythical Meru that was the holiest mountain in Hindu cosmology. The Kurma Purana mentioned its staggering proportions: it was supposed to be 84,000 yojans high and extended deep into the bowels of the earth as well! On its pinnacle was the abode of Brahma and its prodigious slopes housed the guardians of the four directions.

To make sure his visit was not considered an act of aggression he decided to leave his army that was now composed of various tribes and clans, right from Nabhi-varsh to Ilavrita, behind as he headed to the North Pole, the fabled location of Mount Meru.

He had expected to see a mighty structure, taller than even the Himalayas, rising up to the heavens but the reality was completely unexpected. As he walked around the snowy land, he could not find any mountain, not even a tiny hillock; all that existed was a flatland, barren as the desert but cold to the extreme.

And there on that cold desert, where no man before him had stepped foot, was Dattatreya! The Avatar sat in the lotus position at the exact point where the North Pole would be and Arjun was struck dumb seeing him there. As he came to terms with this new reality, the Avatar beckoned to the new arrival. While Arjun was wrapped in a thick fur coat, Dattatreya seemed impervious to the cold with only a saffron angavastra covering his body. In their last meeting, the guru had told him he would be reviewing his performance soon and the king knew that was the reason he had chosen to appear to him now.

The Avatar smiled at his confusion and said, 'I knew I would run into you again some day but you have surpassed my expectations by arriving here in mere years instead of the decades I had assumed you would take.'

Arjun bowed his head and replied, 'It is only because of your blessings that I have been able to do this, my lord. I had never expected to reach this northernmost fringe of the planet or meet you again, yet here I am, seeking your benediction once again! I am glad to be here but also surprised that I couldn't locate the holy mountain that extends so high into the sky so as to provide abode to the Srishti-Karta himself.'

The guru gave another enigmatic smile. 'Meru exists right here my son, but not in a physical form like the description you have heard since your childhood. You have been probably told that Meru extends yojans into the sky as well as the earth; that the cities of the four guardians are located along its four sides; that Brahma resides on its peak and the Asurs at its bottom, and that the entire universe revolves around this holy mountain. Am I right?'

The emperor nodded like a small child.

Dattatreya asked, 'What if I tell you all that is true?'

Arjun looked around him, bewildered. What was the guru talking about? He couldn't see any mountain or city or guardian deity around! Were they all invisible to the eyes of mortals? That would make sense for such a sacred place could not be left exposed for any random onlooker.

Dattatreya saw Arjun's changed expression and realized what conclusion he had come to. 'I appreciate that you have come up with a way to explain my statement rather than doubt its veracity. This faith in your elders is what will sustain your efforts. But, no, Meru is not hidden by spells of invisibility nor does it need protection from anyone who might chance upon it. I shall explain to you how facts become distorted over thousands of years, and descriptions of real places begin resembling fantasies.

'Take the mountain's gargantuan proportions, for instance,' the Avatar continued. 'Have you ever seen any mountain even half that height? No physical structure on this planet can achieve such magnitude and rightly so, since that would put an unrealistic weight on one end of the planet!'

'But all the Puranas clearly describe its prodigious size!' Arjun said confused.

The guru nodded and said, 'What if I tell you that all the measurements mentioned in the Puranas are correct and Meru does extend high above and deep below into the earth. But it is *not* a physical mountain and refers to the axis of the earth!'

'What?' Arjun asked incredulously.

Dattatreya continued explaining, 'The so-called mountain can extend above and beyond for thousands of yojans for it is invisible and imaginary. This spot where I meditate now is the point through which the earth's axis of rotation passes and when you extend this line on both ends and plot the location of the other lokas, you will find that the Brahmalok lies at one end of it and the Asur planets at the exact opposite end!'

Arjun looked at the Avatar in astonishment as he continued, 'The lokas of the four guardians of the cardinal directions similarly exist on its four sides—Yamraj's hells lie in the southern direction near the bottom of the universe, Indra's Swarglok is located in the east in a different galaxy, Varun's abode is in the western ocean of this very planet and Kuber's city Alkapuri exists just further north of here. He has made it his permanent abode after Ravan threw him out of Lanka.

'As for the entire universe revolving around Meru, you will notice the movement of the stars yourself as evening sets in in a few hours. They do not rise in the east and set in the west like other places on the planet but revolve around this point. You have been told that the sun always circumambulates Meru, as does the moon with its attendant constellations, and it's only at the poles that you can witness such a phenomenon.'

'Incredible!' said the emperor. 'I can't thank you enough for sharing this information with me, my lord! You have opened my eyes to the idea behind the fable and I realize that behind all these fantastical legends there is a deep scientific basis!'

'I am glad to be of help,' Dattatreya said graciously and then added, 'You are one of the few humans who will see the entire globe with his own eyes and it would be better for you to keep an open mind, for most of what we hear about other countries and the people residing in them is incomplete and quite often biased.

'You have covered the southern direction riding up here from Nabhi-varsh. Now, you need to head in the opposite route traversing through the Ramyak-, Hiranyak- and Kuru-varsh which shall bring you to the diametrically opposite side of your own kingdom on the globe.'

Arjun listened to the directions attentively as Dattatreya further enlightened him about the vast tract of land west of Meru known as Ketumal-varsh where the people were of golden colour, and the country to the east called Bhadrashwa-varsh that extended right to the saltwater ocean and from where he could proceed back to Nabhi-varsh.

'I wish you all the best in your endeavour and hope for

your success,' Dattatreya said, 'and once you have united the entire world under your banner, do not fail to appoint capable generals to look after each of the kingdoms so that every part of the globe can be developed to its true potential.'

Arjun lowered his head to the Avatar's feet and promised to follow his directions. Blessing him for the final time Dattatreya declared, 'If you continue to follow your dharma and look after your people, the day won't be far when Avanti's citizens will include not just Manavs, but also Kimpurushas, Nagas, Vanars, Kinnars, Gandharvs, Yakshas and Asurs just like the kingdom of Maharaj Prithu, in whose honour the planet is still known as Prithvi. If that happens, you will have fulfilled the prophecy at the time of your birth and rewarded your parents' efforts.'

Arjun knew what that meant—if he did as directed, he could become the second man in the history of humanity to rule the entire world and become a Chakravarti, a universal monarch. Nothing could stop him from fulfilling his parents' dreams now.

Adhyaye 28

Lankapuri glittered like a diamond in the bright sunny afternoon. Strategically located on top of a mountain in between its three peaks, it was an idyllic metropolis with lush gardens, gurgling fountains, towering palaces and a huge fort wall that encompassed the entire population.

The city had been created by Vishwakarma for Lord Shiva on the occasion of his marriage to Goddess Parvati but the lord was reluctant to live in such an opulent house and had passed on its ownership to the young grandson of Brahma, Rishi Vishrav. Being in possession of a dwelling constructed for the gods made the rishi an extremely eligible bachelor and soon he took a wife—Ilavida, the granddaughter of Devguru Brihaspati.

They lived there happily, regularly entertaining guests from the other lokas who came to see the splendour of the magnificent city created by the divine architect. Ilavida's father, Bharadwaj, and her brother Garga Muni, who was now the kulguru of Kartavirya Arjun, often organized grand yagnyas there with Vishrav's father, Pulastya, and the city of gold became famous all over the three worlds as Tamraparni, the golden vessel.

The news of Vishrav's prosperity and growing clout soon reached the Asur leader Sumali. Together with his wife Tadaka, he decided to entice the young rishi into an alliance with their own daughter for that would strengthen their own political status tremendously. Accordingly, they arranged a not-so-chance encounter where Kaikesi bumped into Vishrav and seduced him into an amorous relationship that unfortunately pushed Ilavida out of his heart completely. The day, soon after, when they got married marked the beginning of the end of Lanka's glory.

Vishrav's eldest son from Ilavida, Vaishravan, fondly called Kuber, inherited Lanka when his parents took sanyas and was made the lord of riches by Srishti-Karta Brahma because of his scrupulous honesty. Everyone was happy with Kuber's appointment except Kaikesi, who wanted her own son to emerge from his stepbrother's shadow. In time, Ravan staged a coup against Kuber using the very Asurs that had earlier guarded him and threw him and the Yakshas out of Lanka, forcing them to flee to the North Pole.

The same usurper now sat in Lankapuri's royal court, watching the proceedings with the focus of a predator as his uncle Marich shared the latest developments in Dandak-Aranya. Since the time he had met Karkotak, Ravan's demonic genes had kicked in and he had matured into a full-grown Asur. He was taller than any human now, almost touching eight feet and possessed the muscular build of a mountain lion. Thick whiskers framed his fair face while his brown eyes looked upon his uncle enviously. He admired Marich's fabulous antlers for he himself could boast only of two tiny horns growing out of his temples that he kept covered under his golden crown.

His uncle Marich was a pure Rakshas, skilled in the art of shape-shifting; Ravan had seen him turn into a golden deer many times and that was another reason for his envy.

Because of his half-Rakshas parentage, he himself could alter his appearance only to a limited extent—he could modify his basic look quite convincingly but not transform into any other species.

Shaking his head with the only regret he had, he brought his attention back to what was being said. 'Kartavirya Arjun has brought under his banner not only the kingdoms south of the Himalayas but also the ones on other continents. He is well on his way to becoming the emperor of the entire planet and obtaining the title of universal monarch. It won't be long before he sets his eyes on Lanka, and when he comes we will have to bow to him . . . at least till we figure out an effective plan to deal with him.'

Ravan cursed under his breath: that old Naga had been right all along. He should have dealt with this Chandravanshi *before* he garnered all the armies of the known world under his banner. He looked around at the council, which was made up mostly of elderly generals from various clans. The various Asur tribes were man-eaters who often arrived on battlefields in the aftermath of human conflicts to devour their prey, but they were not averse to luring live humans as well. Occasionally they served as rank-and-file soldiers in the service of one or the other warlords on the planet but now that Arjun had spread his dharmik influence all over the globe, they had rushed to Lanka to take refuge under Ravan. Their leaders now sat in his octagonal hall, discussing the rapid progress Arjun had made and the danger he posed to their way of life.

Marich was continuing his rant, 'The man has almost become a legend, hounding all our tribes to the corners of the globe. Lanka is the only place where they can be safe. Unknowingly though, he has joined us all in a mutual hatred for him, a feat that many mighty Asur leaders of yore couldn't accomplish!'

Ravan sneered. 'So let me understand this correctly, Uncle, you are implying that all of them are here just because of their enmity with Arjun, that their presence here has nothing to do with me?'

'Not at all, my lord,' said the older Rakshas hesitantly. 'Without you to show us the dream of a united Asur empire, who could have imagined that my Rakshas tribe would sit at the same side of the table as the Pishachs or the Danavs would ever break bread with the Prets! It is undoubtedly your leadership that has brought us all together for a common cause.'

His ego satisfied, Ravan said haughtily, 'A fact that you would do well never to forget, Uncle, for I am the fruition of the dream your own father had dreamed when he married his daughter to my father. I shall take the Asurs to new heights and you'll watch this global empire of Arjun give way to a worldwide Asur kingdom!'

The assembled leaders of assorted Asur tribes cheered lustily in unison. When the commotion subsided, Marich said, 'May that day come soon for all of us. As things stand right now, Arjun doesn't seem to be letting down his guard and our spies haven't been able to identify a single chink in his armour that we can take advantage of. Because of the boon given to him by Avatar Dattatreya, no supporter of the Asurik way of life could ever defeat him in a fair battle.

'So that leaves us with two options,' he continued after a dramatic pause. 'Either we abandon the Asurik way of life, for then we would at least stand a chance against him. But if we were to do that, why would we need to fight him? Or, our king, who, as he himself pointed out, is the son of a Vedic rishi and the most powerful Asur on the planet, can challenge him to a duel and defeat Arjun, thus acquiring the Chandravanshi upstart's global empire and ushering in the Age of Asurs in one stroke.'

As the gathered crowd joined Marich in demanding the second course of action, Ravan admired the way his uncle had turned the tables on him as a fitting reply to his earlier insult. These bloody Asurs wouldn't hesitate to feast on their own leader's dead body. Fine, he would show them all what he was capable of.

Adhyaye 29

The kingdom of Avanti now stretched all over the globe.

Arjun had performed massive yagnyas for peace and
prosperity in each of the conquered territories, which were
governed by his chosen representatives. These generals, who
numbered slightly more than a thousand, were fiercely loyal
to their emperor, earning them the epithet Sahastra-Arjun, the
thousand hands of Arjun. All of them had arrived to attend the
Dev Deepawali ceremony that night—a celebration of Arjun's
own victory against the Asurik elements, just like Lord Shiv's
triumph over the three demon sons of Tarak-Asur.

The morning had begun with a victory parade by the
thousand generals, dressed in the ceremonial garments of their
own countries, followed by a contingent of their respective
armies that besides men included marching horses, elephants,
camels, bulls and, in one instance, even lions and ostriches!

It was a veritable treat for the citizens of Mahishmati as they
hosted the biggest congregation in the history of the world.
The preparations for housing so many people and making
provisions for their food and entertainment required lot of
planning, and had begun well in advance. Guest houses and
inns had mushroomed all over the city and the visitors were

having the time of their life, mixing with the locals as well as other foreign contingents.

Arjun and Manorama were discussing the evening's plans with Kulguru Garga, ensuring all the details were double-checked, particularly for the special event the emperor of the world had planned for the evening.

'I am so glad, Gurudev, that you gave your approval to this suggestion, and thankful to my wife for coming up with this brilliant idea in the first place. I hope this will bring us closer to the citizens of Mahishmati and they won't feel their king is only keen on travelling the world, forgetting his own citizens.'

Kulguru Garga nodded. 'There was no reason not to approve this idea, my king, for it promises to emancipate the poorest of the poor! The credit indeed goes to the queen, nay the empress of the world for having a heart big enough to share her husband with so many women!'

Manorama laughed and said, 'Well, kulguru, you know I would never let my husband do anything that involves so many women unless it benefited the kingdom! This is just a symbolic ritual to declare that we follow the same customs as our subjects. As I understand, our family hasn't followed it for obvious issues of paternity but we can serve two great purposes by at least accepting it nominally.'

'Yes,' Arjun agreed, 'the unacceptance of polyandry by the royal family has generated some resentment against us over the years and I don't want to give the people any grounds for rebellion that the Asurs could use against me! Hence, starting from today, five-hundred already-married women of Mahishmati shall be able to claim the king as their second husband by participating in the ritual bathing in the River

Narmada tonight thereby bridging the divide between the customs followed by the masses and the royal house.'

The kulguru smiled, 'And the fact that all of them have been chosen from the poorest of households shall simultaneously help in the upliftment of the condition of these women as well as their families. Ingenious idea indeed!'

Arjun was proud of his wife's plan. Their relationship had been strained in the aftermath of his throwing Karkotak out of the kingdom, but he knew that Manorama understood the necessity of that step and that she was grateful to him for having spared her father's life. It was a testimony to their love that she was able to suggest this idea that involved him getting married to five hundred married women who would now also have the honour of being recognized as the king's wives.

Accompanied by the kulguru and other advisors, the royal couple made their way towards the ghat, all the while being showered with rose petals by the people who were happy with his decision. The new queens of Mahishmati followed them, fanning out on both sides of the couple, bedecked in the auspicious colours of red and gold and wearing the precious jewellery they had been presented with from the king's household as befitting royal brides.

As all of them stood on the banks of the Narmada, Kulguru Garga recited the story of Lord Shiva's victory that the night commemorated for the benefit of the newcomers from other countries. 'After Tarak-Asur was killed by Shiva's son Kartikeya, the demon's sons Tarakaksha, Kamlaksha and Vidyunmali, fled from their own planet, finding refuge on its three satellites. Here they began an intense penance to obtain immortality and avenge their father's death.

'Srishti-Karta Brahma was pleased with their tapasya but

told them he could not provide them absolute immortality. They could live for long provided they never got together at the same spatial coordinates. This boon of conditional invincibility spurred the three demon princes into developing their outposts to the extent that they began to rival Swarg in their opulence. Once they had gained enough followers, the brothers began to take revenge for their father's death. They would mount swift attacks on their sworn enemies, the Devas, and return to their individual cities before any action could be taken against them.'

The entire gathering listened in silence to the story of the origin of their favourite festival.

Garga continued, 'Fed up with their menace the Devas ran to Shiva for succour. He agreed to help but declared that they would have to wait for the time when the three demons were together at one place. Knowing that the brothers would never gather at one particular place if they could help it, Shiva decided to target them when their three satellites were aligned in one straight line during the course of their revolution.

'Now this wasn't a common occurrence and took place only once in a thousand human years, that too for just a few moments when the Pushya nakshatra was in conjunction with Chandra. Brahma sat about calculating the exact moment and Shiva, taking position at the base of Mount Meru, strung his missile launcher Pinak and mounted the dreaded Narayan Astra.'

Arjun knew this story by heart for he had heard it repeated every year in the same words, but he never bored of it. And today, when he himself had managed to defeat Asurik influence all over the globe to establish a global empire based on dharma, he felt each word touch his heart. He could almost imagine the lord of destruction straddling the North Pole, aiming his celestial Pinak towards the three satellites, biding his time for the exact moment when he would launch the powerful missile of Lord Vishnu.

'As the opportune moment began to approach,' the kulguru was saying, 'Shiva fired Vishnu's supreme projectile, timing it in such a way that it would reach the three cities at the exact moment they lined up. The Devas watched with bated breath as the terrifying missile shot through the stars and finally found its mark, destroying the outposts in one massive explosion that created a new asteroid belt around their planet. Overjoyed, the gods declared the day as a celebration of light and thus began the tradition of Dev Deepawali that all worshipers of Shiva celebrate even today.'

The motley gathering burst into cries of 'Har Har Mahadev' and Arjun stepped into the river holding Manorama's hand with his other honorary wives in tow. The priests blew conch shells and the royal band sounded bugles and drums to announce the beginning of the festivities. As the sun set over the city, the newly extended royal family took a dip in the sacred waters and bowed with folded hands while the priests standing behind them chanted the aarti to Lord Shiva.

No sooner had they turned around to step out of the river than the water seemed to rise dangerously. There was a shriek from one end as some women lost their footing and went under. Even as Arjun shouted to his soldiers to help those who had fallen, his sixth sense told him that this sudden surge was not natural. Someone had dammed the river ahead which was causing the water to accumulate here. Within moments, the river was lapping the top step of the ghat, leaving everyone floundering in the water and scrambling to get out.

Arjun closed his eyes and realized that an Asur was behind the damming of water, and using the power given to him by

Dattatreya's boon he began to break the spell. Immediately, the river began to recede and the excess water surged forward, flooding the place where the Asur was, taking him along with it.

Ravan could not believe a mere human had negated his spell and turned it around on him! When Arjun had visited Lanka on his way back from the eastern lands, his uncle Marich had pretended to accept his sovereignty as the senior Rakshas leader while Ravan observed him from a safe distance. He had overheard the plans for this celebration, his devious mind forming its own nefarious strategy to get rid of him. He had thought it would be easy to attack Arjun secretly but now that his plans had been thwarted, he swore angrily and began swimming against the current to where Arjun was to teach him a lesson with his bare hands.

The emperor was still in the water making sure all the women got out safely when he felt his feet slip as something attacked him underwater. The Asur! Ravan had grabbed Arjun's legs taking cover of the darkness and had pulled him with all his strength. Arjun lost his footing on the slippery steps and felt the Asur dragging him deeper into the depths to drown him. Chanting a mantra to remember Dattatreya he felt pure Brahman power flowing through his body, filling his brain, heart and muscles with raw physical strength. He bent forward to firmly grasp the hands that were dragging him down, and started rising towards the surface. Ravan realized he was being outmatched in strength, so the moment they breached the surface, he let go of him and created an illusion to scare the emperor.

The Asur grew in size and produced ten heads that were looking hungrily at the assembled humans. His torso sprouted twenty arms that began to grasp the onlookers as meal for his multiple mouths and the panicked populace began to scamper.

Arjun saw through the deception and gripped Ravan around the midriff with his left arm while planting a heavy blow on his spine with his right elbow. The Asur buckled under the impact and doubled over. Without breaking sweat, Arjun turned, using his body weight to push his adversary's head underwater. Ravan gasped for breath and tried all his magical powers to escape but nothing seemed to work. As the water began filling his airways, he mentally chanted a mantra to call for Pushpak.

With a deep rumbling sound and flashing lights the viman appeared right above its owner, a portal opening in the base of the craft to allow him entrance. Ravan quickly muttered another spell and there was a collective gasp of surprise from the crowd at the ghat as the Asur rose in the air with Arjun dangling from his waist. As soon as Ravan grabbed on to the edge of the entrance, the viman lifted off with such force that Arjun lost his grip and fell down into the water with a loud splash.

As Arjun's soldiers dived into the river to secure their king, Ravan zoomed off towards Lanka thanking his stars for his lucky escape. This human could turn into a big threat indeed!

Adhyaye 30

The ashram at Janapav wore a deserted look as its inhabitants gathered at the banks of the River Chambal to bid farewell to Ruchik and Satyavati. They had spent the last decade enjoying the bliss of family life but it was now time for them to leave behind family ties and work towards attaining salvation as prescribed in the Varnashram, one of the founding principles of Arya society. The first twenty-five years of a person's life were meant to be spent in the pursuit of knowledge and a similar number of years were designated for the pleasures and responsibilities of marital life. After that, it was time to start distancing oneself from society by leaving the cities and moving through the forests for the next quarter-century and thereafter, retire to a remote place where one could be away from all known trappings of the material world and focus on the Supreme Lord alone.

This system ensured that every human being could, within one lifetime, achieve the ideals of dharma, artha and kama—good conduct, monetary pleasure and conjugal bliss in equal measure without having to sacrifice the fourth and the most important, moksha or liberation from the cycle of birth and death.

Raam was old enough to understand he could not force his grandparents to stay but he couldn't imagine how life without them would be. He had never felt alone in their presence for even when his parents were busy, he had always had his grandparents, who had been more like friends with him than elders. He stood there now hugging them hard—too old to shed tears, yet too young to accept it stoically like his father.

Ruchik looked at him and said, 'It is our destiny to leave, my child, so do not grieve for this parting. The trees around us would have been seeds before the wind or birds carried them here and water helped provide them roots. Our karma works much the same way. I created the potion and blessed it with magic but Satyavati exchanged it with her mother, thereby changing the destiny of the two children to be born. All that you are today, and all that you will become tomorrow, is a result of all that has happened in your past. You have great things waiting for you in the future and our blessings are always with you.'

Satyavati did not have the heart to say anything to her grandson for parting from him was the most difficult thing she had had to do in her life. From the moment she had abdicated her royal duties this child had become the reason for her life yet she was leaving him behind at the cusp of adulthood, which would be the most difficult time for him. She wanted to see him get married and have loads of children but she knew how convoluted this web of desire could be—one could get entangled in it, going deeper and deeper and never finding contentment. That she had spent the past years watching him grow and bask in the love of her husband, son and daughter-in-law would have to be enough. All the turmoil in their lives was in the past now and this was the perfect time for them to leave on the journey of self-enlightenment. She choked down tears and addressed

Renuka, 'You know about the magic potion prepared by your father-in-law that had helped me give birth to your husband. I was too scared to face the prospect of raising a child with a warrior's temperament and so requested Ruchik to modify the effects in Yama. These will soon become dominant in Raam.'

Renuka nodded in understanding; she and Yama would have to ensure that their son didn't turn into a violent warrior and that his inherent traits could be controlled through the knowledge of scriptures.

Satyavati then took out her prized manuscript and, giving it to her daughter-in-law, said, 'I hand over to you my chronicles of the lunar dynasty and hope you keep adding new chapters to it. Spend your time well, pursuing your passions, for you have the support of an extremely faithful husband and a devoted son who thinks the world of you.'

Renuka couldn't control her emotions any more and hugged her mother-in-law who had been the only mother she had known since she had lost her own. Yamdagni broke away from them, discussing the preparations of the journey with the oarsmen who would take his parents further northwards towards Ujjain. He was as affected as Renuka, who was now shedding copious tears, and Raam, who was putting up a brave front, but he had to be strong to take care of his family and thus could not let the feeling of abandonment engulf him.

The arrangements made, Yamdagni walked towards his son and patted his head affectionately, 'Raam, your grandfather and grandmother have experienced all the happiness this world can offer. It is time for them to move on and pursue the most important goal of life now. Instead of being sad and filling their mind with doubt, we should be happy that they have chosen to walk this path and wish them the best in their endeavour.'

He then turned to his father and grasped his hand gently. 'Father,' he said, 'I know life is an arduous journey to a solitary destination, but I am glad we had the good fortune of your company for so many years. These people shall take you to the other bank to a point from where you will be able to commence your journey to Ujjain, the abode of Mahakaal. I wish you and mother the best in your sacred endeavour though I don't know how Renu and I shall manage life here without you.'

Ruchik gave a sad smile and said, 'Yama, every day that I have spent with you in this forest has filled me with regret for all the time I lost not being there with you. Sometimes, it feels as if we are victims of causality and free-will is just a charade created by the gods to mislead us into a sense of having control over our lives. But I know every action performed by us counts. Each man's journey in life does lead him to a lonely goal but you need not walk it alone.

'You are a wise, intelligent man, and perfectly capable of doing justice to your role as a householder as well as acting as a guide to your son without any supervision from me or your mother. I want to leave you my most prized possession—the Bow of Vishnu, which was given to me while I was in the Himalayas. Combined with the two quivers Rishi Kanav blessed you with, this bow will help you ward off any evil that comes your way!'

A sudden flash of lightning illuminated the riverbank at this declaration and everyone shielded their eyes from the brilliance. When Raam managed to open them a bit he was astounded to see a thick longbow resting in Ruchik's outstretched hands, glowing with an ethereal blue radiance. It seemed to be made of a tough material, yet was intricately carved like wood, and he looked at it mesmerized as Ruchik presented the divine weapon to his father.

Ruchik noticed his look of curiosity and said, 'If you prove worthy of it, Raam, the Bow of Vishnu might very well choose you as its next caretaker. Before we depart, there are two things I wish to tell you, my child, which, if you follow, can take you to your destined future. One, do not disobey your father even though you may disagree with some of his decisions and, second, never let your mother out of your protection for she is the most vulnerable of all three of you.'

Raam nodded in acquiescence and his grandfather continued cryptically, 'Even though our lives are fated to reach a predetermined destination, we still possess the power to decide how we reach there. Don't worry about what is yet to come. Just follow your karma.'

The two departing elders looked at them with a smile of satisfaction as their own karma towards their family was fulfilled. Ruchik wanted to spend the remaining years of his life in the sacred city of Ujjain which housed the Mahakaaleshwar Temple dedicated to Shiva. Satyavati had agreed to accompany him; it would be the first time since the early days of their marriage that the two of them would be together again and she was content to follow where he led.

She had to find happiness for herself as well, and let go of the fear in her heart about leaving her children by themselves. They were grown-ups, all three of them, and she knew they would take care of each other, but her heart still beat faster at the thought of never seeing them again. The only solace she had was the thought that Ruchik's potion had transformed Vishwamitra's life for the better and she hoped it would do the same for Raam.

Later though, as she slept fitfully in the boat that was taking them to their destination, she had a vision that disturbed her equanimity. Her cherubic grandson, who in her dream was reading scriptures with a beatific smile, was replaced by a well-built man covered in mud and gore. The book in his hand had transformed into an axe and his mouth twisted into a snarl as the rivers on the earth turned red with blood.

Raam

Adhyaye 31

He was on a wide road lined by pine trees on both sides and a view of mountains that almost touched the sky. The sunlight was weak and a haze obscured the path but, once in a while, a chariot or a horseman would pass by and the fog would dissipate a little, though not enough for him to know where exactly he was headed. He was tired but his heart beat with excitement for there were new places to visit, people to meet, cultures to explore and languages to be learnt. He was about to take a ride from the carriage trudging along when someone shook him lightly and a soft voice sounded in his ears.

'Wake up, it is almost time for morning prayers!'

Opening his eyes to slits to see his father sitting beside him Raam realized sadly, it was only a dream! He rubbed his eyes and stifled a yawn so that he could tell Yamdagni about it, 'Father, I had this glorious vision about travelling to some unknown city with huge snow-capped mountains on the horizon and it seemed so real that I could feel the cold wind on my face!'

Yamdagni smiled and said, 'It's the call of the Himalayas, my son! Perhaps you need to make a trip to the north soon. We have kept you sequestered here for far too long save the occasional visit to your grandfather's kingdom of Matripur. I feel maybe it's time for you to visit Kanyakubja now and see the northern cities.'

Raam absorbed his father's words and said innocently, 'I don't want to go anywhere without you both! How would it be fun if I didn't have the two people I love the most with me?'

Yamdagni replied with a smile, 'Do you know why we named you Raam? Because it signifies someone who is always providing bliss. I don't know whether it is the cause or the effect but there it is and I'm glad to have a son like you; you are the most loving child I have ever seen in my life. But it is also my responsibility to make sure you make the right choices in your life and there is nothing better than travelling alone to gain new experiences and form your own opinion about the world.'

He ruffled Raam's long untidy hair and added, 'Pick up the brush if you love to paint, jot down the thoughts swirling in your mind, sing the song you hum in the river . . . Don't hold back, live! Travel to the towns, cities and capitals of our great kingdoms; ride the roads and float in the streams, feel the wind in your hair and the earth below your feet. Only then will you be able to decide for yourself what and who you wish to be.'

Saying this Yamdagni stood up and left for the river. It would be time for classes soon.

Raam went about his daily regimen, studying the scriptures and practising the martial arts routine with the Nishadh boys who were his father's students and, after lunch, left to join them for their regular dose of physical activity. They ran away chattering to the river and after endless games of hide-and-seek wound their way home, climbing trees, grasping overhead branches and swinging like baboons.

This had been their regular pattern for some weeks now

and Raam was delighted to see that his body was becoming more muscular as he kept at it. The initial sprint along the river was like a warm-up and the run through the forest helped develop better quadriceps. The climbing helped take care of his back and arms and the falling down, lifting up and hanging from branches strengthened the pectorals and deltoids. Since his grandparents' departure he had devoted more and more time to his physical training, trying to fill the void that their absence had created.

Yamdagni made sure though that he did not lose touch with the scriptures and provided him the daily dose of study while his mother kept him grounded by making him help her take care of the pets and plants that numbered in hundreds now. With Renuka's efforts, over the past few years Janapav had turned into a veritable sanctuary with a lush green bamboo grove that gave shelter to deer and rabbits while flowering shrubs brought in butterflies of varied hues. Raam seemed to love animals too, especially their cow Suraḅhi whom they had named after the celestial Kamdhenu.

He often wondered why cows were considered so sacred and Renuka had explained their importance patiently. The cow was not just an animal but the provider of milk, the major source of proteins and essential minerals like calcium for all vegetarians. Its calf provided the labour required to till the fields while its dung was used as manure to enrich the fertility of the very soil that provided food for all mankind. Its urine possessed antiseptic properties and even after death, its hide gave leather to protect human feet from the harsh terrain and cold weather.

Renuka's emphasis on non-violence towards animals had worked its way into Raam's consciousness slowly and she was glad to notice that his predicted Kshatriya nature was still dormant.

She often told him that nature or Prakriti was wild and sometimes even cruel for it did not help the weak survive. The weak could survive only through civilization or sanskriti that helped provide equal opportunity to all irrespective of their physical prowess.

As Raam swung along a branch now to land at the entrance of his mother's favourite grove, his companions dropped in after him. 'You won again, man!' complained Lakshya, a dark burly guy with budding whiskers.

Raam looked at the sullen faces of his friends and broke into a grin, 'Yes, I did, losers!'

Hearing the word everyone pounced on him and there was a mock scuffle to bring him down while he laughed in merriment. If he wished, he could have thrown them off easily, but he let them have the satisfaction of beating him for they were his friends and he enjoyed their camaraderie.

As they pinned him down and piled on top of him, Renuka stepped out of the grove admonishing them, 'Boys, behave!' she said, making them scamper off the prostrate Raam, who got up with a sheepish grin on his face.

Renuka had aged beautifully just like Satyavati and her radiant face still reflected the honesty of her youth. There were a few lines of course that proclaimed her to be more mature than her petite frame would suggest but there was beauty in those lines as well.

'How many times have I told you to start acting your age?' she chided them, 'Tridev only knows when you boys will become more responsible!'

'Come on, mother,' said Raam making an innocent face,

surreptitiously gesturing to others to disperse, 'we were just having fun.'

His friends scattered as suddenly as they had appeared and Renuka couldn't help supress a smile—boys would be boys no matter how old they grew. Her son was almost eighteen, yet he still behaved like a teenager. He was a good boy and helped both her as well as his father in the daily chores but she had to at least try to discipline him, however fruitless that endeavour may be. She shooed him away to clean himself up before entering the grove and he happily obliged.

Raam loved swimming and needed to take a dip to cool himself after the exertion of the past prehar. After spending an appropriate length of time in the river, enough to convince his mother that he had rid himself of all the dirt, he returned to the ashram where his father was preparing for the evening yagnya. Yamdagni was becoming more and more accomplished in his craft and was turning into a Siddha just like his father. He had already attained control over the five basic elements which helped them face any kind of adverse weather conditions without any problem. However, the bigger achievement would be when he gained control over the five inner senses; it was a work in progress.

Raam sat down quietly beside his father, helping him light the fire using the sacred arani wood. Once the holy fire was lit, he chanted the evening mantras along with his father and Renuka who joined them once she finished tending to her animals. As the embers on the ground began to die, stars began to appear in the night sky like embers of some long-forgotten fire. Raam lay down on his back and stared at them while his mother busied herself with supper and Yamdagni cleaned and safely stored the scriptures he had been reading that day.

Looking at the glittering jewels in the sky, Raam tried to

differentiate the planets from the stars. His grandfather had told him that planets or *grahas* were closer and therefore didn't twinkle while stars were thousands and thousands of yojans away. Because of the deflection of light along that great distance, they appeared to twinkle to someone watching from earth. He quickly recognized the three easily identified planets, but after that his thoughts drifted and he found himself thinking of Swarg, which existed in a different galaxy.

He had heard stories of how his grand-uncle Vishwamitra had helped a Suryavanshi king reach Swarg without any physical help, and he marvelled at the feat. He hoped to meet Vishwamitra in person some day and obtain more knowledge of the universe, for his father never seemed too excited about what was out there. He firmly believed that doing a good job in this world was better than dreaming of another utopian realm.

Raam saw the way his parents helped the locals advance by teaching their children, and helping and protecting the weak. Clearly, Renuka and Yamdagni had found a way to make the world a better place and he wondered how he could contribute towards the universe. Living in the middle of the forest, there was only so much one could do and he didn't see himself venturing out for any reason anytime soon. Sure, he would love to travel to various cities and see the world but what would be the fun in that if the only two people in his life did not accompany him?

Sometimes he fancied himself as one of the superheroes of yore who slayed demons and fought dragons to make the world a better place. But the chance of that happening was remote now since Kartavirya Arjun had established his dharmik empire in even the farthest corners of the world and the demons themselves had taken refuge under him! Well, it was all for the best, he thought. After all, he was still a teenager—there would be time enough for him to choose what he wanted to do later in life.

Little did he know, time and the proverbial tide do not wait for anyone.

Adhyaye 32

Ravan emerged from his bedchamber with a satisfied grin on his face, having spent the night with three nubile Rakshasis. Man, they were talented! He decided to add them to his growing harem of concubines and queens though Mandodari would always occupy the pride of place in his heart. He sleepwalked towards his own chamber when he remembered that he was supposed to host the Chakravarti Samrat in Lankapuri later that day.

After that ignominious defeat at Arjun's hands on the banks of the River Narmada, he had accepted defeat and tendered an unconditional apology. Marich had negotiated on his behalf and managed to convince the emperor that the new Asur king was just a boy and had acted impulsively. Arjun had decided to forgive his transgression but with a firm warning that the next mistake would be his last. In addition, Ravan had had to surrender his viman to the emperor and that was the biggest blow to him. He hated being separated from his prized possession and finally understood some of the resentment Kuber must have felt towards him for snatching it away. He imagined his stepbrother laughing his heart out at the North Pole, his potbelly shaking with pleasure knowing that even

Ravan had to part with the prized Pushpak! The sense of superiority that flying afforded him couldn't be matched by any other accomplishment in the world. The feeling of floating gracefully above the clouds, looking into the eyes of the sun, while the rest of the world crawled far below him like ants was unparalleled.

Arjun held a different view about the plane; it provided him a bird's-eye view over his kingdom, straddling mountains, oceans, valleys and gorges as it did. For him, using the Pushpak was just a matter of convenience and nothing more than that.

Given the vastness of the empire, it was only natural for Arjun to allow considerable freedom to the individual rulers, and Ravan exploited this to strengthen his dark powers and plot his revenge. He had surreptitiously restarted his agenda to regroup the Asur tribes including the fierce Daityas, the giant Danavs, vampire Pishachs and ghostly Prets, seeking help from their Asur brethren living in other lokas. His brother Kumbhakarna was turning into a wise pundit himself and he hoped to groom Vibhishan into a worthy minister. He just needed to be a little patient so that they would all understand his ambitious plans for the Asurs in the time to come.

For the emperor's visit, he had taken care to camouflage all his fierce warriors as workers and gardeners. He couldn't use dark magic to hide them for Arjun would see right through it, so he had spent the past week fitting everyone in their new roles in preparation for the ultimate coup in history, planned for that evening.

While Ravan relaxed in a hot, scented bath and went over his plans for the evening, the Pushpak was on its way carrying the emperor, his principal advisor, chief of intelligence and the army chief. Arjun was now in his late thirties and his handsome face had acquired new lines that gave him a stern, determined look. His body had gained more muscle due to his relentless campaign to create a global empire and he was more experienced in the ways of the world now.

The craft landed smoothly at the airstrip of Weragantota, located in the middle of the island of Lanka, where Vibhishan waited for them. A mild-mannered, pleasant-looking boy, he greeted the visitors respectfully and led them to the chariot that would take them to the royal palace. After a short ride, the entourage arrived in the palace courtyard where they were met by Ravan himself. The Lanka king escorted them to the chamber for visiting dignitaries so they could freshen up before getting down to discussing the affairs of the principality. They spent the day reviewing the army and navy, the functioning of the royal court, and addressing the problems of the common citizens. Convincing the emperor of the fair dealings that everyone in the principality of Lanka received Ravan took him and his aides to the royal gardens for an evening stroll.

This was Ashok Van, Ravan's favourite place to unwind and he knew being here would put Arjun at ease as well. It was a beautiful tropical evening and musicians had been strategically placed so that the melodious notes of the veena floated in the air accompanied by the rhythmic beats of the drums. Sweet-scented flowers graced the entire garden, suffusing the air with their delicious aroma. The entourage walked on the geometrically laid pathways that wound around fragrant creepers, overhanging trellised arches and shady trees leading to a wide portico that provided a beautiful view of the valley below.

The lord of Lanka took them to the edge where luxurious seating had been arranged for the guests and they all sank down to the comfortable cushions, relieving the stress of the day. In front of them were tables laden with fruits of all varieties and goblets full of wine. Ravan clapped twice to summon gorgeous dancers for a performance and soon the garden was filled with the tinkle of anklets and notes of accompanying music. Arjun really felt at peace after a long time. He let down his guard, and bit into the luscious fruits that melted in his mouth. Combined with the excellent wine, the lilting music and the ethereal performance drove out all thoughts of suspicion from his mind. He wondered if he had been wrong in his assessment of Ravan and if he ought to give him the benefit of doubt.

Ravan knew the time to strike was now for he would never be able to catch the emperor off-guard like this again. 'Samrat, I am sure you are aware of the boon that Rishi Ruchik had bestowed on the erstwhile queen of Kanyakubja and her daughter?' he said. He had recognized the growing powers of Ruchik and his clan, for they were the ones who had exposed Karkotak and had decided to kill two birds with one stone by planting suspicion in the mind of Kartavirya. He continued when the emperor nodded, 'While the first boon shook the established notions of this world in the form of Vishwamitra who has risen to the level of a Brahmarishi, the result of the second is Yamdagni's boy Raam. I wanted to know if you had any thoughts on this issue.'

'What are you getting at, Ravan?' Arjun asked, perplexed.

The Asur didn't want to offend the emperor knowing his close relations with the family, so he said tactfully, 'Nothing, my lord, I just wished to know your opinion about the possible future achievements of the son of Yamdagni. You have established the rule of dharma all over the globe and have become the first Chakravarti Samrat since Maharaj Prithu, so I don't see what he could do to help the situation any further.'

'Hmm,' Arjun said thoughtfully. 'Well, he is the scion of

the Bhargav clan. Whatever he does I am sure he will make his forefathers very proud.'

Ravan nodded along but very slyly added a hint of misgiving in his words, 'Vishwamitra made it possible for Kshatriyas to attain the highest state of Brahmin-hood and I can't help but wonder if Raam might do something similar for Brahmins. Rishi Ruchik no doubt helped you in your initial days but could it be that by doing so, he was just preparing the ground for his own grandson to take over after you?'

Ravan knew from the look on Arjun's face that his words had hit the mark. 'Together, the two men born of his boon shall stand as shining beacons for people who want to break down the Varnashram dharma and disrupt the fabric of society. I shudder, thinking of the day when no one would adhere to their prescribed duties any more and society would be run by the will of individuals. God forbid such a day comes when they think of replacing you, our emperor, who has spent a lifetime creating this empire, with that young boy Raam!'

Arjun's facial expression changed as he thought about what Ravan had said for it did make some sort of twisted sense. The notion that a Brahmin boy could replace him, the universal monarch, was appalling, especially since he had three sons of his own but given what Vishwamitra had done, it might not prove too difficult for Raam as well! He would have to think about this in detail after reaching Mahishmati. As Ravan plied Arjun with some more wine, he signalled to his attendants to move to the second stage of the plan. Numerous Rakshasas began shape-shifting into microscopic worms, rapidly positioning themselves in the folds of the clothing of the emperor and his companions.

Noticing the emperor's thoughtful look, Ravan smiled inwardly. Every human being clung to the limited authority they had on the people around them and Arjun was not just any man but the Chakravarti Samrat of the whole world. As the guests took their leave, Ravan hoped that Arjun would not be able to identify the tiny beings clinging to his clothes and those of his aides since the Asur stench was too powerful here and would camouflage their presence. He might become aware of them in Mahishmati, but by then, hopefully, it would be too late.

He had utilized innocuous words to instil doubt in the emperor's mind without using any Asurik maya or dark magic. True, Dattatreya's boon enabled the emperor to fight tangible threats, but would Arjun be able to fight his own thoughts?

Adhyaye 33

The guests aboard Pushpak sped towards Mahishmati, oblivious of the impending doom they were bringing back with them. As the emperor and his aides slipped into a deep wine-induced sleep, the shape-shifters began their work. Multiple tiny worms now slowly crept out of the folds of their angavastras and made their way to their victims' bare upper bodies, positioning themselves above the spinal column. Two pairs of sharp teeth extended from each proboscis and one by one they bit into the skin, tearing the epithelium and boring their way into the subcutaneous tissue. Arjun felt a burning sensation on his skin and scratched his back dislodging many of the Rakshas worms but they had been sent on a mission by their leader and would not be dissuaded.

Like a determined parasite, the worms climbed upwards again and once they were back in position, started releasing tissue-dissolving enzymes on the emperor's skin to make their entry easier. Within moments they had eaten their way into the subcutaneous layer of his back and reached the spinal column. The same was being done by their counterparts to the other three humans on the craft as Vibhishan flew them back.

Each tiny Rakshas then dug its way to the nearest

intervertebral disc, since it was easier to penetrate than bone, and bored into it with the diligence of a desert dweller digging for water. After a few minutes' efforts in which they chewed through cartilage and fibre, they finally reached the epidural space right above the spinal cord.

The next step was tricky because, by now, their host body's immune system had detected their presence and was sending its minions to strike. The breach of outer tissues had caused a massive release of protective cells and by the time the parasites had invaded the outermost of meninges, a variety of multi-limbed macrophages had identified the intruders and begun their attack.

The Rakshas trespassers though had come prepared for this eventuality and secreted more chemicals that immobilized the cells, effectively putting them to sleep. Once this threat was contained they bore into the middle layer of spinal coverings, gaining access to the cerebrospinal fluid that would facilitate their movement towards the brain. They swam vigorously to their destination, lodging into the brain tissue, and began the process of transforming the human neurons into Asurik ones.

As the infestation spread, the men's brains would come under direct control of the Asur leader. Meanwhile, the worms would keep on multiplying and spreading into every nerve of the body, ready to claim their next victim whenever there was close contact of any nature. With a little luck, the entire army that Arjun commanded today would eventually come under Ravan's control without even lifting a finger.

However, unbeknownst to the worms, the Brahman power coursing through Arjun's body as a result of Dattatreya's boon helped repair the damage to his body, sealing the nicks and reactivating the suppressed immune system. The resurgent protective cells identified and disposed of most invaders one by one, though the change they had caused in his neurons could not be reversed. Fed by the Asur lord, Arjun's sleeping brain was inducing fancy dreams in his head, in which Kshatriyas and Brahmins were fighting amongst each other using Divya Astras, destroying the entire world in the process!

His logical brain knew that the relationship between Kshatriyas and Brahmins hadn't always been smooth and he was reminded of the enmity between Brahmarishi Vasishth and Vishwamitra that had now become the stuff of legend. He recalled the fate of the corrupt King Vena, who was one of the earliest rulers of this land and who had been killed by the rishis with their yogic powers to rid his subjects of his tyranny. They had churned his body to create a new ruler and now his dream presented that same scenario, replacing the dead king with him.

The two classes had been at loggerheads many times before and the reason for that wasn't too hard to fathom. It was human tendency to get drunk on the authority their positions afforded and this was as true for the Brahmins as it was for the Kshatriyas as both held sway over the masses, though it differed in nature. While the kings and their armies were responsible for securing the borders and keeping antisocial elements in check, it was the pundits who held the door to heaven open for the other castes, connecting them to the gods.

When the viman landed, they bid farewell to Vibhishan and headed to their respective homes. Arjun's mind couldn't shake the feeling that his eyes had been opened by this visit albeit in a different manner than he had expected. He had gone to Lanka hoping to discover some subversive activities that Ravan was participating in; instead he had become aware of the possible sedition being hatched under his very nose. He didn't know whether Vishwamitra, now that he was a Brahmarishi, would also be a part of the conspiracy with Maharishi Ruchik but then one could never be too sure!

The caste system was a division of labour that helped society function to its optimal limits. When it started, the members of any caste could follow any profession but few were actively encouraged to do so to maintain a reasonable number of people in each profession in every generation. If each person started to negate their duties, it would compel Shudras to take up arms or Brahmins to till the land and Vaishyas to assume kingship. Nothing was more important for a king than maintaining the fabric of society, and Arjun would ensure it didn't break, at least under his rule.

Reaching his palace, he began listing down the names of the important rishis in Nabhi-varsh— Kulguru Garga and his father Bharadwaj, who was rather aloof from the world of men; Rishi Gautam, who had once cursed Indra; Brahmarishi Vasishth, who had returned to Ayodhya; Rishi Kanav in the west, who was taking care of Vishwamitra's daughter; Vishwamitra himself in the east, who possessed the knowledge of divine weapons and had even challenged Indra at one time; Agastya in the south, who was developing a form of martial art; and of course Ruchik and his clan, who lived practically next door to his capital.

As he thought about them, Arjun saw a pattern emerging. These so called ascetics held between them complete mastery over physical, mental and spiritual powers. Perhaps there were other Druids and seers outside the country who were in on the plan as well. He immediately decided to take a detailed tour of his entire kingdom with his three sons. It was time to introduce them to their future roles and secure the kingdom of the world for the Haiheyas.

Adhyaye 34

The winds of change had hit Arjun's global realm and the empire that prided itself on following the principles of dharma began losing its sheen slowly but steadily.

While Arjun's body had been able to contain the insidious invasion of the Rakshas worms, the infection had spread from the three top officials who had accompanied him, to their families and subordinates. From them, it moved to the foot soldiers, security guards, their families, and in time widespread animosity against Brahmins began to emerge amongst the warrior class.

It started innocuously enough with sporadic instances of harassment faced by local pundits in one or two towns but gradually metamorphosed into a civil war–like situation with Brahmins revolting against the mistreatment meted out to their brethren in other parts and Kshatriyas using that as a justification to keep them in place, forming a vicious cycle of hatred and mistrust.

The worst incident that had occurred was when Arjun's own men attacked an ashram of Brahmins and set fire to their property. All the men were killed including the babies, and the women physically abused. One of the women who had been pregnant at the time of the attack, used all the merit generated through her penance and hurled a curse on them—since they had not spared even the newborn babies suckling at their mother's breasts, their entire clan would be wiped off by the hands of a Brahmin no older than an adolescent.

On their part, the Brahmins were not completely blameless either. Their knowledge of the ancient language of the Devas in which scriptures were written made them indispensable in any major ceremony in one's life, from birth to death. There were some who even prided themselves on this ability and considered all other classes subservient to them, which naturally created resentment in others.

Ravan knew it was only a matter of time before the very fabric of Arjun's empire unravelled. He decided to hasten the process by fostering the animosity in Brahmins, and who could be a better candidate for this manipulation than Ruchik's own family? He made a surreptitious visit to Janapav and set the wheels for the second part of his plan in motion.

Using his limited shape-shifting capabilities, he took the guise of a sadhu and wandered among the Nishadhs living around the area, taking their offerings and blessing them cursorily, figuring out what would be the best way to influence Yamdagni. It tickled Ravan no end that this art of illusion, inherited from the maternal side of his family, could be used in so many innovative ways. His Rakshas brethren had infected half the military of that arrogant emperor of the world and here he was, the king of all Asur clans, being worshipped by the same people who owed their allegiance to Arjun.

He was nearing the edge of the village when he chanced upon Renuka and was dumbstruck by her beauty. He hadn't seen her before but recognized her by the appellation that the locals referred to her with—Rishi-patni Rajkumari. For them she was the princess who was also a rishi's wife, and Ravan knew that no other woman in the vicinity fit that description. She was dressed simply yet gracefully in a white sari with a golden border, and as he watched her a plan began to take shape in his mind

Making an excessive show of blessing the people around in a loud voice, he tried to catch her attention and soon enough he saw her walking towards him. When she reached him, she bent and touched his feet as etiquette demanded. Ravan patted her head and asked for her introduction.

'Rishivar, I am Renuka,' she replied with folded hands, 'the daughter of King Prasenjeet of Matripur, and the wife of Rishi Yamdagni of the Bhrigu clan. I wish to seek your blessings for myself and my family.'

Hearing her sweet voice, Ravan felt an animal urge to ravish her right there and then take her to Lanka to add to his harem, but he realized her beauty could be put to much better use here. He had already formulated a fake identity for himself, so he said, 'I know about the greatness of both your father as well as your husband and it is a pleasure to meet you today. I am Yoginath, one of the few men fortunate enough to be a disciple of Guru Dattatreya!'

Renuka's face registered a surprise and she said enthusiastically, 'Then it is our good fortune that I met you here, Rishivar! I'm sure my husband will be delighted to spend some time with you for he too was taught by the Avatar as a child. Please honour our humble abode with your presence and bless us with the chance to serve you.'

'Of course I shall be delighted to pay you a visit but not right now, for I need to spend some time with these village folk as well,' Ravan replied. 'Please convey my regards to your husband till then and tell me how things are with him and your son.'

Renuka welcomed the question for she wanted to share her worries about her son's future with someone older and more experienced in the ways of the world, and in the absence of Ruchik and Satyavati this elderly rishi was a stroke of luck. She spoke excitedly, 'Rishivar, my son is now a grown man but hasn't lost his teenage exuberance and I worry about him sometimes. He doesn't seem to have interest in any particular field and I really don't know how his future will shape up.'

The rishi smiled, 'Well, we have all been through that phase, haven't we? Once the burden of responsibility lands on his shoulders he will mature in his thoughts as well as behaviour. But, my dear, looking at you I could have never imagined you to be the mother of a grown-up son!'

Renuka blushed at this open appreciation. Before she could respond, the rishi commented again, 'It must get lonely for a lovely lady like you in this wilderness. You should be living in a palace surrounded by admirers who would do anything to bring a smile on your face. Only a fool would leave the beauty of such a bewitching woman at home while he was himself lost in the forest praying to unappreciative gods.'

Renuka was shocked! She must have misheard. In Arya society, a married woman was akin to a sister or mother for all other men, yet this Sadhu had said something that was completely unacceptable and not befitting his status! Her breath quickened and she turned crimson with embarrassment. 'Rishivar, I am completely devoted to my husband and do not require other admirers, either in a palace or here in the forest!'

Saying so, she strode away in a huff while Ravan watched her retreating form with a pleased expression. He had intended to stir some emotion within Renuka's heart and he knew that the thought that she, as one of the most beautiful princesses of the royal family of Kanyakubja, was deserving of more appreciation would stick in her mind for a while. And a while was all he needed to complete his plan. Now that he had ignited a reluctant spark in Renuka's heart, he had to find a suitable candidate to give her the admiration she was unknowingly craving.

Adhyaye 35

Flustered by her encounter with the sadhu, Renuka stormed back home. Since Raam was out with his friends as usual, and Yamdagni was busy with his evening meditation, she couldn't pour her heart out to anyone immediately. She sat down, took several deep breaths to regain her composure, and replayed the entire incident in her mind. She should have left the moment that sadhu had complimented her the first time. But she had given him the benefit of doubt, only to be proved wrong later!

As the daughter of a king and then the wife of the principal advisor of Mahodayapur, she had never really encountered the lascivious behaviour of men. It saddened her that in some men, the sight of an unaccompanied woman gave rise to an urge to exploit rather than protect. She sighed, ruing that even those whose outward appearance marked them as men of dharma could actually be harbouring Asurik tendencies.

As she calmed down, a tiny voice reminded her that the compliment, even if underhanded, was at least a reflection of the man's admiration, which was more than what she had received from Yamdagni in a while now. Her anger devolving into resignation, she decided not to mention the incident to her husband for he could be extremely jealous. He used to frown upon her time spent in the Kanyakubja palace, surrounded by handsome guards, and Tridev only knew how he would react to the hermit's outright advance.

Shaking her head to banish images of that lecherous man, she decided to head to the river to take a dip and fill the pot of water she would need for cooking dinner. The cool river water rid her of all the anger and as she let go of the negativity inside her, she began to hum her favourite song. When she was done, she changed her clothes and filled the amphora she had brought with the flowing water.

As the gentle breeze caressed her untied hair, she walked towards the grove she had nurtured over the years and that housed her favourite animals to spend some time before heading home. She had barely taken a few steps, lost in the melody that was playing in her head, when she bumped into a stranger and dropped the vessel in surprise.

For a second she thought the sadhu had followed her here and felt afraid but when she looked up, it was the handsome face of a younger man full of apology. Seeing that the pot had broken, the stranger conjured up a new one just like it and murmured a few words to magically fill it with water. Renuka was amazed and looked at him appraisingly. He had the chiselled looks of the god of love, and his body seemed to be carved out of white marble, each muscle well defined without seeming bulky. Golden hair framed his handsome face like a halo around the sun and his blue eyes danced with a naughty expression. It took her a moment to collect herself and ask him with trepidation, 'I have never seen a mortal man perform magic of such fine quality before. Who might you be, sir?'

The stranger bowed and replied, 'Devi, I am not a mortal man but the prince of Gandharvs. My name is Chitrarath. Our clan lives not too far from here yet I haven't ventured out of my part of the woods for some time now on account of certain reasons that I no longer wish to dwell on. Today, after many months, I thought of taking a walk to the beach but stumbled upon this grove. May I ask whom it belongs to?'

'This is the fruit of my labour!' Renuka answered proudly. 'I personally selected and planted each tree here to create a sanctuary for those animals crippled by hunters or predators.'

'Oh, I see,' said Chitrarath, 'beauty with a kind heart.'

Renuka blushed for the second time that day and the memories of her encounter with the sadhu returned. Chitrarath sensed her discomfort and sought to allay it. 'My apologies if my words have offended you in any way, Devi! I just wished to convey my appreciation for the good work you have done which is a reflection of the goodness of your heart.'

She acknowledged his effort with a gentle nod. 'I have to return home now. Please feel free to spend some time here but you must promise not to harm the ones I seek to protect.'

Chitrarath bowed in agreement and watched as she gracefully made her way to the ashram at the top of the hill. He blessed the strange sadhu he had met earlier in the forest who had come from the southern seas. While his clansmen had been busy enjoying with their mates Chitrarath had been brooding over his broken heart. In such a scenario, the sadhu had been a godsend, encouraging him to break out of his stupor and seek new interests to help forget old ones.

The sadhu had suggested Chitrarath take a walk along the riverbank and meet the gentle lady of the grove who might just be the cure for his heartache. For some reason he had felt compelled to listen to him and now that he had seen her, he knew his quest had ended. A human who cared for the lower species of life as much as the Gandharvs did was rare to find.

Concealed in his hiding place, Ravan sniggered as he watched the encounter between Chitrarath and Renuka. Encouraged by their interaction, he decided to keep a watch on the proceedings for a few days. And while he was at it, he thought it best to also take a look at what Renuka's son was doing. Locating him using his dark powers, he arrived at the spot where the boys were wrestling and blessed them with a vague *Ayushmaan bhava* for a long life.

Although this wasn't a part of his original plan, he realized it was too good an opportunity to miss. 'You are a Brahmin boy yet you train like a Kshatriya,' he said to Raam, hoping to poison the lad's mind against the emperor. 'Why? I mean how would this help in your life unless you decide to join the imperial army?'

The boy laughed, 'Rishivar, I don't have any plans till now to join the army but it does present an interesting line of thought. My father has taught me that our disposition decides what caste we belong to rather than our birth and since I am equally inclined towards both scripture as well as arms it's hard for me to say which of these I will choose eventually.'

'Well,' Ravan said, shaking his head, 'your father may have these liberal views of Mahodayapur but here in Avanti things are a little different. Our emperor does not condone such caste-hopping for he believes that maintaining the fabric of society is more important than catering to individual aspirations! No one living in the global empire of the Haiheya emperor has any freedom to choose his career any more.'

So saying, Ravan walked away with a satisfied smile, leaving Raam to ponder over what had just been said. The spark had been lit and it would be interesting to see what would happen in case Yamdagni's boy actually came face-to-face with the man Ravan hated the most—His Royal Highness, Lord of the Thousand Generals, Emperor of the World, Karta-bloody-virya Arjun!

the Legend of Kschu-Given ...214

man Ravan hated the most—His Ivyal Highness, Lord of the
Thousand Generals, Emperor of the World, Rama-bloody-Raya
Arjun.

Adhyaye 36

The not-so-chance encounter engineered by the Asur king had yielded limited positive results. Every day for a week now, Chitrarath had waited for Renuka near the grove, and once she came, they spent the evening talking about their common love for animals and discussing their vastly different lifestyles.

Gandharvs were like vagabonds, living wherever they wished to, shuttling between Swarg and whichever other loka caught their fancy. Currently they were residing in the central forests of Nabhi-varsh, restoring them to their original glory after Arjun's campaign had destroyed significant stretches. Chitrarath understood that any development came at a certain cost but he did believe in trying to limit the damage. Listening to his passionate arguments for inclusive development and admiring his physical beauty, Renuka knew that had they met in a different situation at a different time, she and Chitrarath could have had a life together. But they hadn't, and she was married so no such thoughts could be entertained.

She told him about her experience with the sadhu and he was amused at her reaction, wondering how someone could follow monogamy so steadfastly that they would consider even admiration an affront. Gandharvs believed in free love and any appreciation was taken positively. There was no entitlement that any Gandharv held over his or her mate and a couple stayed together only till the time they could sustain their love. She countered with her firm belief in being devoted to one person for whole life. Arguing in favour of her reaction she mentioned that what the sadhu had said to her *had been* an affront, and pointed out that she hadn't reacted the same way with him because of the difference in approach. The Gandharv gave in to the argument, not wanting to upset her.

Since Yamdagni and Raam both were busy with their own pursuits, Chitrarath's presence filled a void Renuka hadn't even realized existed, providing her with a friend whom she could share her thoughts with and Chitrarath reciprocated in the same manner wishing to know her better.

Watching them now, as he had been for the past week, Ravan realized that there was a very real possibility that nothing scandalous would come out of their meetings. Deciding to hasten things along, he sought Yamdagni who was meditating in a remote part of the forest. He introduced himself as an erstwhile disciple of Dattatreya which helped break the ice and after a few moments of false reminiscences of the time spent with Guru Dattatreya, he steered the conversation towards other topics. 'And how are your spouse and child? Now that you have told me your story I believe the graceful lady the locals were addressing as Rishi-patni Rajkumari must be your better half! I believe I caught a glimpse of her when I was roaming around the Nishadh village a week ago but was unable to seek an introduction.'

Yamdagni acknowledged the compliment on behalf of his wife and replied, 'Yes, I dare say it may have been her! The locals adore her and it serves her well since Raam and I spend a lot of time away from home. Visiting the village allows her to meet the parents of her pupils and catch up with the latest gossip.'

Ravan nodded in understanding, 'Well, that is only expected! Besides, gossip is a harmless way of exchanging information for women though I daresay I know many men who follow the practice no less than the fairer sex!'

While the two sat gossiping like old women themselves, Renuka and Chitrarath had ambled together towards the river to fill her amphora. It was hot and Chitrarath began urging her to take a dip in the water. When she refused, he shrugged at her reluctance and, throwing off his upper garments, ran barefoot through the pebble-strewn bank, jumping into the river. Renuka sat on the bank watching the water roll down his handsome form with feelings that were decidedly not platonic and a hot flush began creeping up her neck. Yamdagni had increasingly become asexual in the past few years and while she understood his commitment to his goal, she hadn't realized that her repressed sexuality would become so unbearable in the face of such an alluring proposal! She found herself unable to take her eyes off Chitrarath's glistening body and the Gandharv, realizing her turmoil, stopped cavorting in the water and stepped out, taking slow purposeful steps towards her. Renuka's breath caught in her throat seeing him emerge from the water like the moon god, water dripping off his muscular physique, his angavastra clinging to his powerful legs.

Ravan, through his Asurik maya, realized what was happening and wished he could have witnessed in person as the two took the plunge into the forbidden. But he had to make sure Yamdagni was in the right frame of mind before Renuka returned, and asked him, 'Since I never married, I would like to ask you one question, if you don't mind my inquisitiveness that is!'

'Sure, brother,' Yamdagni said, referring to the bond they shared through their guru.

Pretending to hesitate a little, Ravan asked, 'I have always wondered how the wives of rishis deal with the forced celibacy that is thrust upon them by their husbands. I mean if you practise complete abstinence from all types of sexual union, wouldn't your wife feel deprived? Does she accept it meekly or does she protest for her right to the conjugal bliss that matrimony guarantees.'

Yamdagni was taken aback by the question but gave him the benefit of doubt since the sadhu had clearly never been married and could be genuinely curious. 'Well, as per the Varnashram dharma, once you enter Vanprasth and start living in the forest, both husband and wife must understand that they have to gradually move away from frequent copulation towards complete celibacy, which is what the next stage of life demands.'

They had begun walking towards the ashram now and Ravan asked thoughtfully, 'Pardon me if I'm mistaken but aren't you still in the second quarter of your life? I don't mean to intrude but I was wondering: If someone moves to the forest before the time set by the Varnashram dharma, do you still behave as you would in the Vanprasth stage?'

Yamdagni was beginning to find this line of questioning annoying, and just gave a non-committal nod to which Ravan replied succinctly, 'Ah, that must be difficult for your wife!'

The two walked in awkward silence till they reached the entrance to the bamboo grove. Finally Yamdagni said, 'I am sure she doesn't mind and knows it's for the best.'

He had barely completed the sentence when there was a sound of dry leaves being trampled under running feet and Renuka appeared on the scene, flushed with emotion. Shocked to find Yamdagni standing there, she dropped her water pot, which broke into smithereens. Having filled Yamdagni's mind with distrust, Ravan quietly slipped away to intercept Chitrarath from barging in on a family situation that could potentially rid him of one more adversary.

Adhyaye 37

Renuka and Yamdagni stood face-to-face, each wrestling with conflicting emotions.

The sadhu's persistent questions had rattled Yamdagni and forced him to worry whether he had been neglecting his wife's desires. To compound matters further, Renuka seemed to be wrestling with some difficult emotions herself. He decided to calm his own mind as well as hers and walked forward to embrace her. However, when Renuka did not return the gesture, he realized something was very wrong. There was a faint hint of a masculine scent on her person and her troubled expression gave birth to a doubt he just couldn't ignore. He decided to find out what had happened using his yogic powers and as the events of the previous prehar flashed in front of his eyes he recoiled from his wife in horror.

He pushed her away and asked incredulously, 'How could you!'

Yamdagni's distress spurred Renuka into action and she hurried to calm him down. 'Yama, please don't jump to any conclusion! Nothing happened between me and that Gandharv. I ran away the moment he touched my hand!'

'What do you mean nothing happened?' Yamdagni shouted

in anger, 'I sifted through your thoughts and saw you ogling his body; I *felt* the emotions that coursed through your heart when he touched your skin! Does all that amount to *nothing*?'

Renuka didn't know how to respond. She had experienced a gamut of emotions that even she had not been able to understand. A part of her had wished for Chitrarath to do the unthinkable but she had stopped herself well in time, knowing that by taking this step she would be closing all doors on her present life.

Out of the corner of her eye she saw Raam burst on to the scene. Panic overwhelmed her; she could not bear for her son to think of her in the same twisted way that Yamdagni was describing her in.

Raam was speechless for he had never seen his parents argue like this. Of course they had their share of arguments like any married couple but those were generally much less spirited and easily fizzled out. His father was shouting things he couldn't even begin to grasp.

'Cheating is not just being physically intimate with someone other than your spouse! If you so much as even *think* about another man lasciviously or flirt with him with desire in your heart, it is tantamount to duplicitous behaviour. Such a person is not worth living with!'

Both Raam and Renuka were stunned by Yamdagni's vitriolic outburst. Raam had never thought about his parents' sex life for he found it difficult to imagine his mother as a woman who might have physical needs just like anyone else. He tried to speak on behalf of her but Yamdagni stopped him with a fierce look. The situation had the intensity of a maelstrom and he could only watch from the sidelines as his entire world began to collapse around him.

Yamdagni's heart felt shattered. It didn't matter to him if his wife had actually slept with someone or not. The very fact that she had harboured those thoughts in her bosom for someone other than him was an intolerable blow to his pride.

Renuka gathered the courage to speak, and said, 'Yama, I know you feel betrayed but think for a moment: If I had truly wished I could have had a clandestine affair with him but I didn't! I could have easily run away with him to another loka. Instead I came back to you, for my heart lies here with my family and I would never do anything to jeopardize what we have!'

Her words moved Raam for he could sense the desperate situation his mother had got caught in but they seemed to have absolutely no effect on Yamdagni, who stood with disappointment and anger writ large on his face.

Seeing his obstinacy, Renuka felt annoyed herself and said, 'You are judging me for a crime I haven't even committed but you readily accepted the situation your own relative Vishwamitra had been in with Menaka! We women have more wisdom than you men give us credit for—I stopped myself before anything could happen unlike your uncle who couldn't control his senses even after years of penance!'

At the comparison with Vishwamitra, Yamdagni finally lost his temper for more than an uncle he was like a brother to him. As Ravan's manipulations took effect, he looked at her with a determined expression and said, 'If you came back just because of me when you could have easily run away with him, I declare that from today you are free! The woman who inhabited my wife's body died the moment she let that wretched Gandharv touch her. I don't even recognize the person who stands in front of me now.'

Renuka could not take it any more. 'If you really wish to

think of me as dead, why don't you actually throw me off the cliff and get rid of me!'

Raam knew things were getting out of hand when he heard this and moved forward to hush his mother but Yamdagni's next words stopped him in his tracks.

'So be it!' Ravan's dark magic had seeped deep into Yamdagni's heart, filling it with hatred, and now all he could think of was ridding himself of this woman who had dared to cheat on him. He reached for the sword he used when training with Raam as his son looked on in horror.

'Father!' Raam rushed forward to block Yamdagni's way. 'What on earth are you doing? Mother apologized for whatever she inadvertently did. I implore you, if you have ever loved me or her, do not take her life in a fit of anger!'

Yamdagni's eyes bored into the pleading eyes of his son. He said in a sinister tone, 'I won't. But since you have stopped me in the name of my love for you, in the name of the love you bear me, I order you to behead your mother!'

Raam was stunned. He could not believe his father had asked him to kill his own mother. Renuka slumped to the ground upon hearing this; all the fight was gone from her body. Her husband had grown in his spiritual progress but clearly lacked the self-control that asceticism demanded. Or maybe, the hurt just ran too deep!

Raam knew he had to figure out a way to get the three of them out of this situation. He fell down at Yamdagni's feet. 'I respect and love you more than anyone else in this world, Father! You are the anchor of my life, my guide and my benefactor, but my mother is the light of my life. Please do not ask me to commit a crime as heinous as killing my own mother! You know I shall not be able to live after committing such an act!'

Yamdagni's heart seemed to have turned to stone for he said in an even tone, 'I abided by your imploration not to kill your mother and as a grown man I expect you to fulfil your end of the bargain. Don't make me kill both of you with my own hands and wipe out all future generations of the Bhrigu clan.'

Raam swallowed the sobs lodged in his throat when he realized there was no way out of the predicament . . . Unless . . . Yes, that could work! He wiped his tears and said earnestly, 'If I do as you command will you promise me a boon in return?'

Yamdagni couldn't care less about what his son might want as long as he got rid of the woman who had betrayed him. He nodded, handing over the sword to his son. Renuka looked in desperation at the two men who had been her entire life as they made a pact to end it with their own hands. She knew her son loved her but was helpless in the face of his father's wrath. It was better that one of them die rather than let her revenge-crazed husband kill both of them with his own hands. For the first time she realized how a sacrificial animal felt upon seeing the butcher advance towards it—utterly helpless and trapped. It was ironic, for she herself had never even hurt a rodent; yet here she was, being sacrificed to appease her husband's ego. She looked at Raam who was approaching her, the sharp sword in his hand, and closed her eyes in resignation. Twenty-five years of marriage, countless hours of companionship, dealing with the vagaries and vicissitudes of life, raising a child together, looking after their home and happiness, and in the end it was all wiped out by one wrongful thought that she hadn't even acted upon.

Raam surprised her by not striking but putting his arms around her and breaking into sobs that wracked his entire body. She hugged him back fiercely and whispered in his ear, 'Do what you have to child, I forgive you.'

He marvelled at her forbearance and felt ashamed of his father's excessive outrage. He had to be strong. All hope lay with him now. Kissing his mother on the cheek, he murmured in her ear, 'Trust me.' With that he got up and swung the sword, beheading her in one stroke.

The moment the deed was done Yamdagni snapped out of his trance and ran to her headless body, gathering it in his arms with the loud wails of a madman. Raam knew what he wanted had to be done without any delay for it to be successful. So he shook his father by his shoulders before asking urgently, 'Rishi Yamdagni, the time to grant my wish is now. By my right, for fulfilling my end of the bargain, I hereby demand that you bring my mother back to life this very instant!'

His father composed himself and rose to do what had been asked and Raam looked on, in apprehension. In one cruel stroke of fate, he had turned into a mother-killer and transformed into a man from a boy.

Adhyaye 38

It had been a month since that dreadful episode, yet the nightmares would not leave him alone.

Renuka had woken up as if from a deep sleep and, gradually, the reason why she lay in a pool of her own blood came to her. She pushed Yamdagni away with fear in her eyes and ran to her son for protection. Raam felt relieved at the gesture for it showed that his mother did not blame him for the unpardonable sin he had committed.

Yamdagni was as confused as them: how could things have come to such a pass! Using his yogic powers he realized that the reason for his madness had been the Rakshas who had disguised himself as a sadhu and deluded his senses, channelling all his negativity into him. He blamed his inherent jealous nature that had made him susceptible to Ravan's trickery. He cursed the demon king to meet his end at the hands of a simple forest dweller like him if he ever tried to destroy anyone's marital life!

He had pleaded with his family to make them understand that he had not been in his senses, but Renuka refused to stay with him a moment longer. She urged her son to take her away from the ashram. She didn't want to head to Matripur for that would ruin the relationship between Yamdagni and her father

225

forever, so Raam had taken help from his friends and arranged a boat that brought her to Kanyakubja. As they sat now in the very same veranda that had once been Satyavati's favourite, he rued the turn of events that had broken up his family so violently.

'Mother, will you ever forgive him?'

Renuka looked at him with sad eyes and replied, 'I know in my heart that Yama could never even dream of hurting me on his own. I saw that mayavi Rakshas standing with him when I hurried home that day and should have guessed his role in instilling the doubt in your father's mind. But I can't bring myself to forgive him, for if jealousy could overpower his love for me, how can I trust that it will not happen again?'

Raam understood what she was saying but decided to plead his father's case nevertheless. 'I can't even begin to imagine what you went through but if you could find it in your heart to forgive me, the man who actually struck the fatal blow because I was under someone else's control, can't you forgive the man who merely used words to cause you pain because he too was being manipulated in a similar fashion?'

The argument did have merit, Renuka admitted reluctantly, but said with a sigh, 'Sometimes the hurt caused by words runs deeper than that caused by a sword, my son. You did what you had to do but only after coming up with a plan to save my life, unlike Yama who showed me no mercy for an imaginary transgression. Everyone makes mistakes, but how we make amends for those errors is up to us. And in this case, it is up to your father to fix what he has broken. I know in my heart that things will get better between us at some point, but that time is not now.'

Shrugging off her sullen mood, she said, 'Forget about me. It is time to focus on your future. Now that we are in our own city, you have every opportunity that civilization can provide to choose an occupation of your liking. You have only come here once before in your childhood and it is time you utilized the prospects available here to figure out what you want for your life.'

Raam understood his mother's need to change the topic and went along with it. 'Honestly, I am as clueless as I was before. The only thing I know now is that life is unpredictable at worst and maddening at best and I wish to travel a little before making up my mind.'

Renuka felt a pang of apprehension thinking about the effect recent events would have on her son but she knew travel would help open up his mind. The realization that Ruchik's boon could kick in anytime hadn't escaped her either and she had to be ready to face the consequences. Calming herself, she asked, 'Where do you wish to go? Now that the entire globe is one kingdom, you can easily travel to other countries and visit new places but I suggest you start closer home so that if you require any kind of assistance Deval or I can help.'

Raam accepted her suggestion amicably. 'I don't want to travel with a planned itinerary. I think I'll wander about for a while, going wherever I feel like going. But I promise not to stray too far. I shall keep you apprised of my whereabouts by means of bird couriers and stay in touch while I sort out my mind.'

Renuka nodded. Her son also needed to clear his mind of the horror of the act that he had not only been a witness to but had perpetrated as well. She felt grateful for his presence of mind that had saved both her as well as Yamdagni from parting as enemies for many future lives to come. She gave him her blessings, and requested Deval to help his nephew prepare for the journey. She would utilize Raam's absence to meet Shakuntala, something she had been wanting to do for a long time. While their family had been engrossed in their own lives at Janapav, Deval had convinced Rishi Kanav to move closer to Kanyakubja for the sake of his stepsister and the rishi had established a new ashram in the vicinity.

The able king of Mahodayapur assigned a few trusted soldiers to accompany the lad till the borders of the kingdom and made sure he understood how to send messages across different kingdoms via pigeons and ravens. His heart beating with excitement, Raam took his first step into a new world just as Yamdagni arrived in Kanyakubja to mend things with his family.

While his parents tried to salvage their relationship, Raam rode away from the borders of Kanyakubja, travelling where his heart took him, tired yet full of excitement, not knowing what to expect. He had places to see, people to meet, new cultures to discover and languages to learn. He had grown up praying to Lord Shiva all his life, and recent upheavals, instead of shaking his faith in god, had in fact strengthened it. He believed it was only because of divine intervention that he was able to save his mother's life and decided to head to the Himalayas first to clear his mind. He had always dressed like a Brahmin, just like his father, with his unshorn hair gathered in a knot on top of his head, and had now begun to sport facial hair which made him seem more mature than his age.

Ruchik had told him stories of how he had appeased the gods and the Bow of Vishnu was proof of that. That bow had been the only possession he had taken with him when they left Janapav and he carried it with him now. As he crossed the border of Mahodayapur and asked his uncle's soldiers to return to the capital, he approached the nearest city. The locals he encountered seemed awed by the magnificent bow he carried and helped him find a place to sleep as evening arrived. He spent the night on a bed of hay in a stable that reeked of horse shit. He didn't mind it for this was the sort of experience he had been denied all his protected life; in fact, strangely enough, he was actually *liking* roughing it out on his own. Looking at the thatched roof of his temporary dwelling, he fell asleep dreaming of what he had left behind and the exciting journey ahead.

He was a traveller and he knew now that *that* was his destiny in life.

Adhyaye 39

He woke up to find the stables buzzing with activity. As he stepped out to know what was happening he realized what he hadn't really paid attention to the previous night. He was in Ayodhya, the unconquerable city and the capital of the Suryavanshi kingdom of Koshal.

King Harishchandra, whose father Satyavrat had been helped by Vishwamitra to reach heaven in his mortal body, was the ruler and he had organized a grand yagnya in the palace. As Raam hurriedly got ready, he asked the stable boys what the ceremony was for. The friendly boys were happy to oblige and told him about the past troubles their king had faced in begetting an heir. Even after years of marriage, Queen Taramati had remained childless and the king was too faithful to her to marry again, even for an heir. Instead, he had decided to propitiate Varun, the lord of ocean, to bless him with a son. Harishchandra's wish had been fulfilled but as with most boons given by the gods, there was a caveat attached. Varun had told him that the child could have one of two futures: If he was raised as an ascetic, he would live for a full century, but if he was brought up like a palace brat, he would die on his sixteenth birthday.

Since the royal couple had been blessed with a child after so long, it was unimaginable for the child, Rohitashwa, to not be pampered by his family and the palace staff. Harishchandra knew this did not bode well for the boy's future, and had pleaded with his kulguru, Brahmarishi Vasishth, to find out a way. The learned guru knew the pain of losing a child all too well, having lost his sons in a skirmish with Vishwamitra, and had agreed to help. But rumour had it that he had given his consent reluctantly for it involved a method that was not to his liking.

It was that very procedure which was being performed today, on the prince's sixteenth birthday.

Learning this, Raam hurried to the palace, admiring the beauty of the ancient city whose foundation was supposed to have been laid down by the legendary Manu himself.

The city, shaped as an ellipse, measured more than twelve yojans at its widest part. Well-paved roads criss-crossed the entire metropolis and were sprinkled with water at regular intervals to allow the dust of the vehicles to settle and to clear the droppings of a variety of beasts of burden. Flower-laden trees lined the sidewalks in a veritable carpet of colours. and the royal palace was grander than any that he had seen in his life. The sandstone and pink marble citadel was seven storeys tall as were most other official structures. Inside the palace compound, intricately carved pillars supported massive ceilings that were painted with exploits of the sun god and his brothers. The twelve solar gods known as the Adityas, were represented in massive granite statues starting with the eldest, Indra, right up to the youngest, Vaman. Their powerful presence filled the circular hall, as witnesses to every decision being made within its walls.

The royal throne was shaped like the cosmic chariot of Surya with seven handsome steeds of different colours. Raam realized that it would probably take seven elephants rather than horses to move such a heavy chariot if it were to be used but at the same time, the effect it had on the onlookers was immense. It had one central wheel with twelve spokes, each the size of a full-grown man, representing the twelve months of a solar year and its prodigious carriage was the massive royal throne with lions for its arms and a blazing sun as the backrest.

King Harishchandra sat on this massive throne looking every bit as majestic as a Suryavanshi king. The entire hall was full of people by the time Raam entered and he got the feeling that he was going to witness a major event in Ayodhya's history. Soon after, a rishi of such regal bearing stepped into the hall that Raam knew instantly it could be none other than Brahmarishi Vasishth.

The rishi must have been quite advanced in age yet seemed not older than forty. He stood tall with a straight back and a well-built frame. His long snow-white hair was the only indication of his antiquity and was kept in place by a string of rudraksh sported by Shiva worshippers though he wore the saffron garments and telltale marks of a Vaishnav on his forehead.

Even as Raam watched him with awe, the patriarch walked to the middle of the hall and raised a hand to hush the crowd. Immediately, there was pin-drop silence and the Brahmarishi's voice echoed in the cavernous hall, 'Honourable king, queen, members of the royal council and assembled citizens, we are gathered here today to celebrate the birthday of our prince, Rohit, and I invite him to come to the centre of the hall so that all of us can give him our blessings.'

'Ayushmaan bhava!' the assembled gathering shouted as the lanky teenager came to the nave of the hall and bowed to the assembled gathering with folded hands. Once that was done,

Vasishth asked for a short seat to be placed where the prince stood and another one opposite it.

He looked at the gathering with his fiery golden eyes and paced the room, like a lion looking for its prey. 'We have all blessed our prince with long life yet we all know he may not live to see the light of another day.' He paused dramatically, and looked at the people around him. 'Our just king, like any other father, wishes to avoid such a mishap risking the wrath of the lord of the oceans who, though merciful, is also a strict upholder of the law and swift to punish. For the gods who live for hundreds and thousands of samvatsars human life is ephemeral, but our king would willingly give his remaining life to his son. Unfortunately, the rules of Varun are not that flexible.'

The Brahmarishi turned to look at the king whose face had turned ashen at the thought of losing his child. Queen Taramati, who sat in the high chair immediately on his right, was barely holding back her tears and Raam's heart melted on seeing their state. When he turned his attention back to the Brahmarishi, he was saying something about duty and honour.

'. . . so as the day came closer, our king tried approaching many of his courtiers and relatives for the exchange but none accepted.'

Exchange? What is the rishi talking about? Raam wondered.

As if in response to Raam's question, Vasishth declared, 'Our noble king couldn't order anyone to exchange their child's life to save that of his own son since the sacrifice must come from the heart. Fortunately for the prince, a volunteer has appeared.'

The entire hall burst into a murmur at this declaration and Raam felt alarmed. He had heard of the manner in which some rulers bent the rules of society, but he hadn't imagined that the depravity of the Kshatriya clan had reached such a nadir.

Sacrificing the life of an ordinary child for that of a prince? He couldn't understand how the Brahmarishi could be party to such a nefarious plan. Yet Vasishth's face was impassive as a rock as he continued speaking.

'The Brahmin Ajigarta, in return for one lakh gold coins, has agreed to give up the life of his son in exchange for securing the life of Prince Rohit,' he declared, calling forward a man dressed in rags and the teenaged boy who stood next to him. 'His Highness has entrusted the delicate task of appeasing Lord Varun and convincing him to spare the life of one child in lieu of another to me.'

There was a collective gasp from the audience. Raam felt his heartbeat quicken—how could any father sacrifice his own son's life for money? He was filled with loathing for the man but when he took a closer look he realized he might be judging them too harshly. The man's clothes were shabby and torn and the boy's condition was no better. Maybe he had other mouths to feed at home and saw this as a way to end the misery of his family.

Even as Raam watched, the young cherubic boy, who seemed strangely calm, was made to sit on the seat facing Rohitashwa. Vasishth closed his eyes and gestured expansively, swinging his arms outwards and bringing them together, plunging the hall into sudden darkness. It was as if he had gathered all the light energy around them in a brilliant ball of fire that hung in between his hands which gently settled in between the two children. The entire assembly observed the ceremony in stunned silence. Beads of sweat broke out on Raam's forehead as he braced himself to witness the cold-blooded murder of a Brahmin child to save the life of the Kshatriya prince. He couldn't look away from the boy, who was silently murmuring something with folded hands, unaffected by the blazing flames just inches from his face.

The macabre scenario seemed to last for an eternity in which the only sound in the hushed assembly came from Brahmarishi Vasishth who was loudly chanting a mantra in a language Raam had never heard before. As he finished chanting, the young Brahmin boy slumped to the floor and the ball of light moved towards the prince.

There was a collective groan of dismay from the gathering but what happened after that took everyone by surprise. The ball of energy that had moved towards the prince divided itself in two! While a golden-blue glow lingered on the prince's face, the second part rushed into the drooping body of the fallen teenager who immediately stirred and sat upright!

There was a commotion and the king rose from his throne anxiously asking the Brahmarishi, 'Gurudev, did the procedure not work? This child is alive! Does that mean the gods have rejected the sacrifice and Rohit's life shall not be spared?'

A smile creased Vasishth's face as he declared, 'The procedure worked as it should have, my lord. The gods are merciful and have spared not only your own son but also this child, whose life had been forfeited by his family as well as his king. And now I would like to thank the man who has helped save the life of this child along with my reputation.'

Even as Raam wondered who it could be, Vasishth called out to the said man. 'Brahmarishi Vishwamitra, please step out of the shadows and acknowledge your brilliant effort in saving the day!'

Adhyaye 40

Raam watched in amazement as his grand-uncle stepped into the middle of the hall. Vishwamitra was as tall as the senior Brahmarishi and had limbs as thick as tree trunks with a chest as wide as a barrel of wine. His personality was awe-inspiring and his handsome bearded face glowed with the inner flame of rigorous penance. He came forward and touched the feet of his mentor.

Vasishth bade him to rise, and requested, 'Would you share with us the incidents of the past few days, Brahmarishi?'

Vishwamitra's brown eyes danced merrily as he said, 'I came to know about this unusual procedure on my way to Kanyakubja and knew that I had to intervene. A minister from the royal council had come across the Brahmin Ajigarta in his search for a suitable sacrificial child and the Brahmin's piteous condition made him the perfect catch. Bribing the poor man with gold and cattle, the minister asked if he would sell one of his three boys, and this man, in order to better the lot of the rest of his family, sold his middle son—this child, Sunahshep.'

Raam listened in fascination as his grand-uncle continued. 'Dangling in the middle of life and death, he reminded me of King Satyavrat, and I decided to save him just as I had saved the king. I did not wish for the kingdom to lose its heir but I could not in all conscience let an innocent child die in place of another. It is a sad reflection on our current times that such incidents are taking place even under the benevolent rule of an emperor like Kartavirya Arjun!' While the king shifted uncomfortably in his seat at these words, Vishwamitra shook his head and continued, 'When this child was told of the deal, he understandably ran away to save his life but was caught by the king's men. I knew Brahmarishi Vasishth was bound by his duty towards the king to perform the procedure and couldn't stop him from discharging his responsibility.

'The only solution I saw was by directly approaching Lord Varun. I made a deal with him and assured the child's safety by teaching him hymns that would ensure the merciful lord returned his soul to his body after the procedure was completed, simultaneously granting the prince freedom from imminent death. The result is in front of all to see.'

The gathering burst into spontaneous applause, and King Harishchandra ran down from his pedestal and fell at the feet of the two rishis, begging forgiveness for his selfishness and for putting them in that position. Brahmarishi Vasishth sighed and, looking into the eyes of the repentant king, he said, 'My lord, I was bound by my duties towards my king and the kingdom even though I knew I would be committing a sin by performing a ritual that was nothing short of an Asurik sacrificial rite. To atone for this transgression against nature, I shall have to vacate my position and proceed to the Himalayas to cleanse my soul of this burden.'

The king was flabbergasted by this announcement and tried to dissuade Vasishth but the Brahmarishi was adamant. He continued, 'My decision is made, my lord. But rest assured, your kingdom shall be in safe hands for I have spoken to Brahmarishi Vishwamitra and he has graciously agreed to take on the position of kulguru and guide you in my absence.' ―

Vishwamitra responded, 'It is an honour for me to step into your position even if for a short time, Brahmarishi Vasishth, and I shall endeavour to do my best for the benefit of the kingdom. I daresay our king here needs to be taught a few lessons that I'll be glad to impart in your absence.'

As the assembly applauded this decision he raised a hand to silence them and declared, 'As every person in this hall knows, I had renounced all family ties and become a sanyasi, but destiny has brought me back into society. I wish to change the lot of this child and hereby adopt Sunahshep as my own son and rename him Devrat, the one saved by the gods!'

The crowd broke out into cries of celebration, and some people even showered the rishi with flowers as the boy, who was sobbing uncontrollably, rushed to fall at his feet. Raam's heart went out to the child who had been forsaken by his own family and king and he felt tears sting his eyes as he remembered his own parents whom he had left behind. He would not be seeing them for a while but he was determined to take the blessings of the most distinguished member of their family with whom destiny had granted him this fortuitous audience. Perhaps this rajrishi who had risen to the status of Brahmarishi solely by dint of his willpower could help him chart the course of his life.

As the crowd began to disperse, Raam slowly wound his way towards the Brahmarishi who was patting the head of the child he had adopted. Seeing him approach, Vishwamitra gave a start of recognition and rushed forward to embrace him, surprising onlookers as well as Raam himself. He had heard so many stories about his grand-uncle from his father that he felt he practically knew him and responded with equal warmth.

Stepping away, Vishwamitra exclaimed, 'How good it is to finally set eyes on you, my child, and what an unexpected yet pleasant surprise to see you here!' Putting an arm around his shoulder he guided Raam to the royal grounds, waving away the guards who were hovering around the new preceptor of their king. The heady fragrance of wild roses hung in the air, mingled with the sweet aroma of ripening mangoes, while parakeets and cuckoos filled the garden with their cacophony.

The two selected a quiet corner, away from the fountains with pigeons playing in them. Raam said, 'Pitamah, I had hoped to meet you somehow before my journey concluded, yet witness my manifest good fortune—not only have I met you within days of setting out, but I also got the opportunity to observe you in action! I was worried that you might not recognize me but I realize that I needn't have, for your powers are beyond comprehension.'

Vishwamitra smiled and replied, 'How could I not recognize the son of my own dear Yama? Though I should mention that the bow that hangs on your shoulder did give you away for undoubtedly, it is the Bow of Vishnu gifted to Rishi Ruchik. I have one favour to ask, though: Please don't call me Pitamah since I'm merely your father's age!'

Raam smiled and said, 'As you say, uncle. You may know about the unfortunate events that compelled my mother and me to leave Janapav and my subsequent sojourn to find the direction of my life.'

Vishwamitra nodded. 'Yes, I am aware of what happened at Janapav. I was actually on my way to meet the three of you, for you may not be aware that in your absence Yama arrived in

Kanyakubja to ask for Renuka's forgiveness. It was when I was crossing Koshal that I came to know about the situation here and decided to help Brahmarishi Vasishth before continuing.'

Raam nodded in understanding and for a moment thought of going back to his parents with Vishwamitra to help patch up their differences. But going back would not solve his own dilemma; he knew his journey lay ahead.

Sensing the turmoil in his mind, the Brahmarishi said, 'Don't worry, my son, your parents shall start a new life soon, but for now *you* need to find your path. Do not forget that you are the fulfilment of the prophecy that began with me. I have had my problems with rules and authority and even confronted Indra once but I am sure you shall do something even more significant when the time comes.'

Raam fervently hoped that would be true though he did not know how and when it would be possible. Vishwamitra gestured to the bow he was carrying and said, 'This bow in your possession is not any ordinary longbow but one of the most effective missile launchers that exists in the universe! You have been given its custody because of your parentage but you need to earn the right to put it to use. I think it would be best for you to head to the Himalayas and spend some time praying to Lord Shiva, and seek his help in unlocking the true potential of this Astra.'

Raam thought about the proposal and asked the question that was forming in his mind: 'The emperor has the global empire well under control, then why would I need to use this weapon in the future?'

Vishwamitra clapped him on the back, saying, 'I see troubled times ahead, my child. On the surface things seem fine, but you saw what happened in the royal court of the Suryavanshis today! You may not be aware of the atrocities Arjun's men have committed in recent times but I am. Asur sorcery has spread its tentacles all over the globe and I can feel it pulsating through ordinary men and women. I know who is responsible for this but the time to punish him has still not arrived. I will make sure that day comes soon but till then, it would be advisable for all of us to gear up for the confrontation that is inevitable. I see you playing a big role in shaping up that future.'

Raam paused to think about this and asked, 'Uncle, I honestly do not know how I fit into this scenario. Why do we have to have some trouble whenever there's peace in the world? Why can't peace and prosperity remain forever?'

Vishwamitra smiled at the naivety of the boy and explained, 'Because that is how the cycle of life works, my son. Samrat Kartavirya has ushered in the first global empire based on dharma but every empire, like any individual, has a life cycle. When he began, there were numerous warring kingdoms not only in Nabhi-varsh but all over the globe and his single-minded focus was to stop those wasteful wars and usher in prosperity for all the inhabitants of this planet. This initial phase of growth was followed by years of peace and prosperity and matters have reached a plateau of sorts. The only way forward from here is downhill!'

'But why does it have to be that way?' asked Raam, still confused.

'Well, everything that goes up has to come down,' the Brahmarishi answered pragmatically, 'and that is true for each individual, family, kingdom and empire, even if it be of a global nature. We are meant to toil and earn our daily bread and a culture where everyone lives in plenty is bound to become decadent. In a society that reeks of abundance, no one wants to do the menial jobs even if they are essential for the very survival of that society. If the sweepers stop cleaning the garbage collected every day it would lead to an outbreak of diseases and if the doctors stop treating the people affected there would be widespread mortality. If the priests refuse to perform the last rites for those who have passed away, their corpses would rot on the streets, adding to the morbidity; and if the king neglects to help the families whose bread-earners have died, their children would be forced to work as slaves while the women end up in whorehouses. You see how each one of us is tied to the other?'

Raam nodded, so Vishwamitra continued, 'Just take the situation that arose today in the court. If we try to find the reason behind the poverty of the man who sold his son we will find a neglect of his vocation. An ordinary Brahmin's only source of income is the voluntary donations received from people who utilize his services. If the other castes were to decide they can do without him, all his knowledge of the scriptures would not help him feed the mouths of his family. The same goes for artisans or soldiers or doctors or any other vocation there is.

'Think of your body as society and different organs as the castes. If the lungs are damaged you won't be able to breathe, if the heart stops pumping you deprive each cell in your body of precious oxygen, if the nervous system malfunctions your life can drown in hallucinations, and if the reproductive system doesn't work you cannot ensure continuation of the species. And that is not all!'

Raam was beginning to get the drift of the Brahmarishi's words and he asked the next question, 'I understand how each caste is important and how a society steeped in indulgence can lead to injustices to some of these vocations. But how do the Asurs and their sorcery fit in it?'

Vishwamitra replied evenly, 'I'll explain using a similar example. From the invisible strands of fungi waiting to sprout between your toes to the bacteria in your guts, the body is a complex conglomeration of not only human cells but also opportunists that are always on the lookout for a way to spread and multiply. Imagine this on a much grander scale in the form of the global organism that is Kartavirya's empire and you will realize why things cannot remain the same forever.'

Looking directly at his grand-nephew, Vishwamitra said grimly, 'Taking advantage of the unfortunate circumstances of the current social unrest, the Asur virus has spread so insidiously that I see no way to get rid of it except by using the medicine of Divya Astras. The presence of the Bow of Vishnu in your hands is an indication of your future role in purging this menace and now you need to obtain the blessings from the lord of destruction himself. Only then can this global menace be wiped out.'

Parshu-Raam

Adhyaye 41

He was riding the horse on a wide road lined by pine trees on both sides. Ahead he could see mountains that almost touched the sky and he instinctively knew it was the same place he had seen in his dream all those months ago.

The sunlight was weak and a haze enveloped the path but once in a while, a chariot or a horseman would pass by and the fog would dissipate a little. However, it was not enough for him to know exactly where he was headed.

The plan was to ride as far as the royal highway would take him, exchange the horse for a pony for as far as the dirt roads extended and thereafter go on foot till he arrived at Kailash, the abode of Shiva. He had understood why Vishwamitra wanted him to pray to the Blue Lord. Shiva was not only the annihilator of the world but also the destroyer of ignorance and his blessings would be crucial in ridding the land of the Asur sorcery that had destroyed many lives including those of his own family.

Vishwamitra had confirmed what Yamdagni had claimed: the root of the affliction that had hit his mind that fateful night was Ravan who was seeking revenge on Ruchik's family for exposing Karkotak's plan to Arjun. Though Raam had believed his father's words, he hadn't understood why Ravan would manipulate him into harming his own family but now that he knew, his determination to rid the world of his sorcery had become even stronger.

Reaching the foothills of the mountains, he decided to spend the night at Nepalaksha, the first town he encountered, to feed and bathe his steed that was in desperate need of rest after the long journey. He took up a room at the travellers' inn using some of the money that he had carried from Kanyakubja and after bathing and changing into fresh clothes, joined the other guests in the courtyard for dinner.

The town was the last stop before the mountains began and he felt as excited to see the melting pot of cultural diversity in that quadrangle as he did looking at the hot curry and stew being served with rice and freshly made bread. The spicy aroma reminded him of how hungry he was and he dug into his food with gusto while checking out the other occupants of the room.

In one corner, a group of soldiers was cracking bawdy jokes under the influence of copious amounts of wine; he knew they were trouble the moment he set eyes on them and decided to stay alert. Soon enough, one of them grabbed the hand of the innkeeper's daughter who had been serving them food. A heated argument broke out between the owner and the soldiers who, in their drunken state, began beating up the old man.

Raam could not take it any more. Pushing away his plate, he ran to his room to grab his bow and was back in a flash, pointing an arrow at the nearest soldier. 'Stop this instant!' he shouted at the men.

A couple of them turned to see who the fool who had dared to challenge them was. Taking advantage of the interruption the old man limped away with his daughter.

Raam roared with indignation, 'How dare you molest a

woman in the land of Emperor Kartavirya! What kind of soldiers are you that you would gang up on an old man and beat him to a pulp? If you have even an ounce of Kshatriya blood in your filthy veins, come and face me instead!'

His heart beat wildly inside his chest as he realized that he had never been in an actual fight before, except his shenanigans with his friends. Still, he didn't feel afraid; the blood in his veins appeared to have been replaced with pure adrenaline. The bow seemed to throb with a life of its own. Raam realized it was the essence of Lord Vishnu in it that had recognized his adversaries as the enemies of dharma and was helping him deal with them.

The soldiers saw the determination on the young Brahmin's face and the magnificent bow he held but they were drunk and had faith in their own collective strength. They were the emperor's soldiers. No one had ever dared to cross their path.

The leader of the gang, a heavy-set man with dark beady eyes and a luxuriant moustache bellowed at Raam, 'How dare you insult the soldiers of the emperor? We can arrest you for treason! Or perhaps we shall just slice your puny head off right now. You bloody Brahmins are leeches on society, taking money in the name of god for every small ritual you perform. Clearly, your father trained you to be a more professional thug than the others of your kind because that bow certainly cannot belong to a cowardly Brahmin!'

'Silent, Kshatriya!' Raam's voice boomed in the courtyard and seemed to bounce off the walls till it echoed in every ear. 'I am Raam, the son of Rishi Yamdagni, whose counsel even your emperor deeply respects, and you dare call him a thief? Your arrogance stems from your uniform and I can see that the power it signifies has corrupted you in more ways than one.'

He glared at the moustached brute and challenged him, 'A

true soldier of dharma would never have molested a woman, for our values teach us to protect, not exploit those weaker than us. You are not even worthy of being called a man for your actions identify you as the lowest dregs of humanity, perhaps just a notch above the Asurs.'

'How dare you!' shouted the incensed leader as his gang picked up their weapons to strike at the impudent Brahmin.

Even Raam couldn't describe what happened next for he himself was dazzled by the speed and ease with which he let loose his arrows! Within moments the soldiers lay writhing in pain and their leader, who had dared to mock his father, desperately clutched his wounds as his life's blood oozed out. The owner of the inn fell at Raam's feet, thanked him profusely for his help and begged him to run away before other soldiers came to seek revenge for the carnage he had caused.

Raam was no fugitive but he realized this wasn't the right time for him to get embroiled in local politics or power games. Requesting the owner to send a pigeon to his parents detailing his welfare and whereabouts, he packed his bags and prepared to leave. He had felt invigorated while fighting and was ready for more. If these soldiers were any indication, he had to gain the knowledge of the Divya Astras soon so that he could come back and teach others like them a lesson they would never forget.

Adhyaye 42

Snow had begun falling softly on the pine trees and life had come full circle for Ruchik's family. Yamdagni and Renuka had mended their relationship and Raam was following in his grandfather's footsteps diligently.

Oblivious to the outside world, he had spent the past several months meditating at the base of the Kailash mountain, gazing at its snow-clad peak with adoration. When he had arrived here, he had been wrapped in clothes and fur but, gradually, as his yogic powers grew, so did his tolerance for the vagaries of weather.

He had been coached by his father and grandfather in the science of meditation since he was a little boy yet it was only now that he truly grasped the concepts he had been learning since childhood. With the gradual awakening of his chakras, he had felt the realization of the mystical law of karma fill his mind and he understood now that the vicious cycle of birth and death could only be brought to an end with the wisdom born of its understanding.

Our lives were like the canvas used in a painting—white and pristine when begun until they were coloured in with the brushstrokes of our actions. What form the final painting took

251

was completely in our hands for our karma decided whether it would turn out to be a masterpiece that could inspire others or a hideous monstrosity. As he had grasped this basic concept over the past few days, he had begun feeling a sense of calm confidence engulf him—he, and no one else, was the master of his destiny.

There was a sense of well-being that came with the practice of austerities and detachment from sensory gratification and he could feel a definite positive effect on his neurological, endocrine and immune systems. He now sat at the base of the mountain on a rocky outcrop, concentrating on the mountain as one would on a stone lingam, focused on the *Nirgun* symbol of Shiva.

As a child he had always wondered how a mere stone or idol could represent god but his grandfather had cleared those doubts from his mind by making him realize the imperfection and limitation of human vision. Our visible spectrum couldn't even enable us to see the wide range of radiation around us, then how could we observe god with these eyes? Man needed a symbol or medium to channel our prayers to god and this could be anything from god's own creation.

The Supreme Soul existed in each and every atom of this universe and a devotee could worship a leaf, a tree, stone, river, mountain or even an abstract symbol like 'Om' and seek the divine. There was no need for elaborate rituals or grand temples to obtain His mercy; a softly uttered prayer said with a pure heart did as much.

Raam closed his eyes, shutting out all external sensory inputs, and began chanting the Panchakshar mantra *Aum Namah Shivaya*, simultaneously regulating his breathing and concentration. In his mind's eye he could only see the mountain that was the abode of the lord of destruction, covered with pristine white snow and glowing with a divine aura itself.

As he went deeper and deeper into the meditative state, the image began to change shape and a part of his subconscious noticed the gradual transformation with interest. The mountain seemed to be growing taller with each successive recitation of the mantra! Externally his body was frozen in the lotus position but in his subconscious, he was raising his head higher and higher to look at the growing peak. The white snow was fading away and he could see stars glittering in the blackness of space as the mountain continued its upward movement, piercing the earth's atmosphere and heading towards the moon. In his vision he was now sprawled on his back, looking at the peak in bewilderment and awe as it rose higher and higher into the darkness until it stood, framed in the light of a crescent moon that made the snow glisten.

He felt an intense vibration pass through his very being as he realized he was witnessing a vision of the lord in the form he had been worshipping him. Faced with this immense Shivalingam, a crescent moon adorning its forehead, he lost all capacity to think; his only wish now was to see the lord himself!

Hardly had the thought crossed his mind than a current of anticipation rushed through his mind. His breath caught in his throat and his eyes widened in awe as he saw the silhouette of the lord of yogis on top of the peak. The twenty-eight nakshatras swirled around him in the background and the lord's shadowy face was framed by dreadlocks of asteroid belts that extended in different directions. The serpent Vasuki adorning his neck had turned into a swirling galaxy and the blue throat of the lord was the glow of a nebula. His tiger-skin clothes had been replaced by a volley of meteor showers and Raam saw the dark frame of

Shiva limned by scores of twinkling stars. Even as he watched in amazement, the lord seemed to open his eyelids and his three eyes turned into brilliant suns that blinded him completely. His entire body felt electrified as the spark from Shiva's third eye hit his pineal gland and sent a shiver of excitement down his spine.

The damru in Shiva's left hand began swinging, creating a dull rhythmic beat that reverberated across the universe, sending a ripple of exhilaration all along Brahma's creation. This was unlike anything Raam had experienced before and his heart now beat in time to Shiva's drum. His trepidation turned into astonishment and then relief as the lord raised his right hand in the Abhay mudra intended to calm the fears of his devotee. Tears of joy sprang from Raam's eyes as his consciousness finally registered that he was receiving a vision of the great lord himself! His attention was caught by an object swirling in Shiva's raised hand and he squinted to see what it was. As if in response to his efforts, his vision magnified and he was stunned to see a reflection of himself sitting on the Himalayas watching the vision of Shiva in the hand of the lord in a seemingly endless reflection!

He gulped nervously as he saw the entire globe revolving in the hand of the lord. His vision shot upwards, crossing the higher planetary systems of Swarg, Maharloka, Janaloka and had soon crossed Tapoloka to reach Brahma's own abode. Raam had barely caught a glimpse of the four-headed creator god sitting on his golden lotus, before he was zipped towards the outer reaches of the universe. He had left all his fear behind and felt only contentment as he reached the shell of Brahma's Cosmic Egg—the Brahmand.

There he saw Shiva in all his glory, bathed in a golden glow, his lips curved into a smile that overwhelmed him with its mercy. Raam realized that he was suspended at the edge of material creation beyond which was the permanent abode of Shiva. Kailash was a temporary resort that had come into existence only when the earth's colliding upper plates formed the Himalayas about fifty million years ago but this eternal Shivaloka, called Manomaya by rishis and learned men, was where the lord had lived since before Brahma began creation. The lord of destruction lived as a householder on Kailash and Kashi but here he was the Primeval Rudra, destroying each world as its life cycle came to an end, providing the innumerable Brahmas of the countless universes with the raw material with which to begin creation anew.

Raam couldn't have imagined in his wildest dreams that he would get a glimpse of the lord in a vision so grand. He folded his hands and prostrated himself before the lord, with a silent prayer to show him his destiny. Shiva merely smiled and gestured him to open his eyes. As he did as commanded, he found himself back in the Himalayas. A gleaming golden axe lay in front of him.

Adhyaye 43

Things were not going well for the emperor of the world and he couldn't understand why everything seemed to be unravelling in his kingdom.

He had returned the previous day from his tour of the world with his three sons aboard the Pushpak and had felt the definite presence of Asurik magic all over the globe. He couldn't understand how that could have happened without him noticing. Could it be that the Brahmins were conniving with the damned demons to upset his rule? Dattatreya was nowhere to be found and Arjun didn't trust any other Brahmin in the realm any more.

To relieve his mind, he decided to make a quick trip to the Himalayas for he loved hunting the mountain lion. Stalking the powerful animal and seeing the fear in its eyes as the predator became the prey gave him the confirmation that he was the most powerful man on this planet and boosted his ego.

Mounting his craft, he headed to the mountains alone, stopping at the inn at Nepalaksha for some freshly brewed fruit wine before moving ahead. Seeing the royal vehicle, a crowd gathered to greet the emperor. The moment he landed people came rushing with flowers to greet him and receive his blessings. Arjun spent some time mingling with them and in the course of his interactions learned all that had happened at the inn a few weeks ago.

He went inside to meet the battered and bruised owner, still recovering from his wounds, and offered sympathy for him and his daughter. Even now there were telltale marks of the scuffle in the shape of the broken pieces of furniture that lay in the corner and faint bloodstains on the floor. The clientele had also been affected for he saw very few people residing there unlike on earlier visits when he had always found people thronging it.

Arjun was shocked to hear the behaviour of his soldiers. Clearly they had been at fault and would be dealt with in an appropriate manner, but he was more surprised to hear about the Brahmin boy who had confronted and bested his men. Whatever the provocation, no citizen was allowed to take law in his hands and the boy would have to be disciplined. He gave the innkeeper some gold coins as compensation and promised action against the errant soldiers. Then he asked the description of the Brahmin boy who had destroyed a group of his soldiers single-handedly. There was nothing remarkable in the innkeeper's account except the mention of a bow that glowed with a blue hue which the boy had used to loose off arrows like a wizard. Such a powerful weapon could only be in the possession of an extraordinary man. With some trepidation Arjun realized that this boy could very well belong to the faction of Brahmins who were plotting against him.

He was told that the young man had left immediately after the encounter and would have gone far away by now. Arjun decided to explore the area himself aboard his craft, covering a radius of about fifty yojans. Tall conifers blocked his way so he decided to go higher and get an aerial view. Hovering over the area, he decided to focus his limited spiritual powers in finding out if there was an unusual source of energy nearby that could give him an indication of the Brahmin's location. His eyes popped open in surprise when he found an extremely powerful pulsating source of spiritual power. Either this young man was extremely gifted or he was hiding with a coven of other advanced Brahmins!

The second option seemed more likely since according to his own theory, the boy would definitely be a part of a group. Arjun was excited to think that he may have chanced upon their secret hideout. It was the ideal spot for it was quite far from Mahishmati and well hidden in the mountains. For all he knew the Brahmin boy was holed up there even now. He was lucky he had decided to stop at the inn for he may never have learned about the existence of such powerful weapons or secret getaways otherwise. Within moments he was hovering above the location and guided the machine down in a nearby clearing.

Sunlight barely managed to filter through the thick canopy of trees and the grass was littered with bursting pine cones. As he got out of the viman and inhaled the thick aroma of wild rose in the air, he was momentarily distracted. To his surprise, no young ascetics rushed at him, arms raised to strike. The only sound was that of a variety of birds chirping in agitation at having their tranquil peace breached by the intruder.

Arjun turned towards the small ashram that was the only man-made structure visible and shouted, 'I know you are hiding in there, Brahmins, but your carelessness has exposed you. Did you honestly believe you could stay hidden after what you did to my men? The time for your reckoning is here; come out and face me in a fair fight!'

In the absence of a response from the thatched hut,

Kartavirya Arjun felt even more enraged. How dare they ignore his challenge! They were probably busy chanting secret mantras to create some new nuisance for him. He shot a few warning arrows around the hut, hitting rocks that broke under their impact creating a loud sound. When no one appeared, he fired at the roof almost bringing it down. Again no response. Filled with annoyance, he took the Agneyastra loaded with gunpowder and fired it at a spot a few metres away from the hut. The missile hit a big boulder, shattering it with a loud roar. Adrenaline pumping, Arjun waited. Splinters fell on the dry grass and pine cones, immediately setting them ablaze. The king watched in satisfaction as the fire rapidly engulfed the hut.

At last, from the smoke and fire, emerged a rishi with fury written on his face and eyes like molten lava. Arjun's heart stopped; it was Brahmarishi Vasishth. And he was alone.

'Samrat Arjun,' the patriarch shouted in anger, 'what are you doing? I came here to meditate and rid myself of the sins of my past actions. Yet you, in your mistaken zeal to find the conspirators your delusional mind has led you to believe exist, have broken my deep trance and caused me great anguish.'

Arjun realized that the intense aura that he had detected from the hut was not because of a group of Brahmins holed up together but one extraordinary rishi who possessed more spiritual merit than a score of Brahmins put together. Arjun's heart told him to apologize immediately but the suspicions plaguing his mind were not allayed yet.

'Why didn't you come out when I demanded?' he asked.

Vasishth's face was contorted in anger as he replied, 'Because I was in a deep state of samadhi, you fool! Even a little ego can develop into a huge tree of ignorance, and I can see it has already spread its roots deep into your heart. The attachment to *your* kingdom is its trunk, your dependence on your possessions its branches and your obsession that the throne should pass not to the most eligible person but to your own sons is its ripe fruit!

'Clearly your attachment is making you blind to the Asur ploy to destabilize your empire. For the benefit of future generations, it is of utmost importance that this tree be felled. I am forced to punish you for this impudence; I hereby declare that you shall lose the very possessions that make your heart fill with conceit and that no one who bears your name shall ever become a king in the history of mankind!'

Arjun felt the ground fall away beneath his feet as the ascetic took a deep breath and pronounced the very situation he had been trying to prevent from happening.

'You shall lose everything you have at the hands of the very Brahmin you set out to pursue today! You dared to doubt the loyalties of Rishi Ruchik who saved you from Karkotak's Asurik magic and now his own seed shall destroy you,' Vasishth announced.

Arjun realized now that the young man he had been pursuing was probably the son of Yamdagni but felt angrier than ever before. Why couldn't the senile rishi have come out in the first instance and saved him all the firepower and melodrama? After all, he had given fair warning to whoever was hiding inside. Had Vasishth come out on his own Arjun wouldn't have had to attack and destroy his ashram. And on top of that, he had the audacity to pronounce a curse on him!

The Brahmarishi had overstepped his boundary and needed to be taught a lesson. However, the emperor knew it wouldn't be wise to confront him directly. Vishwamitra had tried that and lost everything he owned. Arjun would have to find some other way to get back at him. The old man had threatened him with

Ruchik's spawn, so the first thing to be done was to neutralize the threat. He didn't know what had brought Yamdagni's son so far but he had some inkling of the probable motive now.

Brahmarishi Vasishth was close by, Vishwamitra was settling in Ayodhya, Ruchik was last heard of in Ujjain and Yamdagni had just returned to Janapav with Renuka after visiting Kanyakubja. Surely there was a plan afoot to destabilize his empire! He decided not to apologize especially after the curse that had been hurled at him and turned around to climb his craft and head towards Janapav. He would teach such a lesson to these Brahmins that they would never forget the power of Kartavirya Arjun, emperor of the world.

Adhyaye 44

Raam's homecoming was devastating.

Flushed with the triumph of his maiden penance, he had returned to find rubble where his home had been. The ashram that his grandfather had built with his own hands had been razed to the ground, and his mother's beloved grove had been reduced to ashes. Shocked, he walked through the charred remains of plants and a few animals that probably couldn't escape the fire. Fearing the worst, he desperately called out to his mother and father. When there was no answer, he rushed to the Nishadh village where one of his old friends found him in a state of agitation and calmed him down: His parents were safe and had taken shelter in the temple complex, where he took Raam to meet them. Though he was relieved to find his mother and father unhurt, Raam couldn't keep his fury at bay when he saw the telltale marks of their struggle. After an anguished reunion, Yamdagni and Renuka told him what had transpired at Janapav.

Kartavirya Arjun had come looking for Raam to avenge the attack on his soldiers and not finding him there had burnt down the entire ashram, slaughtering the innocent animals in the grove and destroying their home with his missiles. He had not spared a moment's thought to the relationship between them and the happy times they had spent together, and had attacked them with the viciousness of a madman.

The Nishadhs had rushed to the hill seeing the flames leap to the sky as the ashram burned and found Yamdagni buried under the rubble. Renuka, who had been desperately trying to save her animals, unmindful of the danger she herself was in, was rescued from the grove and both of them had been brought here. Their only possession which was spared was their cow Surabhi who had been yoked to Arjun's vehicle and taken to the capital.

Raam's blood boiled as he heard the account of the unwarranted attack on his family and he rose with a determined expression. 'Father, I had returned home with pride to share my achievement with you and this senseless attack by the emperor has shown me the real significance of the benediction that I have received! Lord Shiva Himself blessed me with his divine axe and now I know how to put this to perfect use. I cannot let this carnage of innocent animals and the destruction of our home go unpunished. I shall challenge the emperor to a duel.'

'No, Raam,' Renuka said in a worried tone. 'What Arjun did was abominable but challenging him to settle the score will only start a chain reaction that could make things worse; an eye for an eye only turns the world blind!'

Raam marvelled at the composure his mother had even after losing the home they had lived in for more than two decades and the plants, birds and animals she had nurtured in her grove. He wasn't that magnanimous though, and looked at his father for support. Yamdagni had a dark bruise on his chest and another one that extended over his left arm, but to his disappointment, his father agreed with her. 'Your mother is right, Raam! I acted in haste earlier and caused immense pain not only to the two of you, but also to our family in Kanyakubja. I do not wish for you to make the same mistake. Violence is not the answer to the problems facing this world, my son.'

'How can you say that after all that the emperor has done?' Raam asked, his voice rising. 'You always taught me to protect the innocent and meek for only then can a society thrive, yet today, when this madman comes and demolishes our home and burns to death injured animals, you want me to sit back on my haunches and watch what comes next?'

Taking a deep breath, he tried once more. 'How many times have you yourself asked me to find my own direction in life? This bow that grandfather gave us belongs to Lord Vishnu; I have felt its power when it faces those who thrive in adharmik practices. The quivers that Rishi Kanav gave you and this Divine Axe that possesses the power to cut through any Asurik maya have found me for a purpose!'

Renuka looked at Yamdagni helplessly and in a bid to talk some sense into her son's mind said, 'I agree, the possession of the weapons of the Preserver and Destroyer must have some greater meaning. But how do we know that *this* is the reason for which you have been granted their use?'

'Have you thought of how and on whom you are going to use these divine weapons?' Yamdagni added. 'What if the emperor sends his army to fight you? Would you be able to tackle them single-handedly? Have you given a thought to what would happen to the global empire if you attacked or, worse still, killed him?'

Raam countered the argument by explaining, 'I do not wish to kill the emperor! I just want to teach him a lesson by destroying his home, and bring back Surabhi, the only surviving possession that we can call our own. Besides, how can you forget the earlier attack perpetrated by Ravan who lives under the shelter of the emperor as one of his trusted generals? If he is as much of a believer in dharma as he claims to be, he shall accept the punishment for the crime he and his men have committed.'

His parents realized that their son had changed in the months he had spent on his own.

'Stop talking like a Kshatriya,' Yamdagni insisted. 'You are the son of a Brahmin! I hope you realize that an attack on the emperor will be treated as treason; no one will accept it in the terms you describe. He is guarded by tens of thousands of soldiers. You won't be able to breach even the first ring of protection around him. If, by some chance you do succeed, it is more than likely that with the inflated ego that Arjun has he will not rest till he has hunted you down!'

'Have some faith in the capabilities of your son, Father,' Raam retorted with a confidence they hadn't seen in him before. 'I have spent years training and learning about the value of justice and responsible citizenship. Do you think I would ever let mere paid soldiers hunt me like a wild animal? And as for my caste, it does not behove you to remind me of it when you yourself have never believed in the concept of birth-defined castes. I met grand-uncle Vishwamitra in Ayodhya who told me how *you* supported him in his journey, so please don't stop me in mine.

'Lord Shiva has given me his blessing. I am no longer the boy Raam who had embarked on this journey with uncertain steps. I am Raam, the wielder of the axe that can cut down all bondages of material existence. My life's actual journey begins here, Father, for I believe the fulfilment of the second part of grandfather's prophecy is upon us!'

His parents realized the decision was out of their hands and nodded reluctantly. Yamdagni closed his eyes and summoned the magical quivers gifted by Rishi Kanav. As soon as they appeared, he handed them over to his son. It was time for their Raam to become Brahmakshatriya Parshu-Raam!

Adhyaye 45

Raam marched into the capital of Mahishmati, taking long purposeful strides towards the royal palace. As he stepped through the wide gates of the avenue, he was stopped by two burly guards who demanded the purpose of his visit.

He requested them to inform the emperor that the man whose house and family he had destroyed had come to seek damages and an apology. The guards listened to his words incredulously, then burst out laughing. 'Are you insane, boy? You, a mere Brahmin, have come here to challenge the emperor of the world and make him beg at your feet?'

'Yes,' Raam replied, 'if someone commits a grave crime, what does his stature matter when punishment is meted out? Are we living under a despot who isn't answerable to anyone but whose tyranny we must quietly suffer?'

'Shut up, Brahmin!' said one of the guards. 'How dare you call our emperor a tyrant?' he challenged and rushed at Raam with his sword raised high.

Raam simply raised his right hand that held the axe to block the incoming blow. The soldier who had rushed at him was stunned by the impact and fell down. Raam turned to the other soldier and said, 'My weapons are of divine origin and can easily defeat whatever you throw at me. Unless you want me to use them on you, either let me in or call your emperor out to face the consequences of his actions.'

Enraged by this direct challenge, the second guard also attacked and within moments was spouting blood from his right shoulder. He could not believe that a mere boy could have injured him so and called the other guards for help. Soon a whole troop of soldiers was rushing at Raam from all sides, taking aim at him with their swords, javelins, clubs, scimitars, arrows and whatever they could get their hands on.

Raam took a deep breath and prepared himself to use the celestial bow. He began firing arrows with the swiftness of a seasoned archer and soon enough the soldiers lay in a circle around him, groaning and clutching their injured bodies.

The commotion could not have gone unnoticed and soon the emperor, who had been in a meeting with his thousand generals, became aware of his presence. Ravan, who was also present, rubbed his hands in glee for at last someone had dared to challenge the emperor. His Asur minions had successfully infiltrated the imperial army and now he was able to control the minds of most of the assembled generals to varying degrees. He knew the emperor had signed his own death warrant by attacking Vasishth earlier and then destroying Yamdagni's home. It seemed that today was the day he would get to see the mighty Kartavirya Arjun fall.

Seeing the condition of his guards and the threat Raam posed to his reputation, Arjun growled with anger and ordered an entire platoon to attack him. An army of foot soldiers proceeded to neutralize the lone man who had put the emperor on edge. As they surrounded him from all sides, the assembled generals laughed at the absurdity of the situation: a solitary Brahmin boy challenging the might of the imperial army!

Raam was ready for the onslaught and, as the first soldier rushed at him with his sword raised, he started swinging the axe. Rotating a stick is a defensive move taught to any young boy learning the art of combat, and Raam was no different. His hands moved lightning-quick as he deflected the weapons thrown at him, causing more damage to the attacking soldiers than they could to him. He was able to see the tiniest movement of each and every soldier and intercept their weapons as if they were caught in a time warp and couldn't move faster, as if the entire world had come to a standstill and only he was in motion. He realized that the divine weapons he held in his hand were providing him the superhuman agility he had suddenly seemed to have acquired. In no time there was a pile of injured soldiers around him that effectively gave him protection from the ones further behind.

The emperor roared in irritation and ordered the soldiers still standing to clean the mess and renew their attack on the boy. Raam quickly moved from a defensive stance to an offensive one and switched to his bow, unleashing a volley of arrows around him that sliced through the armours of the imperial soldiers, effectively incapacitating them.

The mood in the hall had turned from boisterous to disbelief to anger. As his frustration mounted, Arjun commanded his generals to go and kill the little pest themselves. Ravan watched in amazement as the boy he had met just a few weeks ago in the forest routed an entire platoon by himself. He was in no mood to risk his own life and quietly slipped into the background while the other generals grabbed their weapons and went out to prove their loyalty to the emperor.

Raam watched in amusement as elephants were brought to drag the fallen men away. He felt a twinge of guilt for having hurt so many people, but then all this could have been avoided had the king just come out himself instead of sending his men. Surprisingly, he did not feel tired even after such a gruelling fight and was as fresh and excited as he had been when he had first arrived at the palace gates. In fact, though he had never faced such an onslaught before, he was amazed to find no fear in his mind. The thought brought his attention back to the present and he realized that Kartavirya's generals were closing in on him slowly in a circular formation.

Someone shouted at him, 'Go home, boy, run back to hide behind your mother's skirt or play with your heavy books. These are not toys for you to brandish about.'

Raam knew this was all fake bravado for they had clearly seen his skill with the weapons, and responded calmly to draw out the person who had said the words, 'Have I got you pissing in your angavastra, general? Are you too scared to face a mere boy?'

The affronted general pushed forward, his hands holding a long bow with an arrow aimed right at Raam's heart. 'I have fought more wars in my lifetime than you may have even read about in your books, boy. We are the leaders of the global principalities of this massive empire; not mere soldiers you can dispose of easily.'

Moving around constantly to intercept any sudden attack, Raam retorted, 'Kings and generals can be called leaders only when they listen to their people. I have seen first-hand how your soldiers behave with the weaker sections of the society; I have seen the contempt for lower castes as well as Brahmins in the eyes of the Kshatriyas; I have met a king who was ready to sacrifice a poor man's son to save the life of his own. Those who are busy filling their coffers with the hard-earned earnings of their citizens and taking the lives of their people to save their own are no leaders of mine.'

The barb hit home for the next instant he saw an arrow flying towards him. He easily deflected it with his axe, and as more arrows and spears came zipping through the air, he jumped high and let them neutralize each other. Some, with the force of their momentum, stayed on course and went right through to the diametrically opposite end hurting other generals. Before the outraged militia could recover, Raam jumped again and shot hundreds of arrows from the air into the ground, creating a protective barricade for him and comfortably landed inside. Numerous weapons were thrown at the temporary fortress he had created and he knew it wouldn't stand for long but it gave him some time to think about how to proceed.

When he had come to Mahishmati, the only thought in his mind had been to make the king apologize but this was turning into a protracted battle involving the generals of the world! Not that he minded. He was enjoying every bit of it and he realized that these men, while adept in facing and defeating huge armies with their strategies, were finding it difficult to handle a solitary fighter. When it came to dealing with a single adversary, there were only two things one could do—fight or run away. Having chosen to fight, the men had to bear being shamed by this lone lad in front of their emperor and the world while they figured out ways to neutralize him. Raam realized that they, more than he, were scared of losing face and began shooting arrows at random to break the circle. Some of the generals hastily procured shields to protect themselves and strategically shuffled their formations, breaking into three triangles that attacked Raam from three different sides. He appreciated their strategy which minimized the target for him while enabling them to shoot at will without any significant danger to their comrades. However it took him less than a minute to come up with a counter-attack.

Standing in his position of relative security he started shooting arrows from his inexhaustible quivers at the feet of the approaching generals, for that was the only vulnerable part visible behind their shields. As the men in the front stumbled and fell with cries of pain the triangles opened up and he could pick and choose his quarry as they ran about to protect themselves. When some of the braver ones rushed at him, Raam realized the barricade would actually hem his movements so he kicked it open and stormed out to meet his opponents. The time for defence was over. Placing the bow diagonally across his body, he started swinging his axe, slicing through the bones and sinew of anyone who dared to cross his path.

The legend of Parshu-Raam had begun.

Adhyaye 46

Kartavirya Arjun watched the bloodbath with incredulity.

He could not believe what was happening to the generals he had groomed himself to be his successors in each of their kingdoms. There were men of all types of skin and eye and hair colour lying on the field, yet all that was visible was a predominant red. He wondered briefly if he could have prevented the slaughter of his soldiers had he just met the man wreaking havoc at his doorstep face-to-face, but the time for such contemplation was long gone.

Manorama came running to stop him from going out for it would surely be a fight to the death, but there was no dissuading Arjun. The citizens of Mahishmati had witnessed the massacre of the Sahastra-Arjun in awe and fear. It was no mean feat for one man, a Brahmin at that, to defeat a thousand seasoned Kshatriya warriors in combat but they had seen it with their own eyes. The bodies of the deceased and the blood of the fallen had borne witness to this dance of destruction meted out by the axe of Shiva, the originator of the Tandav.

Kartavirya had lost his thousand arms, but he still possessed the two he was born with and he was sure they would be enough to deal with this pesky lad. A voice in his head reminded him of Vasishth's curse but he silenced it; Dattatreya's boon would protect him from any adharmik attack, and what was this if not a brutal flouting of the tenets of dharma?

For starters, the young man was a Brahmin who had taken up arms, crossing the first boundary set by dharma. He had not only destroyed the governing leaders of a thousand kingdoms but also widowed a thousand women and orphaned many more children. This was his second act of adharma. He had defiled a city made pure by years of rituals and worship and bloodied the waters of the sacred Narmada. Even now, he waited to fight the emperor of the world who had ushered in a golden age never before seen in history of the world. If this was not contrary to all established rules of dharma, he didn't know what was.

Seizing his weapons, he descended the grand steps of the palace for what he knew would be a decisive victory. Armed with a wide scimitar and a short dagger, he did not bother with a shield for he was sure not a single arrow shot by the infidel would scratch his armour and even if it did, Dattatreya's boon made him invincible. Kicking the gates of the palace open he walked out confidently, vowing to avenge the massacre of his generals. The path to the main gate was littered with bodies and he had to step over many of his own men to reach his target. He realized that the boy could have let loose a volley of arrows at him taking advantage of the situation but Raam stood his ground without raising his weapons.

Climbing over the last obstacle, Arjun roared like a lion and leaped towards Raam, to hit him on the head and finish him in one blow. But the boy was alert and blocked the attack with his axe. The contact between the two weapons sent a shock through Arjun's body and he reeled under the impact. Landing on the ground, he changed his stance to try and slice through

Raam's body in a quick sideways motion but the young warrior jumped backwards and parried the blow easily. Without letting him gain balance, Arjun swung his sword again aiming at his head while simultaneously thrusting the dagger in his left hand forward. While Raam managed to dodge the blow from Arjun's right hand, the shorter weapon found its mark and he felt the dagger lodge in his midriff. Blood gushed from the wound in his abdomen. Arjun sneered. Now that he had gained some ground, he could not let the enemy recover, and so he continued attacking with both his weapons. Raam decided to give back the emperor a dose of his own medicine and began swinging his axe in a wide arc, pushing him away and making room for himself. The moment Arjun backed away, Raam kept the heavy bow down to reduce his weight and enable easier movement. That done, he rushed at Arjun, swinging the axe in a wide arc to hit him in the chest. The emperor tried to block the impact by crossing both the blades in his hands, gripping it between them but Raam gave a heave and freed his axe easily and swung again, hitting the emperor squarely in the chest with its pommel.

Arjun reeled from the blow and staggered backwards, blood gushing out of his mouth. He looked at the scarlet fluid in disbelief: How could this happen to him, the protector of dharma? How could this young man, who had disrespected the bounds of dharma, hurt him so?

Raam looked at the king's bewildered expression and said with conviction, 'Samrat Kartavirya Arjun, the boon given to you by my father's guru has protected you all these years since you followed dharma in all honesty. Its failure to protect you now is a proof that you have left that path far behind.'

Arjun spat the blood that had collected in his mouth and replied, 'I know this is the result of the conspiracy your kind has hatched against me! I was invincible before but you Brahmins have used dark magic to undo the protection given to me by the Avatar! There is a reason why you are not allowed to handle weapons and now you see why I protected the caste divisions!'

Raam looked at him pityingly and said, 'You blame us of using dark magic but your own soldiers and generals are the ones actually controlled by Asurik magic that you couldn't identify! Instead of focusing on weeding out the Asur menace from your army you let them torment innocent civilians. Moreover, your attempt to restrict the vocation of each individual to their birth caste is the biggest act of adharma you could have performed and you dare to judge my actions! Dharma doesn't stop anyone from following their dreams and any artificial structure that forbids people from following their destiny is undoubtedly adharmik.'

Driving home his point further he said, 'My grandfather was a Brahmin, but fought the evil perpetrated by Karkotak like a Kshatriya, my grand-uncle Vishwamitra left his powerful position as the monarch of northern lands to become a Brahmarishi and my father has lived the life of both a Kshatriya and a Brahmin. Yet you wish to curtail this natural freedom granted to us by dharma? If you really followed the Varnashram, you would have retired on your own by now and taken Vanprasth, yet here you are, still clinging to power, hesitating in abdicating the hold you have over the vast resources of this planet.

'Your soldiers abuse their power and molest girls while you defend their right to do so; your generals grow wealthy at the expense of other castes who are reduced to abject poverty; your subordinate kings *buy* innocent children to save the lives of their own offspring and you still believe you're in the right? You shall be defeated today—not because of any dark magic that I possess but only because you, the one who was appointed the protector of dharma, has become its worst abuser.'

Arjun couldn't take the diatribe anymore and rushed towards the blabbering young man to deliver a deadly blow. Raam watched him approach with anger and resentment written on his face and knew that there was no way he could hope to talk sense into the emperor. He was beyond redemption, and under the circumstances there was only one way out.

While still running towards his adversary, Arjun threw the dagger at Raam's head but the boy countered by throwing his own axe to block the weapon. Just as the enraged emperor reached close enough to strike the boy who had thrown away his only weapon, the axe boomeranged and came back to its owner and in one swift motion, Raam sliced through Arjun's thick neck in a single stroke.

The emperor of the world was dead.

Adhyaye 47

Ravan had watched the unfolding drama with unbelieving eyes. He had managed to get rid of one monster only to create another! How on earth could he hope to take over Arjun's kingdom while this man was alive?

Taking care to stay hidden, he fled to the other end of the city where Arjun's sons practised swordplay and hoped to salvage the situation by utilizing their anger. The young princes were practising under their guru when Ravan burst in with the news of their father's death. Overwhelmed by a mix of grief and fury, they prepared to ride back to the palace but again Ravan stopped them. It wouldn't make sense to rush into the waiting axe and arrows of Raam; there was a better way to get even.

Raam's mind was swirling with conflicting emotions as he knelt next to the corpse of the man who had created an empire only few could dream of. Growing up in the protected environment of Janapav he had never imagined one day he would fight so many armed men, let alone take their lives. Even worse, he could not believe that he had slain the very emperor he had grown up idolizing!

As the citizens of Mahishmati began approaching the scene hesitantly, and the queen rushed to her husband's dead body, he decided it was time to head home. Locating the horse he had ridden here, he mounted it and began a soft canter towards the cowshed. He untied his favourite cow and led her away, heading back to the forest.

The battle with Arjun and his military had taken a good part of the day and by the time he left from Mahishmati dusk had fallen. Vultures were circling the corpses strewn on the banks of the Narmada and wails of the queen could be heard for many yojans as he cantered away in silence. He rode slowly through the forest he knew like the back of his hand making sure his horse and the prized cow did not get exhausted with the effort.

When he reached the burned grove at Janapav, an eerie silence greeted him. There was something unnatural about the stillness and he felt a tendril of fear grip his mind. He quickly dismounted and ran up the hill dreading what he would find. The gory sight that greeted him took his breath away. Yamdagni was sprawled face down at the entrance of the ashram he had been rebuilding; clearly he been attacked from behind. Raam rushed to help him up, but stopped dead in his tracks for in the faint light of dawn he saw that it wasn't his father who lay there, but his decapitated body. His heart thumping in his chest, he frantically looked around for his mother. Renuka was slumped in a corner, seemingly lifeless. Raam ran towards her, imagining the worst, but thankfully she was breathing. He shook her awake and sprinkled water on her face, trying hard to keep his gaze averted from his father's dead body. Renuka woke as if from a trance and looked at him with uncomprehending eyes. When her pain-riddled brain recognized her son's face she started crying piteously, alternately shouting at the skies and cursing the emperor. Raam tried asking her what had transpired but she just responded by beating her chest again and again in a hysteria that he just couldn't shake her out of.

His own heart filled with grief seeing his father dead and his mother in this condition and he remembered their words cautioning him to not use violence for it could start a chain reaction, but it was too late for repentance now. Even as his own eyes brimmed over with hot stinging tears of helplessness he gathered the courage to calm her down. Wiping away her tears, he said, 'Mother, stop it, Mother! Father's gone. Tell me who did this and I shall make sure they never dare set their foot in any rishi's ashram ever again in their life.'

Renuka was still sobbing uncontrollably but managed to blabber out a few words, 'It was Arjun; there were three of them! I don't know how he did it but I saw three Arjuns. They killed Yama, Raam, they killed your father, beheading him like a sacrificial animal in front of my eyes and I could do nothing!'

Raam's heart burnt with anger but he knew it could not have been Arjun for he lay dead in a pool of his own blood just like his father. His mother was not able to tell the difference in her delirium but the more he thought about it the more certain he became of the identities of the three men. They had to be Arjun's sons. As he covered his father's body with a cloth, Raam looked for the severed head and realized that it was missing. What kind of savages would take away the head of a rishi as a hunting prize! They were definitely no better than Asurs and deserved a fitting reply. He washed Renuka's face with water, slowly taking her towards the village, whispering words of confidence. Leaving her in the care of the Nishadh women and the local vaidya, he turned back to hunt down the men responsible for this abominable act of cowardice.

Rushing back to the horse, he swiftly rode towards

Mahishmati knowing well that the princes couldn't be more than a few yojans ahead of him for his father's body was still warm to the touch. They did not know the terrain as well as him and they would be slower not expecting him to come after them; hopefully he would catch up before they exited the forest. Soon enough he heard the sound of hoof beats and immediately let loose three arrows in their direction, at least one of which hit its mark. There was a loud cry followed by the sound of a heavy thud and then silence.

Arjun's sons realized who was after them, and quickly dismounted to help their fallen brother get up. They prepared to confront Raam with their weapons, ready to attack the moment he showed his face.

As Raam approached the clearing where the princes had stopped, two arrows whizzed past his head while a third grazed his horse making it whinny in pain. Raam hid behind a tree to avoid the barrage of arrows coming his way and then sent a whole volley of arrows, intercepting the ones fired by the three brothers. As his adversaries' quivers emptied, Raam rushed into the clearing, only to stop dead in his tracks.

The princes were exact replicas of Arjun but that wasn't what had caused him to pause. His eyes were riveted by the sight of his father's head impaled on a spear in the hands of one of them. He snarled with anger as a volcano seemed to erupt inside his heart. Blinded with rage, he steadied his horse with his right hand and holding his axe in the other, rode past them, swiftly slicing off their heads even before they could take aim at him.

The spear bearing his father's impaled head teetered precariously, but Raam jumped off his horse and grabbed it before it could touch the ground. Tears streaming down his face, he removed the head from the spear and then rode back to Janapav for he had to reunite Yamdagni's head with its body before cremating it. There would be no miracles this time since the only man who could have revived Yamdagni was Yamdagni himself.

Time seemed to come to a standstill as he chopped wood to prepare a pyre at the top of the hill and tenderly placed his father's body on it. He had rubbed the arani wood to prepare the fire for his father's morning and evening rituals countless times and his heart grieved as he realized this would be the last time he did so.

Chanting the mantras for the *antim-sanskar*, the last rites, he circumambulated the pyre, lighting it just as the sun climbed up the canopy of trees. The funeral pyre consumed two identities that dawn, father and son—Yamdagni and Raam.

As the smoke rose higher and his father's body returned to the elements, a fierce resolve took shape in Raam's mind. He had seen his mother beat her chest in grief twenty-one times, and he promised to make each one of them count.

Adhyaye 48

There was chaos in the world.

All major leaders had perished in the battle with Parshu-Raam, the Brahmin who defeated a thousand Kshatriyas, and his legend spread like wildfire, as did the pandemonium his actions resulted in.

Many of the surviving kings had nursed the ambition to replace Kartavirya but his boons had made him invincible until an ordinary Brahmin boy had proved otherwise. Raam knew the power-hungry Kshatriyas would not let this chance to become Chakravarti Samrat let go so easily but he was determined to not let a single person hold that kind of power again. He sought advice from the elder rishis including Agastya, Garga, Vasishth, Kanav and Vishwamitra who urged him to don the mantle of universal monarch since by virtue of his defeating the erstwhile emperor he could lay claim to his entire kingdom! Discussing the possibilities with his grand-uncle Raam explained his stand, 'I do not wish to rule the world, Uncle, that is the last of my ambitions. I have seen first-hand how power can corrupt and do not wish to be caught up in its web for a single moment. But I do not wish for another Asur-infested tyrant to take charge of the affairs of the world!'

Brahmarishi Vishwamitra replied sagaciously, 'In the combined opinion of all of us, the best way forward is for you to take on the responsibility that has arisen due to your own actions. Whether you sit on the throne or not, you need to organize an Ashwamedh yagnya to declare your own sovereignty over Arjun's kingdom, not to become a ruler like him, but to bring order back to the world.

'This yagnya would be a declaration that as long as you live, you will not let any unjust tyrant raise his head again. You don't have to sit on the throne yourself if you don't want to. We can figure out a suitable candidate later, but for now we can't let there be a vacuum on the royal throne!'

Raam understood what the Brahmarishi was telling him. Leaving the throne vacant would only invite more trouble as more and more people vied for the opportunity to rule the world. If nothing else, organizing the Ashwamedh, widely recognized as the most difficult of all Vedic yagnyas, would at least rid his mind of the guilt of killing so many people and the grief of losing his father.

Tradition required the ceremony to be performed by a married householder and in the absence of his father, the only other person he could turn to was Ruchik. He rushed to Ujjain to meet his grandparents who welcomed him with open arms and grief for the loss of their son.

As the three of them clung together in mutual misery, Ruchik answered his grandson's invitation by saying, 'I have taken sanyas for the second time in my life and as a renunciate I cannot become a part of the material world once again. The only help I can offer is to provide sanctuary to our daughter-in-law, your mother. We shall accompany you right this moment and bring Renuka back for there is nothing left for either of us in Janapav.'

Seeing the disappointment on Raam's face, Ruchik patted his head and said, 'Even though I cannot be a part of the yagnya, I can still help you by suggesting a suitable replacement. Rishi Kashyap, the father of the Devas and Daityas and indeed most life forms on this planet, is my uncle and I can think of no one better than him and his wife Aditi to perform this grand ritual. The rishi is also the great-grandfather of Manu, the first man of this Age. Imagine the sanctity the sacrifice would gain by the very presence of the mother of gods and the grandfather of mankind!'

Raam readily agreed to Ruchik's suggestion, 'That sounds perfect! Since the Suryavanshi and Chandravanshi lineages are both ultimately derived from Rishi Kashyap, it would be wonderful to have the most senior member of our dynasty perform the grand ceremony himself, simultaneously stamping my efforts with a seal of his approval!'

He requested his grandfather to contact the exalted forefather. Kashyap and Aditi, who were living in the beautiful valley of Kashyap-mir, agreed to be the hosts of the ceremony that would see participation from all the seers and priests present on the planet. With the help of Vishwamitra, Raam was able to arrange everything within a month's time and the ritual began on the auspicious day of Nirjala Ekadashi at the highest peak of the Sahyadri mountains.

Ashwamedh demanded the selection of a stallion, that had to be more than twenty-four but less than a hundred years old, and Brahmarishi Vasishth chose the finest Kamboja horse from the stables of Ayodhya for the occasion. It was sprinkled with water and fragrant flowers as the priests whispered protective mantras into its ear before finally letting it loose in the north-eastern direction.

For the period of one year, it would roam wherever it chose to and all the territory covered in its journey would be claimed by the king performing the yagnya. Normally the horse would be accompanied by the king's army to fight all those who challenged its authority but this time, it would be protected by just one man—Raam, the wielder of the Bow of Vishnu and the Axe of Shiva, while an uninterrupted yagnya continued, awaiting his return.

Raam knew this was the opportunity for him to settle all disputes about supremacy in the territories he would visit and he set about cleaning Nabhi-varsh of all despots, making sure evil would not be able to raise its head in the peninsula anytime soon again. His journey took him over the length and breadth of the country as he rid the tormented populations of their tyrant kings and their progeny, and eliminated all Rakshas-infested warriors.

He did not kill those who still clung to dharma, and Chandravanshi kings like Dushyant and Suryavanshi kings like Rohitashwa, Harishchandra's son who now ruled over Ayodhya, had been spared. As Raam's journey brought him southwards after conquering the north, east and west of the country, Ravan fled from Lanka and took refuge in the Himalayas. The Asur king knew the only hope he had to balance the might of the killing machine that the Brahmin had turned into was to obtain a boon from Lord Shiva himself!

Raam still felt great anger in his heart against the Brahma-rakshas who had caused so much anguish to his own family and spread the Asurik maya in the world. Had Ravan so desired, he could have utilized his mixed ancestry to set a blazing trail for all others of his kind but he had done just the opposite, bringing death and destruction to the globe. Nevertheless Raam knew he had to gain control over his feelings since his campaign against evil was not based on vengeance but justice. He would let Ravan live for the time being but pronounced a cursed that if the Asur king should ever resort to such nefarious activities again in the future, a man bearing his own name would rid the world of his menace.

By the time the stipulated period for the yagnya came to a close, Raam, wielder of the axe, had become a terror for corrupt Kshatriyas and as the rivers of Aryavarta turned red with blood, he returned to the yagnya as the undisputable lord of all of Nabhi-varsh, from the great white mountains to the southern ocean.

He came back to a resounding welcome with his friends and family gathered to celebrate the occasion along with the patriarchs Rishi Kashyap and Brahmarishi Vasishth. Renuka, who had taken refuge with Ruchik and Satyavati, proudly hugged him. 'Your father would have been very proud of you today. You have taken up a responsibility that would not have been easy to take for even the gods, let alone the strongest and bravest of Kshatriyas.'

Parshu-Raam bowed his head and replied, 'Thank you, Mother. I really wish Father was alive to witness this accomplishment today! I parted from him on not so happy terms and still regret not heeding his advice while I had the chance. But now I must finish what I have started. This one success cannot be the end of it.'

The elders looked at him quizzically and he explained, 'Order needs to be restored not just in Nabhi-varsh but the entire world and I want to keep touring the world till I eliminate all corrupt rulers. I saw my mother beat her chest twenty-one times while she cried over my father's dead body and I wish to continue the sacrifice for the same number of years. Bringing down the arrogant Kshatriyas I wish to anoint Brahmins and Shudras and Vaishyas as rulers in their stead. Only then I shall have repaid the debt to my parents and truly uprooted evil from our planet!'

Vishwamitra, the Kshatriya king who had become a Brahmarishi, nodded in understanding. 'So be it! From now on, no evil ruler shall be able to terrorize his citizens and the Brahmins, Vaishyas and Shudras shall be the new Kshatriya rulers of this land ending the monopoly of one particular caste over kingship!'

Adhyaye 49

Returning from the farthest corner of the world for the last time, Raam remembered the parting words of his grandfather: what a man became in the future was the result of his past.

He had grown up in the forest because his father had decided to help his own father fight the gathering of dark forces that were spreading from Dandak-Aranya. Had he been born in Kanyakubja, his life would perhaps have been completely different. From his very childhood he was taught the importance of non-violence but was also made aware of the responsibility the strong had to protect the weak. It was this very notion that had finally urged him to take up arms for the protection of justice. One could afford to stay non-violent only in the wake of a weaker opponent and in the past twenty-one years he had made sure he showed all the opponents of dharma their proper place.

It was a genocide the likes of which the world hadn't seen before.

Thousands were killed and the name of Parshu-Raam became like a death knoll for Kshatriyas. After years of touring the globe, weeding out the Rakshas-infested monsters in human form, Raam returned to his country and washed his axe, soaked with the blood of the Kshatriyas, laying it down at Samanta-panchak.

He had come back to Nabhi-varsh to a welcome grander than any homecoming warrior could have ever received. He was taken on royal carriages to bathe in the purifying waters of first the Saraswati, then the Ganga and finally the Brahmaputra to rid him of the sin of taking so many lives.

The burden of his sins may have been cleansed by the holy water but the weight on his soul dragged him down. He had had to kill fathers in front of their children, husbands in front of their wives, generals in front of their soldiers and kings in front of their subjects. Many hid behind their own women knowing well he wouldn't raise arms against them. To be fair, he had not killed a single woman or child and had even spared the lives of the kings who had promised to mend their ways. Yet the pleas of the dead and the cries of the living haunted his dreams every night. He was no longer the boy who didn't know his destiny, but the man with the burden of twenty-one campaigns of extermination on his shoulders. His innocent face was marked by deep lines of responsibility and maturity.

The final ceremony of the yagnya was supposed to be performed at the same spot where it had first been organized, and needed at least a hundred Brahmins to chant the Vedic hymns. The grandsire of the ceremony, Rishi Kashyap, who had a flowing white beard and a genial manner, informed Raam that most capable Brahmins had been appointed as rulers of the various splintered kingdoms, and there weren't enough left in the Sahyadris to help them complete the yagnya.

Hearing this complaint, Raam knew that after Kshatriyas, it was time to break the hegemony of Brahmins as well. Destroying the shackles of centuries of rigid societal norms, he walked towards the nearby fishing village with determination. The sixty fishermen families inhabiting the village ran to hide themselves, worried that he might have come to take their lives as well but he assured them of his protection. As they gingerly stepped out of their hiding places, he surprised them by inducting them into a new order of priestly class thereby satisfying the shortage of Brahmins required for the ceremony.

Rishi Kashyap gave his wholehearted approval, 'Bravo, my son! Let us cast away convention and create a new world!'

The biggest Vedic yagnya of all time was thus successfully concluded with the help of the Shudras that had been turned into Brahmins by Parshu-Raam. Vishwamitra pointed this out to Vasishth and the two Brahmarishis smiled at this achievement.

As the grand ceremony, presided over by the highest of the high priests of all time came to an end, Raam decided to make a declaration. Addressing the gathering that included his childhood friends from Janapav, his mother and beloved grandparents, Brahmarishis, kings of the world and the forefather of his own race, he announced, 'From the lessons I have learnt over the course of my travels and with the permission of my elders, I hereby lay down some rules for all the new kings.'

The crowd hung on his every word as he continued, 'Just as Indra provides rains to help our crops germinate, so shall be the duty of all kings to help their people's lives blossom. Just as the sun evaporates water slowly so as to provide for the following year's rain, so shall the kings collect minimal taxes and spend them for the welfare of the people in the coming years. Just as the air around us provides the life breath, so shall the kings pervade everywhere through their agents to ensure the victory of good over evil amongst their subjects.'

He looked around as he made his declaration, 'Just as Yamraj ends the lives of everyone at the end of their time irrespective of their affiliations, so shall the kings be impartial in according punishments to wrongdoers even if they be from their own family. Just as the moon provides medicines in the form of life-restoring herbs, so shall the kings take care of their subjects' health. And finally, just as fire destroys all evil within and without, so shall the kings fight and destroy the enemies of dharma, both internal and external.'

The crowd at the yagnya venue cheered joyfully as the new directives for righteous rule were laid down and Brahmarishi Vasishth asked Raam to perform the final step—the sacrifice of the stallion that had been allowed to roam freely for these twenty-one years. As the ceremonial sword was brought to him, Parshu-Raam, the man who had wiped out countless families and nipped many dynasties in the bud, hesitated.

He looked at his mother, remembering her constant admonitions about never to prey on the frail and the feeble. She had spent her whole life saving and helping injured animals, birds and sometimes even poisonous reptiles, nurturing them back to good health with the fierce conviction that this earth belonged to everyone and humans did not have any right to kill for their pleasure or greed.

He glanced at his grandparents who had always emphasized that arms should be taken up by the strong only for the protection of the weak. He hazarded a glance at his grand-uncle who, even though possessing the weapons of the gods, had left them behind for the pursuit of a higher calling and saw him give an enigmatic smile. As he gazed in the eyes of the steed he had been protecting for two long decades, he saw the reflection of his own soul's burden and knew what had to be done.

Slowly, he let the sword drop from his hands and proclaimed in a loud voice, 'I take the liberty to change another convention and declare that from this day onwards, no one will have to sacrifice any animal for a yagnya to be considered complete!'

His mother gave a sigh of delight but the greatest support for his decision came from Rishi Kashyap, who stood up to applaud. The patriarch of all life on earth came forward and declared, 'By the authority that my position as the performer of the yagnya assures me, I give this decision my wholehearted approval! From now on, the offering of an animal shall be purely symbolic and the person conducting the sacrifice shall endeavour to slay the beast within him! No priest can force the initiator of the sacrifice to kill an animal or to partake of its meat. Let this day be the beginning of not only a new era for humanity but also for the other life forms coexisting in harmony!'

There was thunderous applause in response to this declaration. As the noise died down, Vishwamitra stepped away from the crowd and kneeled down in front of Parshu-Raam, bowing his head simultaneously. Renuka followed suit, tears running down her eyes, and so did Ruchik and Satyavati, clutching each other for support. One by one, the entire gathering followed as Raam watched, overwhelmed by their gesture.

Witnessing this grand salutation given to the boy who had done the unthinkable, Brahmarishi Vasishth came forward and declared, 'I, Vasishth, the son of Srishti-Karta Brahma and the chief priest of this yagnya, also provide sanction to this proclamation and decree that what Rishi Kashyap and Parshu-Raam have said shall hold true for all coming ages. With this, I hereby declare this yagnya complete!'

There were sounds of 'Swasti' from all around them to wish auspiciousness and Vishwamitra said to his grand-nephew, 'I have accomplished many things in my life, my son, but what you have achieved is a feat even the gods would shy away from. No one except Shri Hari Vishnu could have taken on such a huge challenge and fulfilled it as well!'

Satyavati came forward to hug her son and gushed, 'I remember the day when Guru Dattatreya blessed Yama and Vishwa for the first time. He had said that my grandchild would be no less than an avatar and I see the result in front of my eyes! You are the saviour of those who have been downtrodden for ages, be it humans or animals, and indeed in that respect, you are no less than the lord of preservation, Shri Hari Vishnu himself.'

Raam shrugged off the praise being heaped on him and touched the feet of all elders before stopping in front of his grandfather, the eldest surviving member of his family. Looking at Ruchik's wrinkled face and kind eyes he said, 'You started me on this path many years ago when you taught me to become the protector of the weak. Did you always know things would end this way?'

Ruchik shook his head and replied, 'No one can predict the exact flow of events, my child. Although I knew the general direction your life would take, even I couldn't have known all those years back that the events set in motion by Marich, the Urags and Karkotak would lead to a confrontation between you and Kartavirya Arjun. I played my part by ensuring I passed on to you whatever skills I had to help you survive any future situation, grooming you into a soldier of dharma. I knew the day I had been given the Bow of Vishnu that I had been selected as its custodian and had to pass it on to someone more capable than me! The success of your campaign though is purely your own karma.'

Vishwamitra nodded, 'Had you not followed your heart

and left from Kanyakubja after Renuka and Yamdagni's estrangement, you would not have bumped into me in Ayodhya. When I met you there I had strong intuition that you needed the blessings of Bholenath but again it was up to you to listen to my advice or not. And when you did pursue the path I had suggested, even I didn't know the effect your prayers would have for that was solely dependent on the efforts you put into it. The very fact that you achieved the blessings of the lord of destruction himself is proof enough that more than destiny it is your own actions that have brought you this glory.'

Brahmarishi Vasishth broke into the discussion and said, 'There shall be enough time for a detailed discussion later, my friends, but right now it is time for you to distribute gifts to the officiating priests. We have been doing it on your behalf for all these years, giving alms to the poor and creating a more egalitarian society but the final donation to the performer of this grand yagnya must be made by you.'

Raam thought about what the rishi had said and walked to where Kashyap, the patriarch of all humanity and the official performer of the yagnya stood. Bowing low he touched the rishi's feet and made a final declaration, 'Continuing the tradition of this great evening, I hereby make one last declaration and donate to Rishi Kashyap all my land, making him the supreme sovereign of this planet!'

As everyone watched in disbelief, Raam looked at his grand-uncle who gave him a nod of approval. The future would remember him as the unlikely legend who won the entire globe with his own military prowess and then gave it all away to the Brahmin who had officiated a yagnya for him.

And yet, the act of donating the entire land to Kashyap wasn't even the biggest event of that day. There was more to come.

Adhyaye 50

Rishi Kashyap accepted the donation with a calm he did not feel internally for his heart was still troubled. He was the progenitor of various species of life and even though he had officiated in the grandest of yagnyas to be performed on earth, he did not approve of the carnage of the past twenty-one years. He lauded Parshu-Raam's efforts in weeding out the demonic elements from amongst the humans; he had surpassed all expectations and would be remembered as a great man. Yet Kashyap rued the price that had to be paid to fulfil the dream of a just society.

Placing his hand on Raam's head, he said, 'It breaks my heart to say this, especially after your stupendous display of magnanimity, but as the forefather of all the species who inhabit this world, and whose benefit I think of now, I wish for you to depart from the land that is now mine and stay away unless there is need for your services again!'

Raam heard the directive with a bowed head. He knew that even though he had saved many future lives by killing a few, he would still have to face punishment for the deaths he had caused. Before anyone could intervene on his behalf he replied, 'I accept.'

Pandemonium broke out in the gathering as people sought to understand the significance of what had just transpired.

What did Rishi Kashyap mean by asking Raam to leave the land that was his for he owned the entire earth now! Did he wish him to end his life? If not then where did he want to send him? Would he be given access to another loka? Vishwamitra had helped Satyavrat reach Swarg earlier; would he now have to do the same for his grand-nephew as well? Or would he create an entirely new planetary system just as he had done to put Indra in his place?

Vishwamitra came forward and raised a hand to put an end to the discussions. 'Raam, my son, you need not go to any other loka, nor think of ending your life. True, there is no land other than what Rishi Kashyap owns currently on this planet but we can always create more!'

'What! How?' Renuka asked incredulously, concerned for her son's life.

Vishwamitra turned around to gesture to the ocean and said, 'Three-fourths of this planet is covered by water and there's plenty of land under the sea. Raam, I urge you to throw your Axe with all its might and let it fall into the ocean. I am sure Lord Varun shall respect the power of Lord Shiva's divine weapon, and grant you access to at least a piece of land that you can call your own!'

Brahmarishi Vasishth came forward to support the suggestion. 'Yes, my child. The very fact that Rishi Kashyap has told you to return to the mainland when there's need for your services is a sign that he wants you not to end your life too.'

Raam looked at the Brahmarishi and then the forefather of his race who nodded. 'I do not have any ill feelings for you and just wish to safeguard my progeny that represents eons of evolution! The suggestion given by Brahmarishi Vishwamitra is completely acceptable to me and I am sure the lord of the ocean will listen if all of us ask him for some land for your habitation.'

Other sages nodded their ascent and Raam raised his Divine Axe for the final time. Using all the power he had gained from years of ridding the earth of its parasites, he flung the weapon, watching it fall far into the ocean.

For a moment nothing happened but then, a loud rumble began from the depths of the ocean and the very earth they stood on began to tremble. The entire range began vibrating and huge boulders began to fall from the mountain, starting a panic amongst the assembled guests. Even as they were adjusting to this sudden tectonic upheaval a large wave rose in the ocean and headed towards the hill! Raam watched in fascination as the massive wave gathered momentum; within seconds it had drowned the coastal parts and instead of receding, the ocean seemed to be advancing further inland! Was Lord Varun upset with his demand and wished to teach him a lesson?

He looked around but saw no fear on the faces of the senior rishis. A light smile played on Ruchik's face while Satyavati and Renuka prayed fervently with their hands folded. He was surrounded by friends, family and well-wishers and felt relieved that even if he was to die today it would be looking at the faces of the people he loved and admired.

The wave loomed over the hill and in that split second he saw scenes from his own life flash in front of his eyes. Tender moments of affection spent with his family—the endless sermons by Ruchik given at the top of another similar hill, Satyavati's affectionate pampering and feeding him his choicest meals, learning to care for defenceless animals with Renuka and the martial training from Yamdagni. His had been a life full of love and happiness.

The wave was almost upon them and his mind jumped to the unpardonable offence he had committed by beheading his own mother. He saw glimpses of the first journey he had undertaken on his own, the thrill of using the Bow of Vishnu for the first time and the ease with which he had tackled the soldiers of Arjun. The vision of the lord of destruction in his original abode of Manomaya overwhelmed him once again and he relived the feel of the Divine Axe as he held it for the first time. The final battle in which he had decimated Arjun's one thousand generals moved around him like a blur and so did the carnage of the past twenty-one years. There were many accomplishments and many more regrets but he realized that these were all the part of a life well lived.

Even if he died today, the fable of the Brahmin boy who defeated the bravest of Kshatriyas and cleansed the earth of the Asur menace would remain. The legend of Raam, wielder of the Axe, would grow and for generations, shall instil fear in the minds of those who strayed from the path of righteousness and abused the power that society provided them.

History would not find it easy to forget Parshu-Raam.

Epilogue

Shiva the destroyer watched the mighty wave as it was about to hit the hill and smiled. He knew Varun would never go against his will and was just using the opportunity to display his prowess before agreeing to Parshu-Raam's request.

Sure enough, as they waited for the crushing impact, the huge body of water turned into a light refreshing shower, bringing relief to everyone's face. The sheets of water kissed the hill side with their gentle touch and began their journey back but did not stop at the original shoreline.

A wide strip of land, thirty miles across, extending from where the Divine Axe had fallen right until Gokarna, was revealed, redefining the western coastline of Nabhi-varsh. This hallowed region, donated magnanimously by Varun would forever be known as Parshu-Raam Kshetra and Shiva gave it his personal blessings.

The world had watched Raam perform the dance of destruction but he had taken on this burden the way only Shri Hari Vishnu could. Shiva wondered if future generations might even consider him an incarnation of the lord. He had been the sole witness to the boy's hurts and happiness, his denial of desires and the devotion to duty, the long tiring days and nightmare-ridden nights, the immense loneliness and an occasional smile of satisfaction. Raam had turned Ruchik's prophecy into a blessing for the entire world and established a new and fair society at the cost of his own personal life.

He had watched him destroy the rigidity of caste and colour, crowning Vaishyas, Shudras and Brahmins as the new kings and turn the lowest of castes into Brahmins of the highest order. He knew humanity would require Parshu-Raam's intervention whenever it strayed from the path of dharma and knew how important his support would be in the times to come.

Ravan had taken shelter in Himalayas and was praying to obtain Shiva's blessings but it would take a long time for the Asur to gain an audience with him. He needed to atone for all his past sins before even starting to build up enough spiritual merit. Besides, the two curses cast on him by Yamdagni and Raam would make sure that even if he was blessed with power for a time, his tyranny would also come to an end eventually.

There were many milestones for Raam to achieve still and if he continued on the path that he had chosen, Shiva could see him become the mentor of the final avatar of Lord Vishnu and join the legion of the Saptarishis. He could certainly benefit from associating with Agastya who was perfecting the Kalaripayattu, the toughest of all martial arts, for that would help him train many future warriors of dharma on earth along with the rishi.

Humans try to escape reality by surrounding themselves with others but the truth is that each person had an individual destiny to fulfil. The path to that destination was a lonely one and Raam had taken really giant steps towards his own personal salvation. The cycle of *Srishti*, creation, *Sthiti,* equilibrium and *Samhar*, annihilation, would continue for another seven Manvantars and Parshu-Raam would be there to take care of his fellow humans as the first Brahmakshatriya, a disciple of Shiva and an embodiment of Vishnu who roamed amongst men.

The reign of illustrious kings would begin again and earth would be witness to men like Janak and Sagar and Mandhata and Bhishma. But before all of them, there was a tiny bud blossoming to life in another blood relative of Parshu-Raam. Vishwamitra and Menaka's daughter Shakuntala had come of age and Shiva could foresee the remarkable feats her child would perform.

Soon it shall be time for another adventure, he thought contentedly.

Acknowledgements

As is true for any story that finds its way into a book, this one also owes its existence to the support provided by many.

First and foremost, gratitude to all the readers of my first book, *Vishwamitra*, for turning it into such a success, which encouraged me to give this second book its final form. I thank all my friends and family who have supported my writing, and especially the readers who sent their thoughts and valuable input to me from all corners of the world.

Heartfelt appreciation for the Penguin team: Vaishali Mathur for thrashing out the story with me, Shatarupa Ghoshal for her brilliant editing, Aman Arora for the marketing inputs and Gopal and Harish for all their ground-level help. The cover art by Jay Thakur brought to life Vishwamitra for the first book and the same has been achieved by the Book Bakers team, Gunjan and Neeraj for Parshu-Raam. The credit for helping me with the maps for both books goes to Umang Revari and the author images are courtesy Saurin Jhaveri.

A special thanks to my friend Nirmit Shah who helped me see for myself the places and sites associated with the two main protagonists of this book. I also thank Aditi Daftary for providing her pleasant company on this exciting journey of discovering the past that Nirmit and I embarked upon. The River Chambal, famous for its erstwhile dacoit-infested areas, is believed to begin at the hill of Janapav in Madhya Pradesh. On top of the hill are a temple and an ashram that belonged to Yamdagni (Rishi Jamdagni as known by the locals) and is believed to be the place where Parshu-Raam was born.

The lush green vistas of the hill-side gave me an insight into what kind of life Parshu-Raam would have had growing up in the region as well as a setting for the major events that shook his life. I was delighted to see that a big temple dedicated to the avatar is coming up at the top of the hill and the opportunity to talk to the knowledgeable priest was invaluable.

While Janapav has a romantic feel to it, Maheshwar (as Mahishmati is known today), is the historical seat of power of the Holkar dynasty that ruled the Malwa region. It was from here that Kartavirya Arjun extended his empire to cover the entire globe and the magnificent Narmada ghat constructed by Queen Ahilya Devi Holkar gave me a glimpse into how things would have been in context of my story. Indeed the gentle River Narmada weaves through the Vindhyas just as it does through my story.

My thanks to the local guide who took me to the exact spot where Parshu-Raam and Kartavirya Arjun fought their final battle. Even today, the temple of Raj-Rajeshwar pays homage to the legendary hero who unfortunately lost his way and turned into a villain. Even the city of Indore has many monuments dedicated to this fabled ruler and it is surprising that his story is not better known since he is only one of the three people in recorded chronicles who managed to defeat Ravan.

As always, I shall appreciate any feedback or comments that

you may wish to share and you can reach me through any of
the following portals:

My blog - www.decodehindumythology.blogspot.com
Facebook page - www.facebook.com/Dr.Vineet.Official
Website – www.drvineetaggarwal.com

I conclude with the amazingly open-minded and liberal view
expressed in the Rig Veda –

एकं सद्विप्रा बहुधा वदन्ति
Ekam Sat Vipra Bahudha Vadanti
Truth is One but the learned know it as Many
Aum Shanti: Shanti: Shanti:

READ MORE IN PENGUIN METRO READS

Vishwamitra

Dr Vineet Aggarwal

He was born a Kshatriya. He became a Brahmarishi. When Satyavati, wife of Rishi Ruchik, exchanges with her mother, Queen Ratna, the magic potion for bearing a child, they change not just their children's destinies, but also the history of mankind. Born of this mix-up is Vishwamitra, the son of a Kshatriya, with the qualities of a Brahmin. The duality in his life soon begins to show as he strives to become a Brahmarishi—the ultimate, the most powerful of all Gurus. *Vishwamitra* is the riveting story of a brave but stubborn, haughty yet compassionate, visionary king of Aryavarta who became one of the most well-known sages of all times.